Corporate Heat

WHERE DANGER HIDES

DESIREE HOLT

Dedication

For my readers, who have hung in there with me.
To Claire and Nicki, leaders extraordinaire of Totally
Bound—you were there in the beginning when I needed
you and you pulled me back in when I needed you again.
My beta reader, closest friend in the world and the woman
of my heart to whom I owe so very much, Margie Hager.
And to my fabulous editor, Rebecca Baker Fairfax, who
teaches me how to make a silk purse out of a sow's ear.
Without you this book would not have seen the light of
day again or given birth to the exciting Corporate Heat
series. I am eternally grateful to each and every one of
you. I am glad we will be taking this journey together.

|

Strike Force

Unconditional Surrender

Corporate Heat

Where Danger Hides

Lust Bites

Crude Oil
Beg Me

Anthologies

Treble
Subspace
Bound to the Billionaire
Three's a Charm

Single Titles

Rodeo Heat

Where Danger Hides

ISBN # 978-1-78686-179-5

©Copyright Desiree Holt 2017

Cover Art by Posh Gosh ©Copyright 2017

Interior text design by Claire Siemaszkiewicz

Totally Bound Publishing

Published in 2017 by Totally Bound Publishing, Think Tank, Ruston Way, Lincoln, LN6 7FL, United Kingdom.

Chapter One

Hell and damnation.

Taylor Scott never swore, but after this week — this day — she'd acquired a number of words not previously found in her vocabulary.

She hitched her five-foot-four-with-heels body onto one of the two vacant barstools. Turning sideways, she looked at herself in the mirror behind the bar. She saw a tumble of auburn hair and emerald-green eyes. The conservative navy suit and silk blouse looked only slightly the worse for wear after the day's confrontation. The heavy gold hoops in her ears shone even in the subdued light the cocktail lounge afforded.

Not bad, she thought, critically assessing herself. *Not a showstopper.* Breasts too small, hips too wide, thighs a little plumper than she'd like. But she made the best use of her assets. Certainly not someone to get tossed out into the street, so to speak.

She wasn't much of a bar sitter — not even a bar visitor, truth to tell — and she'd really wanted one of the small tables, only they were all full. But she needed a drink, something to make her forget the fact that in the short span of seven days she'd learned her entire life had been a lie. The letter from her grandmother was folded in the pocket of her jacket, a slim sheet of stationery filled with words that had destroyed everything she'd believed about her life up until now.

"What can I get for you, miss?"

Taylor snapped her head up. The bartender had placed a cocktail napkin on the bar in front of her. Now he waited patiently for her, this stocky blond with eyes that said he'd seen and heard it all and an expectant look on his face. What did one drink to get drunk? Her experience was limited to a small selection of good wines and Bloody Marys at Sunday brunches. *Wait.* The partners in the investment firm where she worked always drank Jack Daniel's at corporate functions. Black, whatever that meant. She guessed it was as good a choice as any.

"Jack Daniel's Black, please." She tried to sound authoritative.

"Rocks or neat?"

She frowned. *Why does ordering a drink have to be so complicated?* "Oh, um, rocks, please."

She was hyperaware of her surroundings. The walls of the bar were a rich, polished oak as was the paneling of the bar itself. The tables were oak planking, with chairs covered in soft-looking leather. The lighting, discreetly recessed, gave patrons the illusion of a cloak of darkness. Soft music drifted into the air from hidden speakers, an effective sound screen for couples with their heads inclined toward each other in an intimate fashion.

"Your drink, ma'am."

The bartender placed a glass filled with deep amber liquid and ice cubes on the tiny square of napkin and set a glass of water next to it.

"In case you wanted a chaser." He gave her a half-grin.

She picked up the glass with both hands and took a healthy swallow. The first splash of the liquor on her tongue was a sharp bite of smoky flavor, a burning sensation she was unprepared for that brought tears to her eyes and made her cough.

"I wouldn't chug that like lemonade if I were you. Here."

The voice was so deep and rich it sent fingers of heat skittering along her spine and tiny pulses throbbing at the heart of her sex. A strong masculine hand held out a snow-white handkerchief which she grabbed without thinking. She blotted her eyes then picked up her glass of water and drained half of it. Then she looked up to see who'd come to her rescue.

Predator. That was the first word that came to mind. An unfamiliar thrill of forbidden temptation shot through her body at the sight of the man sitting at an angle to her right. Broad shoulders and hands with long, slim fingers. A face full of sharp planes and angles with a straight nose and sensuous lips but a totally unreadable look. Eyes blacker than coal under lashes thicker than hers. Black hair worn long and tied back with a thin strip of leather.

There was something feral about him. Wild. Untamed. Dangerous. Powerful energy radiated from him and battered against her body, all of it barely tamed beneath the civilized cloak of a custom-tailored suit and silk dress shirt. An unbidden image flashed in her mind of him naked, his dark hair loose, the muscles of his bronzed body rippling in the sunshine. A panther, that was what he reminded her of. And for a brief moment she wanted to lose herself in the jungle.

He raised an eyebrow. "Panther? Is that a code word?"

Oh, God, did I say that out loud? "Pay no attention to anything that comes out of my mouth tonight." Heat crept up her cheeks. "My mind isn't functioning properly."

His eyes burned into her and she shivered. Good sense told her to get as far away from this stranger as possible before she found herself in a situation beyond her control. Her lovers had been pitifully few and disappointing and none had made her blood heat and moisture pool between her legs the way one look from this stranger did. She wondered what it would be like to have hot, sweaty sex with him. Muscles deep in her body contracted.

She almost laughed. Her grandparents would turn over in their graves if they knew such a thought had even entered her mind. *Good. They deserve a little grave-spinning after what they did to me.*

Taylor knew she should finish her drink, go to her room and try not to think about how her life had been blown to little pieces. Or about today's humiliating episode. But resentment had been boiling inside her for a week and what had happened today had set a match to all that growing bitterness. The ruthless discipline she'd allowed to be imposed on her all her life had all been for nothing. *For a lie.*

When the attorney handling her grandmother's estate had handed her the letter detailing the monstrous charade she'd been living, she'd received the shock of her life. Nothing had been the way she'd thought. She wasn't even Taylor Scott, really. At this point she didn't even know just who the hell she was. But she did know who she didn't want to be.

Maybe now it was time for her to find out what life had to offer. To taste the forbidden fruit she'd always denied herself.

She handed back the fine cotton handkerchief, noticing his strong, lean fingers as she did so. The brief contact sent heat rocketing through her. "Thank you. I, um, swallowed a little more than I intended."

He nodded toward her glass. "You need to sip that stuff slowly, not throw it down. Good whiskey is meant to be savored."

"I know that." She straightened her back and tossed her hair. "You think I don't know how to drink good whiskey?"

She thought a smile ghosted across his mouth, but the hint of it disappeared at once.

"I think your drinking habits are your own business. I was just offering a little friendly advice." He nodded at the bartender and lifted his glass.

"Well, you can keep the advice but thank you for the use of your handkerchief. I'm fine now." *Liar!*

"Good. Happy to be of help."

Taylor finished the rest of her drink in small swallows and tried to ignore the man next to her. The liquor traced fire through her blood but left untouched the cold spot sitting inside her like a block of ice. She raised her hand and motioned to the bartender.

"Sure you want another one of those?" The deep voice spiked another flash of heat.

"Yes. I'm sure. And thanks for your concern, but I don't need someone to monitor my drinks."

He shrugged. "Fine by me." He lifted an eyebrow as the bartender set another full glass in front of her. "Celebrating? Or drowning your sorrows?"

"Neither. Just…" She searched for the right word but couldn't find one. "Just drinking."

"I hate to tell you, but you don't look like you're enjoying it very much."

Taylor turned to face him and found herself captured again by the darkness of his eyes.

Eyes without a soul. Now, where did that come from? "On the contrary. I'm having a wonderful time." She took a healthy swallow of her new drink and nearly choked again. She grabbed her water glass and drained it.

"Mm-hmm. That's certainly pleasure I see on your face."

He was beginning to get on her nerves. "You sure are nosy." She had to turn away from his penetrating gaze. "I'd say it's distressing to find out after thirty years that your life has been a lie and the one relative you seem to have left denies your existence. Take it from me. Fairy tales don't really exist."

He raised an eyebrow. "Sounds pretty serious."

Anger reached up through her again. *Serious* was hardly the word to describe her sense of betrayal. All those years of toeing the line. Of stifling rules and the short tether. Of a life with little pleasure, striving for approval that never came. Of her mother's deep sadness and her grandparents' autocratic grip on her and her mother's lives. She felt as if someone had stolen the past thirty years from her, years that were gone forever. Now, she wanted rebellion and payback.

"I'm scrubbing away my past and saying hello to the first day of the rest of my life. Creating the new me."

Because the old me was the product of a lie and very boring.

Taylor resisted the urge to slip her hand into her jacket pocket, pull out the sheet of paper and re-read the damning words. It didn't matter. She had them memorized.

I realize now it was a mistake to conceal this from you all these years. You must believe our intentions were nothing but the best. But you know what they say about good intentions. They certainly paved the road to hell for all of us.

The man finished his drink and signaled for a refill. "You don't look like someone with a past they need to be rid of."

"Shows you how much you know." Taylor swallowed the last drops in her glass and the tension in her body eased just a little more. The whiskey was beginning to work its magic on her. The anger still simmered, though. That wouldn't go away any time soon.

"What brings you to San Antonio?"

A bad decision. It isn't every day I get thrown out of corporate offices like some criminal or piece of street trash.

"It's personal." *So just shut up and leave me alone.* She waved at the bartender for another refill. Maybe with enough of the liquor in her system she could forget her pain altogether.

"I take it things didn't go well." He picked up his fresh drink and swallowed some of it.

"You could say that. In fact, you could say not going well is a major understatement."

"That's too bad."

"Sure. Too bad." The whiskey in the glass sloshed slightly as she picked it up and licked the drops off her hand.

"Maybe you'd better make this your last one. I'd hate to see you try to drive home after one too many."

She turned angry eyes on him. "Listen, Whoever-you-are, I'm old enough to know how much to drink. I don't need a babysitter. And I'm staying here in the hotel, so if I pass out, I don't have far to go." She stared at him, then shook her head and raked her fingers through her hair. "Sorry. That was rude of me. I'm just in a rotten mood tonight."

He reached out to lay a hand on her forearm and even through the layers of fabric his fingers felt like branding irons on her skin. A tiny jolt of electricity sparked its way through her body.

He narrowed his gaze. She saw that he felt it, too. They stared at each other for a long moment. He broke the eye contact first. "Maybe talking to someone will help."

Yes. Talk to me so I can find out what's really going on in that pretty head of yours.

He tilted his glass and took another swallow of his club soda. No alcohol for him tonight. He had a mission and he couldn't afford to have his senses dulled. If he wished for anything, it was that she'd been ugly and abrasive. Someone he could easily dislike. *Why does she have to be such an appealing package?*

He was already regretting his decision to come here. There were other ways to accomplish the same thing. He should have taken them. Women like her were dangerous to him. Too soft. Too appealing. Too easy to let in under the barriers. And therein lay disaster.

He'd already been through it once. That was enough for him. No, he needed to keep his walls securely in place and sitting here with this woman wasn't the way to make sure that happened.

Finish your drink and go away, he wanted to tell her. *Leave this bar, this hotel, this city. Hide yourself away from me and don't ever come back.*

For the first time in years, he craved a real drink.

She took another swallow of her whiskey. "You can't do anything about the years I've lost. Or make my own flesh and blood accept me."

"So, this is about family problems?"

She gave a short, bitter laugh. "It would be if I had any family." She downed the rest of her drink and signaled for yet another one. They were going down more easily now.

"I know I'm just a stranger in a bar," he went on, "and no one you should take orders from, so consider this a suggestion. I think you should make this next drink your last."

"Thanks, but I'll decide when I've had enough." *And that might be sooner rather than later.*

Taylor concentrated on finishing the drink, the letter still burning a hole in her pocket. The man just watched her with those deep black eyes. Finally, she swallowed the last of the whiskey and gestured toward the bartender for her check. She had no problem signing it, but when she tried to move off her stool she nearly dumped herself on the floor.

Strong hands caught and lifted her. "How about if I walk you to the elevator? Just to make sure you get through the lobby all right."

"I'm not drunk," she insisted. "Just a little...weak in the knees." And she wanted him to keep those hands on her, to touch her, to bring back that electric spark.

The ghost of a smile whispered over his mouth again. "Understandable if you've had a bad day. Come on. Let me prove that chivalry isn't dead."

He took her arm and led her out of the bar, his impressive height making her feel secure for some reason. They walked to the elevator with his arm around her, steadying her. Taylor leaned in to him and caught his scent, spice mixed with a maleness that somehow reminded her of jungles. Or what she thought jungles would smell like. *Panther.* She felt the taut muscles of his body through their clothing and wondered what he'd be like naked.

As fast as the thought hit her, she tried to brush it away. Taylor Scott didn't entertain images of naked men. She even had sex with all the lights out.

If you can call the few fumbling and embarrassing attempts sex.

"What floor?"

"Hmm?" She raised heavy-lidded eyes to him.

"Floor. Where your room is. I want to make sure you get inside okay."

"Five. I'm on the fifth floor." His nearness overwhelmed her, the masculine heat of his body wrapping around her like a cloak. He was everything she'd denied herself all her life. Everything she'd been taught to avoid. Protect herself from. Now that life was in shreds and she wanted what she'd missed. Wanted him.

And why not? I'll never see him again. One night. What could it possibly hurt?

On the walk to her room, he held her braced against him. At the door, she opened her purse to take out her key card and fumbled trying to slot it in the lock.

"Here. Let me." He removed it deftly from her fingers, swiped it and opened the door. Inside, he flicked the light switch and a lamp came on. "Well, you got to your room safely. I think you can take it from here."

Taylor drew in a breath and for the space of a heartbeat tried to reach for all the inhibitions the whiskey had let loose. In thirty years, she had never done one impulsive thing. Did that make her disciplined or repressed? And if she gave in now, who was there left to give a damn, anyway? Her body was shimmering with unfamiliar sensations and a need she could barely identify was clawing its way up from her core.

Tomorrow, she'd be gone, back to whatever waited for her now in her fractured life. Tonight, she wanted something for herself. Something dangerous, something wicked.

The man stood there, looking down at her, assessing her as if trying to reassure himself that it was safe to leave her. With something close to desperation, she grabbed the collar of his suit jacket and pulled him toward her.

One minute, she glimpsed his startled face. The next, she was pressing her mouth to his and wishing he would open it so she could drown herself inside.

Chapter Two

His body tensed and rippled beneath her touch, and she clutched harder at the fabric of his jacket to keep him from pulling back. She wanted this man in ways she'd never wanted anyone else. Ways that startled her as her body reacted in an unfamiliar manner. She almost changed her mind, frightened at the explosion of desire streaking through her, but determination overrode trepidation. For all the things she'd lost and the ones she'd never had, she deserved this. She pressed her tongue hard against his mouth and, whether from shock or desire, he opened and she tasted him. Whiskey and coffee and mint combined to produce a heady flavor that tantalized her senses. She sucked at his tongue, drawing him into her mouth in a kiss more sensuous than she'd ever permitted herself. Or ever wanted.

He gripped her upper arms tightly as if to push her away, but she had a death hold on his lapels. She was so damned tired of being straitlaced and obedient. The past week had stripped away all the steel bands restricting her life, with today finishing the job. All that obedience had been for nothing. Now, she wanted *wild*, a night that would help her blot out all the dark feelings rampaging through her.

With a groan, the man pulled her closer. He swept his tongue into her mouth, responding to her, leaving no inch of the dark wetness untouched. The slight roughness of it scraped across her sensitive tissues, calling each hidden nerve into play. He pressed his lips hard against hers, bearing down on them, devouring them, as he dug his fingers into her shoulders.

They stood suspended in the darkness, sensations from the kiss rocketing through her and drawing forth reactions from parts of her body long dormant. Her nipples tingled and wetness seeped between her thighs. She would have given anything to stay that way forever, balanced on a precipice.

He was the first to break away, looking down at her with glittering eyes. "I think you've had far too much to drink."

Taylor was trying to find her breath, but all the air seemed to have been sucked out of her lungs. The pulse that beat between her legs was echoing through her core. She knew about 'getting hot' and 'getting wet', but this was the first time a man had made her feel it. The drinks had nothing to do with what was happening to her. It was the man, a powerful jungle animal who called to the hidden wildness within her.

"This is my idea, not the whiskey." She pulled in another breath and tried to drag his face down to hers again.

He tightened his hands on her shoulders, a strangled sound erupting from his throat. "I'm a stranger. You can't just pick me up and take me to your room like this. Don't you know this kind of stuff isn't safe?"

"I don't think you'll harm me," she whispered. "I don't know why, but I trust you."

And wasn't that absurd, when she'd hardly trusted anyone all her life? Yet something in him gave her a sense of security, certainly unusual when locked in the darkness with a caged panther. "Please don't pull away." With slightly trembling fingers, she shifted his tie out of the way and unbuttoned his shirt. She pressed her body against him, rubbing herself against the hard erection that the layers of clothing between them couldn't hide.

"This is insanity." His voice was hard and edgy, his grip on her tightening almost to the point of pain. "There are things about me you don't know."

Taylor licked the bare skin of his chest that she'd exposed and slid her hands inside his shirt. The warmth of his body almost burned her. Beneath the hot male skin, he was harder than steel, with thick, ropelike muscles. She danced the tip of her tongue over his chest and smiled at the hitch in his breathing.

She looked up at him, struggling to bring out words. "Are you a wanted criminal? Do you have a deadly disease? No? Then I don't care about anything else." Her voice dropped to a whisper. "I want this. I want you."

"Listen, you don't know… God damn it, I should have my head examined. I can't do this."

"Why?" She yanked on his tie. "Am I so repulsive?" She dropped her hands and turned away, consumed by equal parts desire and shame. Of course. He was used to women with long graceful legs and ample breasts, tiny hips and small asses. His kind only got turned on by model-thin women. "That's it, isn't it? I'll bet all your women are tall blondes in size two dresses."

"That's not true. Not true at all." He reached for her and turned her to face him. "This is just…" His throat muscles worked reflexively as he swallowed. "I have to get out of here."

She saw the heat in his eyes, felt the desire flowing from his hands into her body and the whiskey empowered her. "But you don't really want to, do you? Or you'd be out that door already." She reached out and pressed her hand against his crotch, a very bold move for her. She cupped the hard, impressive bulge through the fabric of his pants and squeezed. "See? You want me, too. This tells me."

My God, am I doing this?

He sucked in his breath. For a long moment, they stood there, her hand on his crotch as she waited for whatever war he was fighting with himself to resolve itself. Then, as if he'd come to some momentous decision, he pushed her hands away and stripped off his jacket, shirt and tie. "I'll be damned to hell for this."

All the saliva in her mouth dried up at the broad expanse of chest and the soft curls that spread across it and arrowed down to his groin. She stood, waiting for him to remove the rest of his clothing and wondering what to do next.

He came back to her and brushed his lips across her forehead. "You don't look like this is a familiar dance. Last chance to change your mind. Otherwise, I'll lead."

"I'm not changing my mind." *I want this. I need it. Don't turn away from me.*

"I should be shot." His voice sounded strained. "I'm not…"

Impatient at his reluctance, she gripped the edges of her jacket and blouse and ripped them open, sending buttons popping onto the floor. Next came the skirt, pooling at her feet. She stepped out of it and kicked it away, along with her shoes. She was glad she hadn't worn pantyhose. Her grandmother would have been scandalized, which was the very reason why she'd done it.

He gave a sharp intake of breath as his gaze dropped to her breasts and her nipples hardened into tight points.

He ran a finger across the upper slope of her breasts, back and forth as if memorizing the texture of her skin. When he reached around behind her and unclasped the bit of lace and silk, her breasts sprang free and he cupped them in his hands.

"You have unbelievable breasts." His voice was awed. "Magnificent." He bent his head and drew one peak into his mouth, pulling on it, bathing it with wet heat.

Heat streaked directly from his lips to her womb. When he bit down gently on her nipple then ran his tongue over it, she thought she would faint from the pleasure. Just that light grazing of his teeth and the pull of his mouth were enough to make her legs wobble.

He gave a soft laugh and swept her up in his arms. "I think you'd do much better lying down, don't you?"

He stripped back the covers on the bed and laid her on the coolness of the sheet. His hand was warm on her abdomen as he lightly stroked it before moving downward with a gentle glide. The touch of each finger was like a fiery kiss on her skin. Taylor shivered both in anticipation and fear of the unknown. No man had ever looked at her with such a devouring gaze. When he slid his hand inside her panties and teased at her curls with his fingers, the throbbing deep inside her vaginal walls increased in tempo.

She had barely a second for her insecure self to wonder if he found the touch of her pleasing and her curls soft and appealing to him. Then the panties were gone and she was stripped naked.

When she reached to snap off the bedside lamp, he shook his head and closed his fingers around her hand. He spoke in a voice heavy with desire. "I'm not doing this in the dark. I want to see what every inch of you looks like."

She flinched under his gaze, turning her head away from the brightness. No one had ever seen her completely naked except doctors. Her tiny roster of lovers had been more than willing to perform in complete darkness. Her choice, but no one had objected. The darkness had given her a sense of refuge, hiding her flaws and protecting her from the disappointment she'd been sure she'd see in the eyes of her partner. And that was all they'd been — partners. Not lovers. Lovers caressed and worshiped and adored. Her fumbling experimentation had never included that.

But he smoothed his hands down her arms and hips as if stroking fine silk and her skin tingled under the intensity of his gaze, the sweep of his eyes touching her like a caress. There was no hint of the expected disappointment, no indication that he found her body wanting in any way. That in itself eased the painful band around her heart. Without taking his gaze from her, he rid himself of shoes and socks, trousers and boxers. When his cock sprang free, the sight of it made saliva pool in her mouth. It was enormous, leaping proudly erect from the dark hair curled at its base. Below it, his heavy testicles rested against his thighs. She swallowed, wondering if she could fit all that inside her.

As if he read her mind, he said, "Don't worry. You'll be fine. I promise I won't hurt you."

Fine. What a mild word to describe what she wanted to feel.

She devoured his naked body with her eyes. He was a magnificent animal, her panther. The bedside lamp reflected on the rippling muscles and sun-bronzed skin of his sculpted body. *Warrior.* The stalker, not the prey. He would devour and the prey would relish the devouring. She could barely breathe at the thought of being captured by him.

He watched her face intently as he kneeled on the mattress at her feet. Placing both hands on her legs, he bent them up and spread them apart, fully exposing her. Her breath caught as he looked at every inch of her. No one, none of the fumbling men she'd had such unfulfilling sex with, had exposed her so shamelessly or looked at her with such hunger. Or wanted to.

Her first instinct was to cover herself, frightened of the gaze that seemed to see inside her. But the heat in his eyes blew that away and suddenly she wanted more. To expose more. Feel more. With her eyes fastened on him, she spread her legs wider to offer him even greater access, shocked at the ripple of pleasure it gave her.

"You like that, do you? I wonder what else is under that proper exterior of yours." His face gave nothing away but his eyes flashed and he stroked the lips of her sex, probing gently. When he spoke, his voice was almost reverent. "God, your cunt is beautiful."

She jerked slightly at his words and he gave a soft laugh.

"Not used to people telling you it's beautiful? Or is it calling it a cunt that puts that startled look in your eyes? Does it offend your sensitive ears? Get used to it. Whatever polite sex you've had until now is out of the window. Tonight, I'm going to look at every inch of your cunt" — he stressed the word — "your pussy. I'm going to put my mouth on you and suck you then plunge my fingers inside you. When you're good and ready then I'm going to drive my cock into you and fuck you until you don't even know who you are." He bent toward her. "Can you take that, little girl?"

His voice was hard with an indefinable underlying edge. Was something wrong? Had she already displeased him in some way? She was caught in a mixture of inexperience and uncontained need, with no idea how to deal with such a complex man. What did he want her to say?

"Can you?" he repeated, his head close to hers, eyes demanding an answer from her.

"Yes," she hissed at last, pushing herself toward him. Rather than frightening her, his words aroused her to an unbelievable state. Her body was suddenly not her own but an instrument that his words were tuning for the main performance. "And I'm not a little girl. Far from it."

He reached out a thumb and forefinger and gave a light pinch to her clit. "We'll find out, won't we, little girl? You wanted to unleash the panther. This is what you get."

"Taylor." She was struggling to hold on to the threads of her mind which was rapidly sinking into a haze.

"What?" He frowned at her.

"My name is Taylor. Call me Taylor, not 'little girl'."

"All right, *Taylor*." He stressed the name, the tone slightly mocking. "Time to feel the panther's bite."

Her body quivered in anticipation of what his words promised.

He moved up on the bed and cradled her breasts in his palms, rubbing his thumbs and forefingers over her nipples. When he tugged and pinched them, the sharp bite of pain sent arrows of heat straight to her womb. But the heat of his mouth soothed them as he licked slowly. With a slow movement, he rubbed the pads of his fingers back and forth over the heated points until Taylor thought she would come just from his attention to her breasts.

She shifted beneath him, wishing he'd stroke her between her legs again, wanting to feel his hand there touching her, probing, wringing every drop of liquid from her. This was every fantasy she'd ever suppressed coming true with the kind of man she'd dreamed of but who was always far beyond her reach. His hands on her were magical, his tongue hot wherever it touched her. Her body was so aroused she couldn't hold herself still. She shifted her hips and thrust them at him. Whatever was driving him didn't matter, only that he brought her the pleasure promised with every touch of his hands.

"Touch me like you did before," she pleaded, her voice coming from a faraway place. "With your fingers. Please."

"Don't rush me." He spoke the words directly against her lips, his voice liquid in her mouth. "I plan to take my time with this. A gourmet feast shouldn't be hurried. It should be savored and enjoyed slowly, letting the flavors invade your body."

When he touched his mouth to hers again, his tongue stroking inside, heat consumed her, leaving no space bare. This was beyond anything she'd ever experienced, even anything she'd dreamed of. If she had one rational thought left, the blaze consumed it.

Taylor reached up to untie his badge of civilization, the leather thong that held his hair gathered neatly at his nape, and his hair fell loose and thick around his shoulders. She ran her fingers through it, feeling the silken texture, and the strands fell easily away from her touch. She moved against him, pressing her body upward against the heat and hardness of his. He made her aware of him in a way she'd never been aware of another man, his powerful strength wrapping around her.

"Easy, Taylor." With his big hand, he cradled her hip, stilling her, his voice a low crooning sound. "We don't want to miss all the good parts."

He kissed her jawline, under her ear, down the column of her neck, painting her skin with his tongue. He grazed his teeth along the column of her neck and bit gently at the place where her neck and shoulder joined. Then, in the next moment, he soothed the bite with a tender flick of his tongue.

She shivered and the heavy beat inside her core intensified.

When he returned to her breasts, he paused to suck each one again, drawing little whimpers from her. Her chest felt swollen and tight and she was sure her nipples would burst. His five o'clock shadow rasped against the tenderness of her skin, but then the silkiness of his hair flowed over her. When she was sure she would come if he kept it up one more minute, he moved his head and pressed his open mouth on the softness of her belly. The sensation made the muscles in her sheath contract and moisture pour out of her, drenching the curls covering the opening of her sex. God, she wanted him there. Touching her there.

With attention to detail that could only be called reverent, he kissed his way down the length of her body, licking every inch of skin he moved his mouth over. At last, he kneeled and pulled her toward him with her legs draped over his thighs. With his thumbs, he pressed apart her labia, staring intently at her open cunt. Without warning, he leaned down and ran his tongue along her seam, then flicked it across her swollen nub. Her body jerked and she nearly came off the bed. She would have, except for his pressure on her inner thighs.

"Delicious. I knew you'd taste this delicious."

He licked her again and when at last he'd tasted his fill, he parted her lips, slid a long, lean finger inside her and stroked it back and forth.

Her inner muscle clenched at once. Gripping the sheet with her fists, she pushed against his hand, urging him to explore her, wanting to feel him higher, deeper. God, just the simple exploration of her vagina and she was ready to turn herself inside out for him. She wanted to draw him into the deepest recesses of her body. When he slipped a second finger in beside the first, tremors rippled through her.

"Tight and wet. You might squeeze my cock to death. I don't know what to do first with such a banquet spread before me. But I think I'm going to finger-fuck you, because

I want to watch that gorgeous cunt when you come. The first time."

"Mmm," was all she managed as he slid his fingers inside her hot, waiting flesh.

He leaned toward her, his face suffused with lust. "Better than pleasuring yourself, isn't it, little girl? Better than your vibrator." When she didn't answer, surprise flashed across his face, but he wiped it away almost at once. His eyes narrowed. "You've never used a vibrator, have you? Never touched yourself or used your hand to give yourself release?"

She lowered her eyelids as she tried to hide her embarrassment. She couldn't tell him that in the house where she'd grown up, everything was forbidden and nothing was private. There was no place she could have hidden to pleasure herself or hide the toys she'd need. It was nothing short of amazing that she'd managed even the unsatisfying, awkward forays into sex that she'd accomplished without her grandparents seeing the telltale knowledge in her eyes or emblazoned somehow on her face.

Now, she wanted it all. Everything. Fate had dropped this man into her lap. After tonight, she'd never see him again, so she was free to indulge in whatever fantasy played out. She could act with as much abandon as she wanted and never fear censure or gossip.

When he rose suddenly and left her body, the absence of his touch disturbed her. Was he leaving? *Now? Surely not.* "What's wrong? Where are you going?"

"Nothing's wrong. I just saw something here I want." He picked up the hand mirror she'd placed on the dresser then he was back, her legs draped wide again over his powerful thighs. He propped the mirror against his stomach so it was facing Taylor. "I want you to watch me, little girl. See what your gorgeous cunt looks like with my fingers sliding in and out." His voiced thickened. "I'll bet you've never even looked at yourself in a mirror, have you? I want you to see what you've been missing all these years. What it looks like to have a man's hand stretching these tight little muscles and spreading your juices on that soft flesh. Watch yourself as I pleasure you, see your body respond to me."

"I've never…"

"No, I'm sure you haven't." His voice was heavy with lust. "But, tonight, you will."

Her skin grew hotter as her gaze automatically dropped to the mirror and she watched him open her pussy and slide two fingers inside. Dark tendrils of need coiled low in her stomach and reached out their tentacles to every part of her body. Unfamiliar sensations bombarded her, awakening her dormant sexuality.

"Do you want to know what you feel like, little girl?" His voice was thick with desire. "Wet satin. You are so smooth inside and sopping wet. Slick. But tight. Very tight. Let's see just how tight you are." He slid a third finger in and flexed them together to stretch her.

Taylor couldn't take her eyes off the mirror, off his fingers sliding in and out of her, off the slickness that told her just how drenched she was. She was fascinated by the sight of those strong male fingers stroking in and out of her vagina, the knuckles brushing against the curls of her sex which were damp with her moisture. Automatically, she spread her legs wider and braced herself on her elbows to get an unobstructed view of the hand mirror.

As she watched the smooth movement — in, out, in, out — the quivering in her sheath became faster and harder and echoed back into her body.

"Do you like that, little girl?" His voice had just the slightest tremor in it. "Does that excite you?"

She couldn't speak, so caught up in the erotic sight before her eyes that speech was impossible. But when his other hand moved to her swollen nub and massaged it, she wanted to close her eyes and go with the feeling.

"Eyes open, little girl," he commanded in a soft voice. "Eyes wide open. Put your feet on my thighs and bend your knees." He nodded when she complied. "That's right."

Now she saw everything, her entire sex, the core of her, where his fingers kept up their hypnotic motion while massaging her clit at the same time.

"*God.*" The word escaped her lips.

His eyes flashed at her. "Turns you on, doesn't it? I thought it would."

Taylor only vaguely heard him now, even though he never stopped talking to her as he turned her clit into a throbbing nub of tissue and her sheath greedy. Wanting more, needing more, she moved her hands to the insides of her thighs, holding her legs apart so her view of the mirror was unobstructed.

Every sensation in her body became magnified, consuming her until nothing existed except the building of an intense orgasm. She tried to pull back from it, terrified of a place she'd never been before but needing to go there. Her body welcomed it while her mind did battle with it. A fine sheen of sweat covered her and she labored for each breath.

"Don't fight it." His voice was dark and seductive. "Go with it. Just let it come."

Without warning the orgasm broke over her, a violent lifting and tossing, waves of sensation buffeting her body, hurling her about and pounding at her with frightening intensity. Spasms shook her beyond her control. Her blood was hot. No — cold. No — hot.

He moved one hand to press down on her abdomen and hold her in place as her body gave itself over to the orgasm. "Watch," he commanded. "Don't take your eyes off it."

Taylor wanted to throw her head back and scream with the ecstasy of it, but he forced her to watch the mirror. She saw the walls of her pussy grip his fingers, pulse against them and liquid pour from her into his hand. His eyes focused on her face, watching, maybe gauging the strength of her spasms. At the peak of them, he pushed harder inside her and his fingers scraped the sensitive spot that sent her tumbling again, a toy in the wind that was consuming her.

He kept his fingers inside her sheath, stroking the still

quivering flesh until the last aftershock had died away. When he removed them, he brought them up to his mouth and carefully licked each one. His dark eyes glittered. "Sweet cream, little girl. Very sweet."

Moving the mirror out of the way, he also shifted until he was lying beside her. He pulled her against his body, her own still shivering from her climax. He rubbed her back, his big hands gentling her and holding her as her breathing returned to some semblance of normal.

This had to have been the most insane thing he'd ever done. *What in the hell am I doing here?* He had no business in this hotel room with this particular woman. Shooting would be too good for him.

He wasn't a man who let his cock lead him around. Far from it. And passion was a forbidden emotion in his life. The past had taught him what a trap that could be. He had an itch and he scratched it. When he'd satisfied his sexual needs, he was always up front with the women he took to bed. Expect nothing, he told them. He had nothing to give.

Yet here he was, unable to pull himself away from this woman who made him feel things long dead and buried. A woman he had no business being with in the first place.

Considering her age, she was surprisingly untutored, but fire bloomed beneath the alabaster skin and flared in her emerald-green eyes. Her lack of experience was as much of a turn-on as the woman herself. With each response he drew from her, his own body reacted.

His eyes devoured her nudity, imprinting the image of her on his mind. She was a miniature Rubens come to life, all lush curves and voluptuous flesh. Breasts that fit nicely into the palms of his hands. Hips and thighs a man could feast on. Her skin so soft and satiny that touching it made his blood heat and his cock throb.

She didn't trim or wax her pubic hair and he wondered what that tempting cunt would look like totally naked. His cock bobbed as visions of the sight shot through his brain.

Unreasonable anger clawed at him, resentment at the woman for making him feel things when he wanted this to be nothing more than an act of physical satisfaction. Bitterness that he couldn't turn away from her, drawn by the tug and pull of an invisible thread she unknowingly exerted on him. He knew that anger had made him behave appallingly, but he couldn't seem to do anything else.

If only he'd had the strength to walk away before things had gotten this far. But he hadn't had it then, nor did he have it now. Instead, he'd sought to make her despise him by using crude words and forcing her into things like the mirror trick. His sexual tastes and habits were far beyond anything Taylor Scott had ever experienced. Of that he was sure. The women he took to bed knew what he was about and what he expected. They weren't neophytes who could be frightened away.

And she would be if this ever went anywhere, if he let things get out of hand again. Taylor Scott was not into the type of sexual games he was. Nor was she the type of woman a man took to bed for a quick fuck. He knew the unlocking of her sexuality tonight had been a reaction to the chaos in her life. Certainly, no one knew it better than he did. She deserved someone who would seduce her and cajole her, unwrapping each layer with care and attention. He was bombarding her, assaulting her senses to drive her away.

He had his reasons. This woman could reach beneath the surface if he let her and that was not an acceptable option. He had to put emotional space between them. Get his famous control back. When tonight was over, this needed to take up residence in the back of his mind, not tempt him to find her again, strip off her clothes and fuck her senseless.

Or admit the duplicity that he was hiding from her, a truth sure to provide even more fuel for her anger.

Chapter Three

Taylor let the warmth of the big body next to hers soothe her as her pulse rate slowed and regained a sense of normality. She lifted a hand to his chest and ran her fingers through the thick pelt of fur covering the hard muscle. When she grazed his flat nipples, they hardened and she looked up at him, startled.

"You are a novice, aren't you?" He shook his head. "Yes, men's nipples are just as sensitive as a woman's. Get just as aroused. And stimulate other areas of the body, too."

His fully aroused cock pressed against her and without thinking she clasped her fingers around it. The shaft was rock hard, a center of steel with soft skin cradling it. She felt the veins and ridges, brushing her thumb over the wide head to capture the moisture sitting there. Should she tell him she'd never done this before, either? Except for one idiot who'd forced her to jack him off and wouldn't release his grip on her until she did.

This is so different that there's no comparison.

She pushed away from him, sat up and took the heated shaft in both hands. Cradling it, she stared at it in curiosity. His body next to hers was rigid, waiting. She still thought his erection enormous and doubted his ability to get it all into her body, but she reveled in the thought. Heavy veins ran along the sides and the head was wide, a dark purple. A tiny bead of liquid dotted the slit. She swiped a fingertip across it and licked it slowly. It tasted salty with a hint of sweet.

Responding to some primal urge, she bent forward and ran her tongue across the head, touching the tip to the tiny opening.

"Jesus, Taylor." He grabbed her head and pulled her back. "I'd love to come in your mouth but not before I fuck your cunt."

His use of words that had tiptoed around the periphery of her vocabulary until now made the beast within her body stir to life again. He pulled her up to lie on top of him and cradled her face in his hands.

"Long before we get to that, I'm going to fuck you with my mouth and have my fill of tasting the delicious treat you are. I'm going to slide my cock into your very tight cunt and make you come your brains out." He touched one cheek of her buttocks, sliding his fingertips into the cleft and tracing the line. When he touched the tightness of her anus, she jumped. He laughed, a guttural sound. "I'll bet nobody's ever touched you here, have they? You don't know how I'd love to fuck that virgin ass."

Every muscle in her body clenched as a dark thrill ran through her.

Suddenly he rolled so she was on her back, looking up at him.

"You have no idea the things I want to do to you." He paused. "Taylor." He stressed her name. "Too bad we only have tonight."

Yes. Too bad.

He played her body like a violin, doing things she'd never dreamed of. Now, he had her legs up over his shoulders, their width spreading her thighs apart, and his mouth was driving her crazy. He held her open with his thumbs while he used his tongue to taste her in strokes so light she wanted to scream. She tried to thrust her hips at him, but he held her firmly in his grasp.

"I told you." He looked up at her, the moisture from her cunt gleaming on his lips. "I'm not rushing anything."

He bent his head again and resumed licking just the outer lips, holding her wide open to his exploration.

"Please," she begged, her body in a suspended state of

arousal that screamed for release.

He laughed, a low rough sound. "Pick up that mirror."

"What? Mirror?" Her brain was starting to short out on her again.

"The mirror. It's right by your hand. Pick it up. I want you to watch this again. I want you to see what I see when I open you up like a flower."

Feeling powerless to deny him anything, she lifted the mirror and held it out away from her body. He maneuvered her hand under one thigh so she saw every inch of her pussy. She was fascinated, unable to stop looking. He had her totally exposed, her lips drawn wide, the darkened pink tissues pulsing lightly from his stimulation.

"See how responsive you are?" He moved one hand to pinch the tip of her clit and drag it forward.

At once, she saw more fluid wetting her tissue and her throbbing vaginal walls. With her juices coating one finger, he flicked it back and forth across the tip of her swollen nub. A coil of desperate need tightened inside her with every movement of his hand. Watching him do this to her only increased her arousal.

He took the mirror from her and tossed it to the side. "When you go home, wherever home is, I want you to lie in bed at night and remember this. Take this mirror, prop it between your legs and finger yourself. Pretend it's my hand. If we ever meet again, I want you to have that image in your mind."

He bent to his task again, licking her open tissues before sliding his tongue into her sheath and moving it in and out in a steady motion. He lapped at her entire length then took her clit between his teeth and bit down gently.

The intensity built inside her, low in her stomach, deep inside her cunt. But the moment she moved, he drew back, pausing until she wanted to scream. He watched her as if waiting for some sign then he'd begin again.

She tried to hold his head to her, threading her fingers through the black silk that was his hair, but he was too strong for her — too determined. When she thought she'd surely lose her mind, he slipped two fingers inside her, soaking them in her copious liquids.

"Do you want to come, little girl?" His voice was thick with lust, his eyes burning into her like twin lasers. "Do you want me to take you over that edge?"

"Yes, yes, yes," she chanted, trying to urge him with her hips.

She felt his tongue inside her again, and one hand pinching and tugging on her clit. Without warning, he pushed one of his fluid-covered fingers deep into her ass. She screamed and bucked and came with such intensity she thought her bones would break. As he fucked her with his tongue, he moved his finger in and out of her ass in the same rhythm. The dual assault drove her higher and higher until she was sure she couldn't stand it anymore.

He gave her no relief, holding her with her legs hiked high on his shoulders, his tongue and fingers relentless. At last, at long last, as the quivers slowly subsided, he reached for something on the nightstand and she saw him roll a condom onto his huge erection.

God, is he going to do it now?

She was so exhausted she didn't know how she'd handle it.

But then he was there, the head of his cock right at her entrance, right at the tight little opening. He still held her legs over his shoulders, giving him greater access. She curled her hands into fists as he pushed into her slowly, withdrawing then pushing again. In. Out. In. Out. Her body couldn't stretch, she wanted to tell him. And she could hardly breathe, she felt so full.

When she opened her eyes, he was watching her, that same hot glitter burning in the black irises.

"I can't," she tried to say.

"Yes, you can. Take a deep breath, then let it out."

She did as he said and, on the exhalation, he pushed hard once more and he was in her to the hilt. *God!* The feel of him was unbelievable.

"Okay?" he asked, watching her closely.

She nodded, unable to properly form words.

"You have no idea how I'd love to see my cock in your mouth, feel your tongue on it, your lips around me. But I'm too far gone, so I guess this will have to be one of my fantasies. But ramming your cunt will be the sweetest ecstasy, little girl." He shook his head as she opened her mouth. "Taylor. I'm going to fuck you beyond anything you thought possible."

His pinned her with his gaze as he began the slow dance, the steady rhythm in and out, back and forth, the scrape of his cock against the walls of her cunt so erotic she thought she'd come just from that sensation alone. She locked her ankles behind his neck to balance herself then she couldn't think at all. Her world consisted of his shaft as he stroked her in and out, the soft slap of his balls against her ass a counterpoint.

On and on he went, never varying the rhythm. In and out. Back and forth. The sweat on his body was wet beneath the skin of her calves, the muscles in his arms taut as he held himself in place.

"Take your nipples," he gasped. "Pinch them for me."

Desperately wanting him to take her over the edge, she rubbed and pinched them. The sensation was so intense she rubbed and pinched harder, silently urging him to go faster.

"Tell me, Taylor. Let me hear you say it."

Say what? What does he want?

His voice was barely audible to her. She couldn't hear, couldn't think, could just feel that huge cock driving into her, pushing her higher and higher, until she could only concentrate on the need deep in her cunt.

"Tell me to fuck you," he ground out between clenched teeth.

Yes. Anything. Just do it.

"Fuck me," she yelled.

"Now, Taylor. Come now." He pushed hard one last time and, as he began his release, it triggered her own. The orgasm took her with such force she didn't think she'd survive. She throbbed and convulsed and impaled herself on him, using her body to demand he stay in place, deep inside her.

As the last shudder died away and he gently lowered her legs to the bed, she sank into a sleep deeper than anything she'd ever known.

* * * *

He kept all the windows in the car open as he drove away from San Antonio. His intention had been to return to the ranch tonight, but he was sure the man waiting for him would be able to read his sins written across his face.

Fuck!

He'd made a fine mess of everything.

Following her cab to the hotel had been easy. When he'd seen her go into the bar, he'd sensed an ideal opportunity to check her out. Get a reading on her for the old man. Truth be told, he'd figured to find a tramp. Or a conniver looking to score big. Or just a plain, ordinary scam artist who'd staked out the biggest mark of all.

But Taylor Scott had been none of those things. What she'd turned out to be was someone he'd been completely unable to walk away from. It shocked him that he'd been so instantly hard just sitting next to her at the bar. Walking her to her room had been the biggest mistake, a chivalrous impulse that he'd regretted as soon as the words had left his mouth. The second she'd touched him, he'd been undone.

He'd certainly had plenty of women. Maybe more than his share. But they'd been nameless and faceless, a narcotic to blot out the pain that lived in his soul. They'd known the score with him and had willingly offered themselves up to the man whose sexual appetites were legendary.

Taylor was unlike any of them, with a quality to her that

was both earthy and sweet, and the moment she'd pressed her lips to his in that bold kiss, something had slammed into him. A lightning strike would have had less effect on him. The sexual heat was only a part of it. He felt as if he'd been waiting forever for her and that was what scared him.

He hadn't been able to get enough of touching her. Tasting her. Burying himself deep inside her. He couldn't erase the memory of her soft lips on his mouth, on his hot erection, or the feel of her tight, wet sheath clenched around him. She was in his blood, infused in him like a drug. Even now his head was still back in that hotel room and his fully aroused cock wished that it was.

The touch of her hands on his skin had been as soft as kiss of a butterfly, the feel of her cunt around his cock a tight, wet fist drawing every drop from him. He could still feel the slap of his testicles against the firmness of her ass as he drove into her. Feel her satin-smooth skin and her plump nipples, just the right size for his mouth. Inhale the lingering scent of her essence, sweeter than the finest pastry. Her scent was embedded in his nostrils and the feeling of her hair and was skin branded into his hands. If he closed his eyes, the vision of her naked, hair tumbled around her like a hoyden, eyes blazing, made him instantly hard.

But it wasn't just her body that had captured him. He'd looked into those vivid green eyes and felt himself drowning. Anguish had churned inside her and he had wanted to take away her pain. Yet he'd sensed that playing the role of protector with her would be the wrong thing to do. No, this was a woman filled with grit and determination. She might have held it back all her life, but the tiger hiding inside her was about to roar into existence.

There were so many reasons why this whole night had been a bad idea. Yet if he had the choice to make again, he knew he'd make the same one. He wanted to possess this woman almost more than anything in the world, and that was the worst idea of all. Women like her had relationships and men like him didn't. Certainly not with anyone like

Taylor Scott. Why couldn't he walk away from her the way he'd turned from every other woman in the past ten years? He knew as certainly as he breathed air that if he saw her again he'd be stripping her naked and fucking her at the first opportunity.

He was ruthless about keeping a tight rein on his sexual impulses. The women who'd shared his bed had been awed at his ability to give them hours of pleasure before taking his own. He'd never told them that his mental detachment allowed him to control his body and therefore the pace and variety of the evening's activity.

No one had reached deep inside him where he kept the panther caged, like Taylor had in one night. Not even his famously ruthless personal discipline could purge her from his system. How in hell had he let one tiny female blow it all apart in the blink of an eye?

He didn't know if the anger festering inside him was at her or himself. He'd thought to drive her away, make her hate him with the rawness of the sex, his crude behavior. Anything to kill the feeling growing within him. All he'd done was drive both of them to a greater pitch of arousal. And why had he told her over and over to pleasure herself at home and think of him while she did it? Remember his touch and feel?

Jesus!

He was damn glad she was leaving town. If he saw her again, every good intention, every admonition to himself would shatter like thin glass. Tomorrow he'd make his report, reel in the well-defined structure of his life and pray to the heavens that the circumstances would change and he never had to see her again.

* * * *

The first thing Taylor realized when she opened her eyes was that every muscle in her body ached. Inside and out. The second was that she had the mother of all headaches.

The room was still dark, the heavy drapes pulled tightly across the windows. She slid her eyes to the right where the radio alarm clock sat, and blinked at the numerals.

Twelve o'clock?

Noon?

Not possible.

She sat up, then decided that wasn't such a good idea. Her body felt as if a truck had rolled over it, then backed up and done it again. And an entire percussion section was practicing in her head. The room reeked of sex, its aroma clinging to her skin and the sheets and hanging thick in the air. As she fell back onto the pillows, last night came rolling back to her like a frightening dream.

God, Taylor. What have I done?

She covered her face with her hands as images flooded her brain. The drinks in the bar, the sharp bite of the alcohol and its opiate qualities dulling her pain. The man — the predator — drawing responses from her she didn't even know she had. And the words she'd cried out. Was that woman really her? In her brain, her voice was still screaming, *'Fuck me,'* and she wondered now that the entire security forces in the hotel hadn't descended on them.

The memory of the things she'd done and let him do to and with her was enough to send a hot flush creeping over from her toes to the tip of her head. Surely that hadn't been her. Someone else had taken over her mind. Her body. God! She'd let... She'd done... Spotting the mirror on the nightstand, she remembered how he'd used her, remembered watching his fingers slide in and out of her and her cunt convulsing around them. *Well, if that doesn't kill the last vestiges of 'proper upbringing', nothing will.*

It was the culmination of everything — that was her only excuse. The shock of the letter, then yesterday's insulting episode. All of it. Her life had been turned upside down and she needed to lash out in some way. But lordy, lordy, not that way.

Oh no? Admit it. I wanted it more than I wanted to breathe.

She remembered the feel of his body against hers and his mouth on her everywhere. Still felt him squeezing her breasts with his hands. Reaching inside her with those long, slender fingers to the spot that made rockets go off. His teeth nipping at her nipples, her clit. His hands bringing her to one shattering climax after another. And his fingers in her ass, creating a dark hunger she never knew existed within her.

If they could see me now. All those people who knew the uptight, buttoned-down Taylor Scott. The one who never, ever colored outside the lines, who walked around as if she had a stick up her ass. She'd managed to take the stick out of her ass, all right, and replace it with something else. Every muscle in her body clenched at the memory of what The Man had made her feel when he'd fucked her ass with his finger.

Yes, Taylor, say it. Just like that. Fucked my ass.

The worst of it? She'd wanted more. How insane was that?

Is this who I really am? Is this the person who's been inside the tightly wound, impenetrable outer shell all these years, released only with the knowledge of betrayal?

Strangely enough the wild, uninhibited sex had been a tranquilizer, soothing the edges of her life that had been ripped open and left raw and bleeding. He hadn't been a gentle lover, this stranger with the bottomless black eyes, the body and air of a warrior and the sure knowledge to take her to places she'd never thought to go. He'd been rough with her, deliberately crude, unwilling to give anything resembling tenderness or affection.

But that was good. Last night, she hadn't wanted gentle. She'd wanted hard and crude and that was what she'd gotten. A one-night stand with a stranger she'd never see again, where all the boundaries had been cast aside.

She was puzzled by his anger underlying everything, too strong to be missed. She'd sensed it everywhere — toward her, toward himself, maybe toward his inability or unwillingness to turn and walk away from her room. Away from her. As if he was punishing her. Lust had rolled from him in waves even as rage had clawed beneath that granite mask. But why? What was really going on with him? What was he really so furious about?

It didn't make sense. They were total strangers. What difference could the one night possibly make to him? She was sure he did that all the time, a man with his appetites.

Not that it mattered. She'd never see him again. And thank God for that. A man like him would dominate her life and she'd already had more than her fill of that. To learn that all that control her family had exerted had been to perpetuate a viciously contrived lie had left her questioning the blind obedience with which she'd accepted it. For thirty years rebellion hadn't even tempted her. Now it came welling up out of her like a newly tapped spring. She wasn't about to hand over that control to someone else. Not now. Especially to a stranger.

Get it together, Taylor.

She forced her eyes open again and took in the rest of the room. Her clothes were lying neatly on one of the chairs, a pile of tiny buttons carefully stacked on the table next to it. Oh, yes, now, she remembered. She'd been so hot for him she'd ripped off her own clothes, too anxious to let him take the time to do it himself. Well, wasn't she just the seductress?

Except for that neat pile of buttons, there was no sign he'd even been there. No note. Nothing left behind. Only the overpowering scent of their physical activity.

Her purse was where she'd left it. Had he robbed her? She wasn't even sure she wanted to know. Her briefcase sat on another chair and looked untouched. Gritting her teeth, she pulled herself out of bed to check everything else, but nothing had been disturbed.

Thank God. As drunk as she'd been, he could have taken everything in the room much as he'd taken her body and she'd never have known the difference.

She managed to stagger to the bathroom and pry the cap off the bottle of aspirin on the sink. She tossed four into her mouth and ran a glass of water to wash them down. When she was sure her stomach wouldn't betray her, she lifted her eyes to her reflection in the mirror and thought she might pass out.

Her cheeks and jawline were reddened from what she was sure was whisker burn. Her lips were swollen and her eyes had a slumberous look to them. What was that word he'd made her say? Oh, yes. *Fuck.* She looked and felt like a woman who'd been well and truly fucked.

With her headache having subsided to a dull roar, she stood in the shower and let the hot water beat down on her until she was sure her body was fairly ready to function. Closing her eyes as she showered had been a mistake, because immediately visions of The Man—what else could she call him? She hadn't even asked his name—danced before her eyes, the lamplight gleaming on his powerful naked body, his dark hair loose around his face, giving him the look of a wild warrior, his thick erection punishing her nearly virgin cunt. Yes, *cunt.* Another forbidden word.

Maybe I'll just walk around reciting my new vocabulary, she thought as she dried herself with the thick towel. *Fuck. Cunt. Cock.*

But she knew it was defiance. Rebellion. Just as last night had been. With the towel wrapped around her, she padded into the bedroom and fished the sheet of stationery from her jacket pocket. Reading the damning words again only made the anger rise more strongly than ever.

She thought about trying once more to call the man she'd flown from Florida to see, but as her hand reached for the telephone, she hastily drew it back.

No. He's humiliated me enough.

Well, her day had started and ended with two very different men. One didn't want to see her and the other she hoped never to lay eyes on again. Or did she? Yes, she did. She was once and done where he was concerned. That was the way it had to be. Besides, she didn't even know who he was or how to get in touch with him.

And what would she say to him if she did? *Please fuck me again?* In a heartbeat.

No, today she'd get on the plane and fly back to Tampa, finally claim her inheritance from the people who'd cheated her of her life and decide what to do with herself. At first, she'd thought to reject everything that had been left to her, but then she'd decided she'd earned it. She and her mother. And while her mother wasn't around to benefit from it, Taylor could enjoy it for both of them.

What do I do now that I'm suddenly rich, sporting an MBA degree and have no clue how to live the rest of my life? Do I suddenly go wild, like I did last night? Pick up strange men in bars?

She shivered as thoughts of last night again played like a video tape in her mind. No, she wouldn't go back to the same life. She'd make some drastic changes. She just didn't know what.

Chapter Four

Taylor slapped the folder on her desk closed. She'd read the clippings inside so many times the print had begun to blur. The letter from someone named Noah Cantrell, telling her it was urgent she contact him at once regarding Josiah Gaines, sat at the bottom of the pile, out of sight and out of mind. She'd had no trouble deciding not to answer it, but now he'd taken to bombarding her with phone calls, insisting he had to speak to her. She'd refused all of them.

Perversely, she opened the folder once more and the headline on the first clipping jumped out at her. *International billionaire Josiah Gaines killed in ambush.* Someone had waited for the man as he was driven from his offices in San Antonio to his ranch outside the city and had blasted his car, killing both him and the driver. Every alphabet agency in the country — maybe the world — was scrambling to find clues, but in a month, nothing had turned up.

Too bad I didn't do it myself, Josiah. I'm sure you deserved it.

Even with all that had happened in the past few weeks, the shock of learning that her father was not dead as she'd always been told was still fresh in her mind. She'd had some childish vision of walking in on this man, the founder and major stockholder of a multinational conglomerate, and creating a family situation. What a fairytale that had been. She'd never even gotten past the reception desk, escorted out of the building like a criminal of some kind by two unsmiling security guards.

Of course, she'd realized that just as she'd never known about him, he hadn't known of her existence. Her grandmother's letter described in what could only be called venomous language how she and Taylor's grandfather had tracked down their runaway daughter and the malicious manner in which they'd manipulated the end of her marriage to a man they'd considered both unsuitable and unacceptable. They'd brought her back to Tampa, determined to file for an annulment and wipe the incident out of family history, only to discover Laura had had the last laugh. She'd been pregnant and no amount of threats or pleas had convinced her to abort the child. It had been her last act of rebellion.

The myth of Taylor's father had been contrived at once — the son of wealthy Europeans, killed in a plane crash shortly after the wedding. Then Laura had been bundled off to relatives in Maine until the baby had been born, while her grandparents had continued with their diabolical plans to keep the lovers apart and prevent any further contact. No wonder her mother had been so sad and defeated all her life. Taylor seemed to have been all she'd lived for. The day after having seen her daughter graduate from college, Laura Scott had swallowed an overdose of sleeping pills and taken herself out of the misery in which she'd lived.

Josiah Gaines' refusal to see her had been the final swing of the wrecking ball against the structure of Taylor's life, igniting the tinderbox of rage and resentment that had been accumulating since she'd received the letter. How else to explain her out-of-character behavior — getting drunk, picking up a strange man in the bar and spending the night indulging in the most erotic sex she'd ever had? Memories of it still made her blush and squirm.

Memories that, if she were truthful, swept over her on a regular basis.

Far too often for her comfort zone.

Her dreams were constantly invaded by images of Him. The Man. That was who he was to her — The Man who had taken her body and taught her the pleasure of uninhibited sex. The images flashed through her mind over and over like a slide show stuck on repeat. Her naked body. His. His hands on and in her. His mouth on her. Feeling the huge thickness of him inside her. The words he'd used. She awoke each morning flushed and heated and more tired than when she'd gone to bed.

Well, she was done with that, with the man who haunted her dreams, with Josiah Gaines and with this Noah Cantrell, whoever he was. He could go to hell, which was where she hoped Josiah Gaines was right now. They could all go to hell as far as she was concerned.

The past month had been exhausting as she'd gone through the business of settling her grandparents' estate. But it also marked what she'd begun to call 'the emergence of Taylor'. No longer did she go along to get along. She owed nothing to anyone but herself. Her carefully constructed little world had fallen apart and she had no desire to put it back together the way it had been. She had the money now to do whatever she wished. If only she could figure out what that was.

Not what she was doing now, that was for damn fucking sure. Damn. And fucking. Yes, prissy little Taylor Scott had also taken to cursing and using graphic language as her stifled inner self slowly emerged, propelled by resentment that continued to smolder like an underground fire.

Her first step had been to resign from the investment firm where she'd worked. Today was her last day. The partners had taken her to lunch but refused to call it a celebration, asking her one last time to change her mind. But Taylor was adamant. She needed to do something else. Or maybe do nothing for a while. She'd turned into someone she didn't even know, carrying a chip on her shoulder larger than a boulder. Where before she'd been agreeable and adaptable, now she was often hostile. Yes, it was definitely time for a change. She'd lost the person she'd been and had to discover who she was to become.

Not someone who picks up a stranger and allows him to push my sexual boundaries.

The two Bankers Boxes on the floor next to her desk held

the sum total of her years at Clemens Jacobs Financial Services, color-tabbed folders holding personal papers, precisely aligned just as her life had been until a month ago. She was seized by an overwhelming urge to drag them out of their boxes and toss them into a jumble, just as her life had been tossed about. She'd been so regimented for so long—except for her one lapse—she wondered how she would manage without the anchor of routine.

Leaning back in her chair, she closed her eyes and, as always these days, the picture of The Man danced across her brain unbidden. She rubbed her eyes, trying to erase the images that were always there no matter how she wished them away. That night had been at once the most erotic and embarrassing of her life. At least she'd broken out of her shell with a stranger, someone she didn't have to see again.

You want to see him again, though. Quit kidding yourself. You want all those things he did to you, made you do. Maybe even more. That's why you can't stop thinking about them. About him.

A commotion in the reception area broke her train of thought and drew her attention. She heard the voice of Sheila, the receptionist, raised in protest over something and the angrier male voice overriding her.

"You can't go in there," Sheila was saying as the door to Taylor's office flew open.

"I'm in. Miss Scott can throw me out if she wants to."

There he was, standing in front of her.

Him. The Man.

She blinked hard, thinking for a moment she'd conjured up his image. But when she opened her eyes again, he was still there. Alive. In her office. In full alpha mode. The man she'd never expected to see again. The man who'd taken her far beyond the boundaries set by her inhibitions and who beckoned to her in her dreams each night.

He was even more impressive than she remembered, his presence filling her office and surrounding her. His custom suit and silk dress shirt—were they his uniform?—were window dressing for the barely leashed panther beneath the fabric of civilized clothing. Expensive hand-tooled leather boots on his feet. His hair tied back with a leather thong as before. His face still an unreadable mask. The sense of controlled power still there. A man larger than life. The panther was caged today, but just barely. This might be her office but he was definitely the person in charge.

Even as embarrassment and anger warred within her, her nipples hardened, her breasts tingled and her panties dampened with moisture. She felt every bit of blood drain from her face and drop to her feet. Waves of hot and cold rolled through her and she was sure all the air had been sucked from her lungs. Gripping the arms of her desk chair for support, she licked her lips, trying to moisten them.

Quick, lithe movements brought him to the front of her desk where he stood facing her, his face set, dark eyes probing hers. Eyes that for a brief second held a knowing look.

"Miss Scott?" Sheila's worried voice cut through her fog. "Shall I call one of the partners?"

Taylor managed to find a functioning part of her brain. "No thanks, Sheila. It's all right."

"Would you like me to send someone in to carry your boxes for you? Walk you down to the garage?" Sheila wasn't quite ready to let go.

Taylor forced a smile. "No, I can manage. Thanks for your concern. And for all your good wishes today."

Sheila gave her a last worried look before she closed the door.

His eyes burned into Taylor's, mesmerizing her as they'd done that night in San Antonio.

What is he doing here?

As if he'd heard her, he reached into his inside jacket pocket, extracted a card from a small leather case and dropped it on top of the folder.

She picked it up with trembling fingers and stared at it.

Noah Cantrell, Vice President of Security, Arroyo Corporation

Rage fired throughout her system, displacing the sexual hunger that had threatened to explode the minute she saw him. She tossed the card back onto the desk and curled her hands into fists.

"You knew who I was all the time."

He nodded, his face expressionless.

"You tracked me down at the hotel."

Another nod.

Taylor wanted to pick something up and throw it at him, but she refused to let him see how he affected her. A game. He'd been playing a game. What a fool she'd been.

"Well. I'm sure I gave you an interesting story to take back to your employer."

"I told him I'd checked you out and you didn't seem like a hustler or scam artist." His voice was flat, uninflected. "He knew nothing of what happened between us."

"How very kind of you." She was shaking inside, panic and desire clashing wildly. The only protective shield she has was the anger she needed to feed. She had to get him out of there.

His face was a mask of stoicism but his unfathomable eyes glittered. "What happened between us was private and personal. I wouldn't discuss it with anyone."

"I'll just bet." He was standing so close to her she could count his eyelashes.

"When I took you to bed, I broke the trust of a man who was very good to me and who I respected — still respect — a great deal. I've been damned for it ever since. No matter how I try, I can't get you out of my blood."

She stared at him, shocked by his words. Even in her most farfetched dreams of him somehow finding her, she'd never expected the reality or the harshness of the words he'd spat out. Before she could move, he gripped her shoulders, bent his head and pressed his mouth to hers in a blistering kiss. His tongue was hot against the seam of her lips, pressing, demanding she admit him. When she did, he swept inside like a starving man seeking the last morsel of food.

She closed her eyes, barely able to breathe as waves of sensation washed over her.

At last, he released her. When she lifted her gaze to his eyes, they were so heated she was sure his look alone would scorch her skin. She stared at him, unable to move, touching her fingers to her bruised lips, her body thrumming with desire.

"Tell me you didn't feel that as much as I did," he demanded, "and I'll call you a liar."

Finally, she found her voice. "I should just tell you to get the hell out of here, you arrogant ass."

"But you won't, will you." A statement, not a question.

"You seem very sure of that."

Why is he here? What does he want? I can't think when he's in the same room with me. What the hell is wrong with me?

His voice jarred her out of immobility. "You still want to find out why I'm here. And I'm not leaving until I tell you. There's too much at stake." He folded himself into one of the client chairs.

Everything about his attitude said, *'I dare you. To throw me out or to listen. Your choice.'*

"Don't make yourself comfortable. I didn't answer your letter and refused all your phone calls. I have no interest in what brought you here. Josiah Gaines had no interest in me when he was alive. Dead, he means even less to me." She reached for the phone to call security. Getting him out of there had become a priority.

"I don't believe you." Noah leaned forward and placed a hand over hers, gripping it. "And you're going to hear what I have to say if I have to tie you down, little girl."

His fingers on the back of her hand were like branding irons, searing her skin and sending a blast of heat through her body. She snatched her hand away.

"Taylor." She gritted her teeth. "My name is Taylor. I'm not *your* little girl, or anyone else's. And your threats don't scare me."

He shook his head. "I'm not leaving."

"Look, Mr…" She made a show of looking at the card. "Cantrell, we have nothing to say to each other. You happened along at a bad moment in my life and I managed to thoroughly embarrass myself. I'd be very happy if you'd just get out of here."

Noah rested his elbows on his knees. His bottomless black eyes captured hers.

"I haven't forgotten one minute of that night. Or stopped thinking about it. Don't tell me it hasn't been on your mind, too."

"I…" She wet her lips and started again, "That night is best forgotten. So are you and Josiah Gaines." Her fingers played with the edges of the folder.

"Aren't you curious about why I'm here?" His eyes challenged her again.

"I can't afford to be. The message was quite clear when your employer had me tossed from his corporate headquarters by his thugs. All I wanted was five minutes of his time. Five stinking minutes to tell him who I was."

A muscle jumped in his cheek. "Do you think I wanted to come here? The smartest thing I can do for myself is to stay as far away from you as possible. But Josiah made that impossible."

"How did a man who's now dead send you here on a mission you seem to resent?"

"Have dinner with me and I'll tell you all about it."

Have dinner with him?

Just being in the same room with him was dangerous. Sharing a meal would increase that danger. And what could possibly interest her about a man who'd thrown her out of his life?

"I want nothing to do with you or anything that relates in any way to that man." She nodded at the folder. "Especially now that he's dead. Murdered, the newspapers say."

Noah's face hardened. "That's a big part of what I need to discuss with you."

She glared at him. "Why should I even care? The man had

no time for me when he was alive. And why would I want to spend one minute with a man who had no conscience about playing a charade with me?"

The muscles in his face tightened. "I couldn't tell you who I was."

"Oh." She tossed her hair. "But now it suits your purpose to reveal yourself. If I didn't answer your letters or return your phone calls, what makes you think I'd spend another five minutes with you?"

"Taylor. Miss Scott." Frustration tightened his voice. "We have a serious situation here. You must listen to me."

"Give me one reason why I should do that. Otherwise, you can just get out."

A muscle twitched in his cheek as he took an envelope from his pocket and handed it to her. "Read this."

She pulled out the single sheet and unfolded it. Her hands shook as she read it.

My dear Taylor,

There is so much I would like to say to you and I may not have the time. When I refused to see you that day, it was because I had no reason to believe I had a child. Your grandparents saw to that. But I had to satisfy myself and now I have. I loved your mother more than life itself. Losing her nearly killed me.

I hope to see you soon and make amends, but, if something happens, trust no one but Noah Cantrell. No one. He is the only person I would trust to do what I've asked of him.

Your loving father (much too late),
Josiah Gaines

"How touching." She folded the paper and slid it back into the envelope. "Why should I believe a word of this? It's just one more letter screwing up my life."

He was around the desk and lifting her out of her chair before she had time to protest. He pulled her towards him, fingers digging her arms, and his dark eyes bored into hers.

"I'll tell you two things. One. Have dinner with me and

I'll explain everything. Then if you want to walk away, it's on your head, but I don't think you will. Two. If you think that night in the hotel is the end of it with us, you're very much mistaken. Much as we both might want to pretend otherwise, you know I could take you down on this rug right now and fuck you blind and you wouldn't push me away."

She was losing herself in the intensity of those bottomless onyx eyes.

"Don't try to deny you feel the same," he went on. "Your body's already responding to me, even as mad as you are."

Taylor tried to pull away. "You're very sure of yourself for someone who showed up in my life under false pretenses then didn't contact me for a month. You obviously knew who I was. If you wanted me that badly, why didn't you come after me?"

Still he held her in an unrelenting grip, his face so close his breath was like a soft breeze against her skin.

"There are things I can't tell you. Reasons why I wish we could make this…thing between us go away. Coming after you would have been a disaster for both of us."

"Yet here you are, despite what you just said."

Muscles jumped along the line of his jaw. "I have a job to do. I told you. And damn me for it, I can't seem to keep my hands off you. I find myself losing control where you're concerned."

"And you want me to sit down to dinner with you? After all that?"

Taylor was sure her entire body was shaking. The heat and power that radiated from him enveloped her and his touch brought back every memory of every moment in that hotel room. Her nipples were so hard they felt raw as they pressed against the lacy fabric of her bra and her pussy throbbed with instant need.

Damn.

He gritted his teeth. "I think I can manage to keep from attacking you during a meal in a public place. What about you?"

She looked up at Noah Cantrell and knew she was stepping into more danger than she'd ever known. Taking a deep breath, she drew back her hand and slapped him.

He didn't even flinch. "Mind telling me what that was for?"

"For not telling me the truth that night. For letting me get drunk and make a fool of myself. For staying away from me." She jerked herself out of his grasp. "For…for a lot of things."

"We'll let that lie for the moment." The ghost smile danced across his lips. "Feel better now?"

"Yes." *No.*

"Good. Then can I assume dinner is on?" He was still crowding her space. "Hear me out before you make any snap decisions."

"All right. Dinner. Then we'll see."

* * * *

Taylor knew at once she'd made a mistake in her choice of restaurant. She wanted one that was quiet and out of the mainstream, a place where she wouldn't run the risk of seeing anyone she knew. She didn't need to field questions about Noah Cantrell when she didn't have any answers yet herself. But the atmosphere was more intimate than she'd remembered, the corner booth arranged so their knees touched beneath the table.

His presence was still overpowering, sensual, masculine. *Panther* had been a good word to describe him, with his caged power, jungle grace and the dark aura about him. But he also carried the air of a warrior and she wondered idly about his ancestry.

Neither of them had ordered alcohol, as if both were determined to keep things businesslike and operate with clear heads. And after the bomb Noah dropped on her, she wondered if she shouldn't change her mind and make friends with Jack Daniel's again.

"He did what?" She still couldn't come to grips with what she'd heard.

"Made you his sole heir. Period. Oh"—he waved his fingers in the air—"he has a few bequests that have been stipulated for a long time, but the rest goes to you."

"He knows nothing about me." Taylor tried to kick her brain out of slow gear. "Had me thrown out of his building when I came to San Antonio. Why should he leave everything to me?"

Noah handed her a folder he'd brought into the restaurant with him. "He didn't totally ignore your claim. Josiah was nothing if not thorough. That was one of the keys to his success. Read everything in here. When you're through, I'll answer questions."

He watched her through narrowed eyes while she scanned the papers. A lab report. A credit report. A copy of her grandparents' wills. Her college credits. And on and on. A complete record of her life. She was ready to take the folder and tear everything in it to pieces when she came to the last item, a black and white photo of a young couple smiling happily, arms around each other. The woman held a small bouquet of roses and the man had a rose pinned to his lapel. Even as old as the picture was, no one could miss the love that shone on their faces.

"Turn it over," Noah told her.

She flipped to the back and her eyes widened.

I thought you might like this picture of your parents. Laura was the love of my life. Always. Your father, Josiah Gaines.

Taylor wanted to put her head down and cry. For herself. For the young couple so desperately in love whose lives had been torn apart by people who made no allowance for emotion. For everything that could have been and wasn't.

"I think I'll have that drink after all." She signaled the waiter.

"I'd stick to wine, if I were you," Noah cautioned. "We have a lot to discuss."

"And I might lose my head and attack you again?" She curled her hands into fists. "Maybe this was a mistake."

He grasped her hands. "This is no mistake. On any front. And next time I fuck you, little girl, it won't be because you've consumed a week's worth of alcohol."

Her breath caught in her throat. "I'm not..."

"Yes. You are. And yes, we will." His voice was low and intense. "Don't think any of what's going on will get in the way of what we both know is going to happen." He released her hands and sat back, a strangely unsettled look on his face. "Whatever this is between us, we need to tame it and move on. We have business to conduct and more eyes than you can imagine will be watching us."

Tame it. Move on. Like they were exorcising a demon.

If she had any sense, she'd get up and run from the restaurant as fast as she could. Away from Josiah Gaines' legacy. Away from what Noah Cantrell had to tell her. But most of all, away from the man himself. She was angry and frightened and aroused all at the same time. And the erotic lust that he'd awakened deep within her was pressing hard to burst forth again.

With an effort of will, she pulled herself together.

"Forgetting about the personal stuff. What is so urgent about this situation? Couldn't I just sign away any claim to the estate and you can all get on with your business?"

Noah shook his head. "It's a lot more complicated than that. Something happened the week before Josiah was killed, but I don't know what. Nothing seemed to stand out as unusual the day before he left on a trip and he was killed on the way home from the airport the day he returned. He'd called me as soon as he landed to tell me we needed to meet, but he did that often. Whatever it was, we never got to discuss it. He was killed on the way home from the airport."

"My God!" Taylor rubbed her temples, trying to absorb

what she was hearing. "Who's been running the company since then?"

"Kate Belden, Arroyo's executive vice president."

His tone of voice said it all.

"You don't like her," Taylor guessed.

Noah gave his characteristic shrug. "Not my cup of tea. She's a machine in human skin with lofty aspirations."

Taylor raised an eyebrow. "How lofty?"

"She considered herself Josiah's heir apparent. I know she assumed the board would automatically vote her into the CEO position. She's been doing some active lobbying for the past month. You'll be quite a shock to her."

She frowned. "I don't understand."

"Josiah's will gives you ownership of his sixty percent of Arroyo. I have proxies from most of the board appointing you temporary CEO."

Taylor's jaw dropped. "What? You're kidding, right?"

Noah shook his head. "Not for a moment. I owe it to Josiah to keep together what he built and to find out what's wrong. It appears you'll have to be the glue."

She took a healthy swallow of her wine. "What do you think I know about running a conglomerate like Arroyo? What did Josiah think?"

Noah took the folder she'd been looking at, flipped it open and pulled out two sheets of paper.

"I'd say a degree in business from the University of Tampa and an MBA from the University of South Florida aren't a bad starting place. You graduated at the top of your class both times." He flipped over a sheet of paper. "Excellent recommendations from your professors got you an investment counselor position at Clemens Jacobs Financial Services and you're the top producer. The youngest person ever to be fast-tracked for partnership." He looked up. "You probably know a hell of a lot more than the people you're going to meet will give you credit for."

She was struggling to comprehend his extensive knowledge of her. "How did you get all this information, anyway?"

"Most of this material is public record. And money can buy anything if you spend enough of it."

Taylor pushed her hair back from her face. "Don't I just know that." She couldn't keep the bitterness out of her voice. She opened the folder again, studying each sheet of paper. "This DNA test. I assume you used something from my hotel room. Is that what the whole thing was about?"

He gripped her wrist before she even saw him reach out.

"I wasn't the one so hot I ripped off my clothes," he pointed out in a tight voice. "But that isn't important. What's important is that I didn't run away from it, damn me for a fool. And, no, I could have gotten what I needed a number of ways. I didn't need to take you to bed to do it."

Her face heated and she yanked her arm away. The sudden movement knocked over the wineglass and it spilled onto both of them. Taylor jerked and grabbed her napkin, blotting ineffectively at her skirt. She glanced sideways at Noah to see him wiping at his suit jacket with an implacable look on his face.

"I'm sorry." She threw her napkin down on the table. "I'm making a mess of things as usual. This time, quite literally. Why don't you just tell me how we got to this point and what you need, in the least number of sentences possible?"

"Fine." His voice was steady, but when she looked at his face she saw the glitter in his eyes. "As to what's in the folder, Josiah had me check out everything about you. He wanted to be sure he wasn't turning his back on someone who was really his. When I brought him the folder, he locked himself in his den and got stinking drunk."

"Drunk?"

Noah nodded. "I had to jimmy the door to open it the next morning. He was sitting at his desk holding the picture of your mother. He never told me what happened back in the day, but he gave me instructions."

"Instructions." She dropped her napkin over the spot on her skirt.

"Yes. He was in the middle of investigating what was happening with Arroyo or he would have asked you to come back right away. I drove him into San Antonio to a lawyer he's used for private activities before and he had the new will drawn up. He'd already gotten the board's proxies himself by that time, with the vote assigned to me for a new CEO."

Taylor frowned. "Didn't the board think it strange?"

"Maybe. I don't know how he did it. He told me this was his fallback plan. Just in case. I do know he was planning to fly to Tampa to see you when he was killed."

"Have the police made any progress in the case?"

Noah made a sound of disgust. "The police can't find their asses with both hands. If anyone's going to find the answer to Josiah's murder, it will have to be me. All I can tell you is my gut says it has to do with Arroyo, and that now involves you."

She leaned against the back of the booth, trying to make some sense of it all. "And what is it you want me to do?"

"Come back to San Antonio with me. Move into Rancho Arroyo, Josiah's home. Take over the reins of the company. Help me ferret out what's going on and who's behind it. I can fill you in on the key players, help you with whatever you need. I will be with you every step of the way."

"I'll just bet." She gave a short laugh. "Why did Josiah choose you for this? What do you get out of all this, Mr. Cantrell? Forgive me, but I can't see you as being particularly altruistic."

His jaw tightened and he took a long time answering her. "I owe him a great debt. One I'll never be able to repay. I would do anything for him. And he trusted me. This is for him."

"And exactly what—"

He held up his hand. "No. The details are not open for discussion."

"Well." She sipped at her water, trying to make some sense of things. "You don't want much, do you? And when am I supposed to do all this?"

"Tonight. I'll give you all the details and a rundown on the cast of characters on the plane."

Taylor thought she'd faint. *Tonight?* "That's impossible."

Noah turned his gaze on her. "It's necessary. What could possibly hold you back? I know you resigned from your position at Clemens Jacobs. And today was your last day. You have no close associates that you have to explain things to. No…relationships to keep you here."

She jerked herself upright. "You checked out my love life? You are the most arrogant ass in the world."

A corner of his mouth twitched. "Probably. But I had to know if you had any loose ends we needed to tie up. I had to have a complete picture."

She clenched her hands around her water glass. "I'm sure you had a good laugh at how pathetic that picture is. I guess that explained why I threw myself at you in the hotel room."

"I told you. What happened that night is a separate issue." His eyes narrowed. "One we'll definitely get to later."

"And what about my house? Other things? I can't just get on a plane and fly away."

"Yes, you can. I brought people with me to take care of closing up your house and storing your car. We'll hire a security service to keep an eye on things."

She set her glass down carefully and looked hard at him across the table, hands folded in front of her, shoulders stiff. "All my life, people have been telling me what to do. Giving me orders. Setting my priorities. Then I find out these people had quite literally destroyed my mother's life and would have gladly disposed of mine. So the quiet, complacent Taylor Scott has disappeared. No one is going to tell me what to do. Not anymore. Am I making myself clear?"

His answering stare was just as hard. "This is a little more than telling you what dress to wear and who to have dinner with. An entire corporation is at stake here. And all the people involved with it."

She picked up the wine again, sipped the rest of it slowly then replaced it with a hand that shook just slightly. "If these people are determined to hide what they're doing, to take over the company, what's to stop them from killing me? They probably thought they were home free and now I pop into the picture."

His hands tightened slightly then relaxed. "I won't let that happen."

"Really." She laughed, but it wasn't a pleasant sound. "You didn't manage to keep Josiah safe."

Anger flared in his eyes. "We weren't expecting anything that drastic. We are now. We'll be prepared."

She stared at him, sudden knowledge flooding her. "You want to use me for bait."

"Taylor." He leaned forward. "Someone has to take the reins of this buggy before the horse thieves steal it. Josiah chose you. My options are limited."

She fiddled with her napkin. "Do you suppose you'd get further if you *asked* me instead of ordering me?"

A muscle jumped in his cheek. "All right. I'm asking you. Will you please come back to San Antonio with me and do this?"

She sat silently, turning everything over in her mind.

Finally, he spoke again. "Chicken? Afraid to step into something this challenging? Afraid of a little danger?" His voice lowered. "Afraid of me, little girl?"

If anything would have pushed her to it, this was it. The new Taylor Scott wasn't afraid of anything. And he was right. What did she have to hang around here for? Maybe this was a chance to find out about the father she never knew. To explore who she might have been if her grandparents hadn't interfered.

"Damn it. I am not your little girl. Or anyone's." She chewed her bottom lip for a moment. "All right. I'll come back with you. But I want some ground rules."

He arched an eyebrow. "And those would be?"

"I know nothing about what I'm stepping into. I have to depend on you to get me through this, but with one stipulation. We're on equal footing. No orders. I told you. I'm in charge of myself."

She thought she saw the ghost of a smile twist his lips, then it was gone. "All right. What else?"

"I have some things to do before we leave. Packing, for one thing."

Noah was already reaching for his wallet and signaling the waiter. "Don't pack much. We have a personal shopper coming tomorrow with a new wardrobe for you to look at. She'll know what the CEO of Arroyo and a top resident on the A-List needs to wear."

Taylor just stared at him. "A shopper? You were certainly damn sure of yourself. Are you choosing my clothes for me, too? I don't think so."

He bit down on his obvious irritation. "You will need a wardrobe that says who you are. I'm sure there's nothing wrong with the one you have, but you're about to become someone else. Can you just trust me on this and not argue? You don't have to take anything you don't like."

She swallowed her own annoyance. "All right. Point taken. What other surprises do you have for me?"

He shrugged. "Checking account. Credit cards. Other things you'll need."

Taylor slid out of the booth. "I suppose I should thank you for your efficiency."

"I didn't plan to leave without you, even if I had to kidnap you."

For once, Taylor was speechless. As Noah guided her out of the restaurant, her mind whirled with the events she was being thrust into, and her body began to hum in anticipation of what this man might want of her in private. And whether or not she was willing to give it. Her only thought made use of her newly acquired graphic language.

I've lost my fucking mind.

Chapter Five

Noah followed her to her house, where a black Expedition not unlike the one he drove was waiting at the curb.

I wonder if they just order a fleet of them?

As they pulled into her driveway, two men got out of the vehicle and came toward them. Taylor parked her car in the garage and waited for the men to approach her. Noah took care of the introductions.

"Joe Deland, Grant McCoy. Meet Taylor Scott." He held out his hand. "Keys."

"What?"

His face was a mask of patience. "They'll need them to lock up your house and move your car. I think you should probably sell both of them. You won't need them anymore."

"Wait just a damn minute here." She planted her feet and summoned her newly found self-possession. "Are you giving orders again? I want to make sure I have something to come back to. This could all fall apart." She twisted away from him. "Or a month from now, I could no longer be useful and you'll send me back like discarded luggage."

He turned her around and tilted her chin up with his hand. "I don't think you'll have to worry about that."

His face was taut with tension, but that elusive something flashed in his eyes again. He was so close his warm breath whispered across her skin. His tantalizing scent drifted across her nose.

I have to get control here. I can't let him do this to me or I'll lose the battle.

She headed for the stairs. "I'm also not making any changes to my financial accounts or anything else here. According to you, I'll be well provided for in that department. This is my insurance if this scheme of yours falls apart."

"Fine." He followed her up to her room. "Just pack so we can get the hell out of here. Only what you absolutely need. Anything else, the personal shopper can take care of."

Dictatorial ass.

But she chose not to argue again at that moment. She simply marched into her room, opened the closet and pulled a suitcase from the top shelf. A door slammed and when she turned around, Noah was an inch away from her.

No. No, no, no. I can't let this happen.

They stared at each other, heat shimmering between them. Whatever this was, it was stronger than the pull of the most addictive drug. Her earlier anger, which had thrown up an effective shield between them, dissipated the moment he took one step closer to her. The hunger she saw in his eyes matched her own. Her pulse ratcheted up, her breath caught in her throat and hostility fled in the surge of desire that raced through her. She wanted to rip off her clothes as she'd done in the hotel and beg him to take her. Right here, right now.

Jesus, Taylor.

He reached for the buttons on her blouse and began to thread them through the buttonholes. "You'll need to change into something more comfortable for travel. I'll help you."

Taylor shook, undone by the sensations rocketing through her. "You said we had to hurry." *What is the matter with me? Why don't I push him away?*

"My cock is so hard I promise you this won't take long. If I don't get inside you soon…" His voice was thick with need as he deftly removed her clothing.

She was powerless to stop him. His touch aroused her, his heated gaze mesmerized her and rational thought deserted her. "The two men…"

"Are busy doing other things. Tell me you don't want this and I'll stop. Right now." His eyes burned into her.

She was cemented in place by the heat of his gaze, the grip of his hands, the insistent throbbing in her womb. *Tell him no?* That was what she should do, but her treacherous, newly awakened body had other ideas. She wanted him buried deep inside her as much as he wanted to be there.

"All right, then." His hands were shaking. "God, Taylor, I have to touch you. Taste you. I want five hours with you, not five minutes. But I'll take what I can get. Do you have any idea how hard it's been to control myself tonight?"

"You don't seem to be controlling yourself now." Her voice was none too steady.

"You have no idea. The minute I get within five feet of you, all I want to do is plunge myself inside you," he ground out. "I want to rip off every stitch of your clothing and run my tongue over every inch of you. Do you have any idea how unlike me that is?"

She gave a shaky laugh. "That ought to spice up the activities when we get to San Antonio."

He paused as he was about to slide her thong down her legs. "You don't have to worry about me embarrassing you at Arroyo. Even a savage like me can understand the importance of not giving people ammunition. We'll be under a microscope. There'll be no signal from me that there's anything to find."

His voice softened slightly. He cupped her breasts in his palms, rubbing his thumbs gently over her nipples. "But I can't promise the same when we're alone. Be warned. I'll take advantage of every minute we're alone together to fuck you senseless. God help me, you're a craving I can't seem to satisfy."

"You resent that," she said with a shrewd look even as her legs turned weak and shaky and her heart raced.

"Damn straight." His voice wasn't much steadier than hers. "I don't give anyone that kind of control over me."

She was having trouble with her breathing, his nearness overwhelming her. "What's happening with us, Noah? What is this thing between us, as you keep calling it?"

"Let's hope it's not the devil having a good laugh at our expense." He touched a finger to her lips. "No more talking. We have to hurry."

I'm out of my mind.

That was the last intelligent thought she had.

Then they were both naked and Taylor was flat on her back on the bed, knees bent and legs spread. Noah stroked the insides of her thighs, down then back to her open sex. He lightly caressed her folds with one finger and flicked against her clit, sending bolts of electricity stabbing through. Her flesh begged for him to ease the ache that spread outward from her open cunt. But still he stroked, his hands everywhere, finding the sensitive places behind her knees and in the crease of her thighs.

"Still pissed off at me? Having second thoughts? There's danger everywhere, little girl, but none greater than you'll find with me." His gaze pinned her. "Tell me to stop and I will."

Stop? Stopping her next breath might be easier. Just the touch of his hands or the wonderful male scent of him scrambled her brain and set her body to vibrating.

"I thought so. You might try to make the rules every place else, but in the bedroom, I'm in charge. You'd do well to remember that."

If she had one functioning piece of her brain, she'd tell him to get off her and go to hell, but she was powerless in the spell he seemed to weave around her.

His face was taut with the effort of control, but he seemed determined to deny himself—deny them both—until he'd touched and looked his fill, despite the crush of time.

"Beautiful." The word escaped on a puff of breath. "Taylor, your cunt is exquisite."

His words fed the need rising in her. *Do it. Do it. Do it.*

Noah leaned down and slipped one finger into her open pussy. "Drenched. I knew it would be. You're as hot for this as I am."

His touch was like liquid heat, scorching her everywhere

he touched.

He trailed the finger down from her clit past the tight opening of her sheath, leaving a damp trail, until he reached the tight ring of her anus. When he pushed his finger into the furled muscle, she nearly came from that sensation alone.

"Yessss," she hissed, trying to clench around the intruding digit.

"Jesus, Taylor." The words escaped on a gasp. "You're going to burn me alive." He leaned down and placed an open-mouthed kiss on her clit. "Not now, but soon, I'm going to help you get this exquisite little ass ready to take my cock. The preparation will be almost as good as the real thing." His eyes shone with his heat. "Maybe you'll run. Maybe you won't. But if you stay, I'll take you higher than you've ever been."

She had no idea what he meant. She hadn't been anywhere. Right now, all she wanted was to feel him inside her.

He kept his eyes locked on hers while he rolled a condom onto his throbbing erection. Then he cupped her breasts, grasping her nipples as he licked a path along her already weeping sex.

She was torn between knowing she should push him away and wanting his thick cock inside her again.

"Noah…"

"Don't talk." His voice was strained. "I wanted to rip your clothes off and fuck you the minute I walked into your office. I can't wait any longer. I've dreamed about this tight little pussy for a month."

"But…"

"Be quiet."

He did the only thing that could shut her up. He brought his mouth down on hers, hot and demanding, probing and striking with his tongue, scouring every inch of that heated cavern. There was nothing soft or gentle about the kiss and it sent a message loud and clear. He would have her any time, any place and she'd be powerless to stop him.

Did she even want to? She could hardly speak, the flame consuming her body also stealing her breath. There was no question who was in control here.

He shifted to pull her legs over his shoulders, the hair on his chest brushing her thighs. He opened her wide as he rested the head of his cock at her opening. Taking a deep breath, he pushed, once, twice, three times and with a strong thrust, he was inside her.

Taylor was sure every inch of her was stretched beyond the limits of endurance and yet she wanted more. She locked her ankles behind his neck, thrusting her hips at him and trying to suck him even deeper inside her. Then he began to move—not the slow and steady pace he'd set that first night, but a rapid pistoning of his hips, driving her against the smooth surface of the coverlet. He leaned back from her a millimeter and slipped one hand between them to find her clit and rub.

She exploded, the orgasm shaking her like a violent fist, just as he climaxed inside her, his cock pulsing in her tight grasp. She shoved a hand into her mouth to keep from screaming. Noah's big body shuddered as the spasms ripped through him and his heart thundered against hers. His cock throbbed within her, the tremors of her climax milking him. For a month that night had haunted her dreams, leaving her shaken and frustrated in the morning. Now the reality was here and it was even more than she remembered.

Then it was over, like a hurricane that had swept through, leaving devastation in its path.

Noah leaned his forehead against hers, his breathing still unsteady. "I don't like quickies. They're crude and I have far more respect for you than that." His mouth twisted. "Though I'm sure you have a hard time believing that right now. This is not what I want for you. For us."

She just looked at him, trying to gather the tattered edges of her emotions.

"But all I had to do was look at you again and my cock

was so hard I thought it would poke a hole in my trousers. Next time, I'll take longer. Much, much longer. You have no idea the things I want to do to that hot little body of yours." His eyes glittered. "Including fucking that tight virgin ass. Be warned."

He slid out of her cunt, pushed himself to his feet and headed for the bathroom to dispose of the condom.

Taylor was still trying to steady her pulse. "And I suppose I have nothing to say about it?"

He was on her in seconds, his face close to hers, his warm breath a heated breeze on her skin. "Just tell me to stop. Tell me no, and it ends right here, right now." When she didn't say a word, he nodded. "I thought so. Your cunt was so wet for me I slid right into it." He pushed himself away. "Get dressed. We need to get going."

She stared at him, openmouthed, astonished at his audacity. But her body had been all the evidence he needed. There was no way she could deny her arousal.

Damn, damn, damn.

She rolled off the bed and got to her feet, grabbing underwear from one of her drawers. Standing there in her thong and bra—modesty seemed false at this point—she began throwing things into her suitcase. When she turned toward the bathroom, Noah was already back in the room and dressed.

"This changes nothing," she told him.

"Ten minutes," he said and walked out of the room.

Taylor picked up a shoe and threw it at the closing door.

This can't happen again. I can't let it happen again. I can't let him take me over.

She repeated it over and over to herself, like a mantra, as she dressed and finished packing. But even as she said the words, she knew she'd be helpless to resist. Noah Cantrell was like a powerful tidal wave surging over her and swamping her, tossing her about then rolling in again.

Another fine mess you've gotten yourself into, dummy.

But, in less than ten minutes, she was ready, dressed in

linen slacks and a silk blouse, hair pulled back in a clip and makeup repaired. She wished she'd had time for a shower. That would be her first order of business when they got to wherever they were going.

Noah entered the room without knocking and raked his eyes over her with an assessing gaze. He nodded. "Good. You'll do."

She bit back the smart remark that leaped up to her lips, instead grabbing her jacket and following him downstairs. "I'll need my briefcase and laptop, too. They're in my car."

"I thought so," he called back to her. "I had Joe move them."

She waited in the Expedition while he and the two men huddled for another minute or two. Then he was beside her and they were away from the curb.

Away. Away from her house. Her city, the place where she'd grown up. Away from everything familiar, everything she'd known all her life. But instead of feeling trepidation, she was gripped by an incredible feeling of relief. Even excitement.

"When we're on the plane, I'll have several things to go over with you."

Noah's was voice so impersonal she had to wonder if this was the same man who'd just fucked her brains out. Then she realized he was back in his business persona, an attitude she too would have to cultivate and keep in place before the plane landed and she walked into her new life.

That was the end of the conversation.

Thirty minutes later, they pulled up to a private aviation hanger at Tampa International Airport. A man nearly as tall as Noah, in jeans and a T-shirt, walked out of the offices and the two men shook hands. Noah pointed to the SUV and the man nodded and came forward. Taylor watched him take her things out of the vehicle and head toward the plane that stood waiting on the tarmac.

She'd seen one like it before. One of the firm's clients had flown her and Bob Clemens to an investors' meeting last year. A Gulfstream G280, the ultimate in private luxury for small planes. Noah took her arm and led her up the waiting stairway, nodding to a man in black slacks and white shirt who stood at the foot.

"Good evening, Mr. Cantrell."

"Carlos. This is Miss Scott."

"Yes. Welcome aboard, Miss Scott. I'll be ready to serve you as soon as we level off."

Taylor blinked. "Serve me?"

Noah hustled her up the stairs.

"Serve?" she repeated.

"We didn't get any dinner. I'm sure you're hungry. I phoned and asked Carlos to have some club sandwiches and pastries ready. I hope that suits you."

She blinked again. "Oh." Then she got a look at the interior of the plane and almost stumbled.

She might have been in a living room, one carpeted in thick gray shag with furniture upholstered in navy leather and denim tweed. Heavy oak tables were placed for maximum efficiency. When Taylor bumped into one and it didn't move, she realized they, like the furniture and lamps, were bolted to the floor.

Noah led her through a door into a combination bedroom and office. A desk against one wall held a computer, fax machine and an impressive array of electronics she couldn't begin to identify. But what captured her attention was the huge king-sized bed in the center of the room, covered with a thick comforter.

She looked up at Noah.

"In case you need to sleep." His eyes smoldered. "Or anything else."

She cleared her throat. "I don't think we ought to…"

He shook his head. "Not tonight. We have business to take care of. But other times? Who knows?" He pointed at another door. "Bathroom's in there if you want to freshen up. Meanwhile, let's get belted in. As soon as Carlos serves us, I'll fill in the blanks for you."

Captain Sam Leland came back to the cabin to introduce himself, along with the copilot, George Monroe. Less than five minutes later, they were belted into two of the blue leather armchairs and the plane taxied down the runway. Taylor swallowed and watched the runway lights flash past them.

What the hell am I getting myself into?

Chapter Six

Taylor had to force herself to eat half the sandwich Carlos served. In any other situation she would have wolfed it down, but the grumbling in her stomach was stilled by the litany of information Noah laid out for her and the knot of nervousness that kept growing larger.

Carlos cleared the plates and refilled her wineglass before disappearing somewhere into the nether regions of the plane. She'd kicked off her shoes and Noah had stripped off his jacket and tie. If not for the intensity of the conversation or the tension radiating between the two of them, they might have appeared to be two people relaxing during a flight.

Noah was doing his best not to be dictatorial and Taylor was trying not to take offense at the arrogance that seemed to be a normal part of his personality. But the awareness was there, an invisible presence shimmering in the air.

As the plane cut through the darkened skies, hurtling her into a yawning pit of unknowns, Noah educated her on the story of Arroyo. From its start as an oil and gas lease company through its acquisitions and expansion, he was careful and concise. Her business-educated mind absorbed everything, filing bits and pieces away to pull out as she needed them. Josiah Gaines may have started out as a penniless nobody, but at his death, he could have bought and sold her grandparents one hundred times over.

"They didn't think he was good enough to invite into their house." Her voice was bitter. "Do you know they paid someone to get him drunk and take pictures of him in bed with some woman? They showed those pictures to my mother and it nearly destroyed her, but she insisted on confronting Josiah. My grandparents practically locked her away until they got her back to Tampa. Thirty-one years ago, things were a lot different from what they are now."

"I can't believe he just let her go. That isn't his style."

Rage flashed across her face. "According to my grandmother's letter, he tried every way in the world to see her. They shipped her out of the country when they found out she was pregnant, gave him a note supposedly from her telling him to leave her alone and told her he'd married the woman he was in bed with."

"Jesus." Noah rubbed his hand over his face. "They certainly managed to destroy a lot of lives. But he threw himself into building Arroyo and the results are obvious."

"Until all this happened," she pointed out.

"Until now," he agreed.

"I know this is a dumb question and you've probably already checked, but did you look at his calendar for the last day he was in the office?"

Noah grimaced. "Yes, but it certainly seemed a dead end."

"What do you mean?"

He leaned forward, arms resting loosely on his knees, frustration in every line of his body. "I had Carmen send me what was on it. He had lunch with Howard Rivas, an old friend who handles all the insurance for Arroyo. Nothing out of the ordinary there."

"And that was it?"

"Then he ordered the plane and said he felt like visiting some of the plants. Carmen said he was very low-key about it, although he seemed to be hiding some kind of tension."

Taylor crossed her legs and rolled the stem of her wineglass between her fingers. "Did he often take trips like that?"

"Yes. No." Noah spread his hands. "Not as much as he used to. He'd been sending Kate Belden on what he called the look-sees for quite a while. But he was still trying to come to terms with you and with Laura's death. Carmen and I just assumed he wanted some time away from everything to get his head back on straight."

"And who is Carmen?"

Noah actually smiled. "Josiah's secretary. Now yours. A spitfire with a computer for a brain. Sometimes I think she should have been running the company."

"If she was close to Josiah, she won't be any too happy to see me," Taylor predicted.

Noah shook his head. "Not true. She'll see you as his extension." He studied Taylor's face. "Let her help you. She can make your life much easier if you do."

"What kind of plants did he visit?"

"Farm implement and machinery manufacturing. He had contracts to sell all over the world."

Taylor chewed her thumbnail. "That doesn't sound very ominous."

"No. It doesn't. And it's not a division that ever comes under any kind of scrutiny. The plants are all out in states like Idaho and Nebraska. I just figured they were good places for Josiah to do some thinking."

"All right." Taylor leaned back in her chair and sipped at her wine, her mind speeding like a race car. "Let's leave that for a minute and get back to the people. I've got Carmen and Kate. And I can guarantee you I'll be an unpleasant surprise as far as Kate's concerned."

"Probably," Noah agreed.

Something in the tone of his voice told Taylor that Kate wasn't one of Noah's favorite people. She'd want to know more about that later.

"Any other key players I should know about?"

"Paul Hunter, corporate counsel. Kate's lapdog." He sighed. "Josiah refused to acknowledge it, one of his few weak spots. But I saw it and I don't trust it. If there is something going on with Arroyo, I'd put my money on either or both of them."

"And who should know better than you, as head of security?" Taylor hunched forward. "Who has been told about me and this whole setup? Am I just supposed to walk in tomorrow and say 'Here I am'?"

"I've been keeping this pretty quiet while I tried to contact you. But today I had Carmen send out a company-wide memo. I contacted the board members personally."

Taylor tilted her head. "And what did Carmen have to say?"

Noah drained the last of the coffee in his mug. "I checked in when I landed in Tampa. She said the grapevine is working overtime."

"I'll just bet." She thought for a moment. "How did the board take it?"

"Better than the staff. I think Josiah was hoping to bring you onboard with Arroyo once the two of you got together. He'd been preparing them for changes when he got their proxies. They're mostly old friends of his anyway, officers of other corporations on his level of wealth and stature and they had a healthy respect for him. I think they'll be the least of our problems." He unlocked his briefcase and handed her a manila envelope. "Checkbook. Credit cards. Arroyo ID tag. Passport."

Her jaw dropped. "Passport? Am I going somewhere?"

He shrugged. "You might have to. You never know. Better to be prepared."

"How did you get a photo to use? And the information to open the accounts?" She shook her head. "Never mind. I'm not sure I want to know." She got up to refill her wineglass. "What else should I know? For instance, who's taking care of the ranch since Josiah's death?"

"Jocelyn Hart. She and her husband, Tony, run Rancho Arroyo. Your new home."

"My new home," Taylor said carefully.

"Josiah's home. Now yours. It's about forty minutes from downtown San Antonio. The name is more than window dressing, by the way. The ranch runs ten thousand head of cattle."

Her eyes widened. "You're kidding me."

"Not for a second." He shrugged. "There's a full staff for both the ranch and the house. Jocelyn runs the house, Tony heads up the ranching operation. Jocelyn will take good care of you. She knows what she's doing." He hesitated in the act of bringing his cup to his lips, as if debating his next words.

Taylor cocked her head. "Something wrong? Are they going to attack me or anything?"

"No." Noah finally swallowed some of his coffee. "On the contrary. Josiah pretty much left the Harts alone to run things and they're a little nervous, Jocelyn especially, about you."

"But why? She doesn't even know me." She frowned. "What did you tell her about me?"

"Very little. But she wants to make a good impression on Josiah's daughter. She can be a very good friend, Taylor. I trust both of them."

Taylor relaxed slightly. "That's good to know." He trusted the Harts, but did she trust Noah Cantrell? She wavered from one moment to the next.

"We'll figure out time for you to meet with Tony and go over the ranch operation. Maybe take a riding tour." He narrowed his eyes. "Do you ride?"

Taylor wanted to laugh. "Yes. I won't embarrass myself. Or you. My God, I had no idea the scope of things I'd be stepping into." She gulped half of her wine.

Noah removed the glass from her hand and set it aside. "Maybe you'd better cut back on this until we finish talking."

She tried to reach for it to grab it back, but he gripped her wrists.

And there it was again, the heat that flared with the instant combustion of a Formula One engine, so incendiary it could have ignited the cabin. Their earlier encounter, rather than banking the fires, had only fed the flames.

We can't keep doing this.

This wasn't a devil riding only on Noah's shoulders. She

was just as securely in its grasp. She was like a child in a candy store, long deprived and now with a feast spread out before her.

"Noah?" Her voice was questioning, her eyes seeking answers. *Tell him to back off.* But just as in the bedroom, she was paralyzed in the grip of desire.

He stared at her for so long she began to feel uneasy. "God damn it," he said at last and bent his head to capture her mouth.

She opened for him almost automatically and he slid his tongue in smoothly. She responded with a thrust of her own as if it were a given and pressed her body against his. Her breasts were crushed against his hard chest and there was no mistaking the thickness of his erection pressed against the softness of her belly. What was it about this man that made her take leave of her senses whenever he touched her? Made her instantly hot and wet, her pussy quivering for his touch?

He drew back his head and looked at her, his breathing not quite even. "Jesus. You make me crazy. I get too close to you and I lose my mind." He lifted her, carried her to the couch and laid her back against the cushions before she could object.

When he pressed a button in the table next to the couch, the captain's voice came over the speaker. "Yes, Mr. Cantrell?"

"Miss Scott and I are in the middle of a project we need to finish before we land. Can you tell Carlos not to disturb us until I buzz again?"

"Yes, sir."

Taylor looked at him through eyes half-shut. *This is true insanity.* "They'll know what we're doing."

"No. They won't." He raised an eyebrow. "Would you rather we went into the bedroom? Then there won't be any question."

Heat climbed Taylor's cheeks.

"Let's get something clear." Noah pulled her blouse loose from her slacks and pushed it up to her neck. "You might have made the first move in San Antonio, but after that, it was my show."

"I…" She swallowed and tried again. "I don't…"

"Yes. You do. And the sooner you admit it, the sooner we can figure out how to take care of whatever this is between us and get on with business. The next week is going to be high pressure and you'll be on display all the time. We can't hide in a corner and fuck whenever the urge hits us. Which seems to be every five minutes."

She struggled against his hold on her. "I was right. You're an insufferable ass."

A ghost of a smile teased at his lips. "I think the word you used was arrogant."

"Why me?" She struggled to find words to give her some space "Surely you could have any woman you wanted, not some short, dumpy female who can't begin to match your experience."

He clenched his jaw so tightly she was afraid it would break. "I don't know who's been giving you such bad ideas about yourself, but you are more woman than any man should be expected to handle." He traced the line of her breasts, paused at her waist then moved over her hips and thighs. "You have a wonderful lushness that makes my dick get hard when you even walk into a room. Everything about you shouts 'female'. Does that answer your questions?"

He pushed her gently back against the cushions and unzipped the fly front of her slacks. With her legs draped over his lap, he slid one hand inside her lacy bikini panties, satisfaction blatant in his eyes when he discovered her wetness.

"The body never lies, little girl." He slid his fingers into her folds and found her swollen, sensitive clit. He pinched it lightly and pulled.

Oh, God!

Her breathing stuttered and she tried to squeeze her thighs together. "I thought…we were having…a business discussion. You said…no sex while we talked business."

She could hardly get the words out.

"No. I said I wasn't going to fuck you. And I'm not. Next time I bury my cock in you, we'll be taking a lot of time to get it just right." His breathing was ragged, his voice not quite steady. "But I can't keep from touching you. I want to feel that cunt flex around my fingers again. And my cock in your mouth."

Electricity surged through her entire body. "This is insane."

"No." His voice lowered, deepened. "This is what we need."

He pressed the pad of his thumb against her hot, swollen nub and slid two fingers inside her pussy. He began stroking her slick inner walls with a gentle rhythm. The movement of his fingers and the touch of his hand were hypnotic. This man only had to look at her and she was aroused. Touching her set a match to the flame. She loved the feel of his skin against hers and the hard musculature of his body as he held her splayed on his lap. She knew she was soaked.

"Oh, God." She shifted and tried to spread her legs but Noah held her in place.

He increased the speed of his strokes, pushing his thumb harder on her clit. When he raked his nail across the throbbing flesh, Taylor nearly came off the couch. "Easy, little girl."

Don't stop what you're doing.

She wanted to come so badly she ached. She wanted his whole hand inside her. No, she wanted that hot erection inside her.

God, what am I turning into?

"Please," she begged.

But the incredible feeling rolling through her body wiped away all rational thought. She was on a rollercoaster, climbing to the crest of the peak, reaching for the downhill slide. Everything was moving, faster and faster, waves of sensation consuming her.

Noah moved one thigh infinitesimally closer to him.

When he slid a third finger inside her and began massaging her clit in a circular moment, the rollercoaster bumped higher and higher. He increased the speed of his thumb and fingers even more, stroking harder, his eyes never leaving her face. When she began panting and moaning, he pushed her bra up over her breasts and took one nipple between thumb and forefinger. He pinched it hard and she poured into his hand. The walls of her hot channel clenched around his fingers, pulling at them. The orgasm swept over her, shaking her so hard she pressed her fist into her mouth to keep from screaming.

Noah stroked and petted her until the last shudders died away and her head dropped back. When her breathing settled to a semblance of normal, he rearranged her clothes, zipping and tucking and helping her to sit up.

Dizzy from the aftereffects of desire, she took the glass of wine he fetched for her, draining the rest of the liquid. Studying Noah's face, she tried to see behind it, but he wore an impenetrable mask. Why was she so attracted to him? He made her do things she had only imagined in her darkest dreams, seducing her into a world of raw sex she could easily become addicted to. Once they landed in San Antonio, he'd be sticking to her side like glue, leading her through the maze of corporate intrigue that awaited her. And there was the question again. How would they manage to keep from succumbing to the lust that held them in such an inexorable grip? And pretend to the world that it didn't exist?

He had been right about one thing. This thing that burned between them wasn't going away by itself.

"You make me so hard I can barely walk." His voice was almost guttural. "Touching you, making you come, only makes me harder."

He was sitting beside her again, stroking her back, watching her through heavy-lidded eyes. When her gaze dropped to his groin, she saw his fly was open and that enormous cock made her draw in her breath. Noah cradled it in one hand, moving his fingers idly up and down.

Although he had his hand pressed lightly against her spine, Taylor didn't need him to tell her what to do. Or even ask her. She wanted to do what she'd missed during that one night. He was right. When it came to sex, he was controlling her and that very power made her tremble with unbelievable need.

As she looked at him saliva pooled in her mouth and shivers skittered along her spine. Still shaky from the orgasm, she slipped off the couch and kneeled in front of him. Taking his cock in one hand, she slipped the other under his testicles which were lying heavy against his thighs. She'd never done this before. No other man had appealed to her enough, tempted her to taste them. But, somehow, with Noah she wanted to touch every inch of him with her hands and her mouth. As she took possession of him, instinct took over.

She swirled her tongue over the head, licking up the salty bead of liquid shining on the purplish skin. When she pressed her tongue into the slit, she heard the sharp intake of his breath. Slowly, she took him into her mouth, sliding her lips down his immense length. She loved the silky feel of skin over the hardened steel of his shaft. Moving her lips and hand in concert, at the same time she used her fingernails to tickle his balls, lightly tangling the soft covering of hair.

He groaned, a harsh sound, and when she raised her eyes, Noah was watching her. The black pools of his eyes glowed with the now familiar look of lust. She held his gaze as she continued sucking and stroking, teasing and caressing. At first, she gagged as her throat tried to close against the intrusion but she made herself relax and his cock slid in more easily. As he'd done to her, drawing out the sensations, refusing to let her reach that plateau, so she did to him now.

He groaned again and wound his fingers through her hair, holding her head and moving it, increasing her speed.

She squeezed his balls and felt them tighten up.

"Jesus Christ, Taylor. Do it." His voice was harsh with need.

She wanted to laugh at the power she suddenly realized she had over this powerful man. Guided by the pressure of his hands, she pumped faster and sucked harder and increased the pressure on his balls. When he pushed down harder on her head, she knew he was ready to come. In seconds, the first splash of liquid hit the back of her throat. She pumped and sucked until the spasms stopped, swallowing every bit of the semen he shot into her.

At last he moved his hands from her head and she sat back. Carefully, she zipped his fly, tucked in his shirt and fastened the button at the waistband of his trousers.

Noah reached down and pulled her up to him, pressing his mouth to hers and sliding his tongue inside, licking every inch. Then he sat back and held out a hand to her to help her up.

"I wanted to taste myself in your mouth." He rubbed a thumb over her lips. "It's almost enough to make me hard again. God, Taylor. You're in my blood." He kissed her very softly then got up from the couch, picked up his briefcase and extracted a folder. "Your schedule for tomorrow. Starting with the personal shopper at eight-thirty."

Taylor groaned. "Can't we hold off on that for a while?"

He shook his head. "Appearance is everything. You are what you wear in this circle of people." He was careful to take a seat far away from her.

"Then the executive staff? The board? All in one day?"

"Get it over with all at once." He narrowed his eyes at her. "You and I need to carefully plan how we handle this. What you say. How you say it. It's important that everyone believes you're in control from the beginning."

"In control." She stared at him. "Don't worry about me. I can handle it."

"I have no doubt about that. You have the necessary brains and determination. I'll see you have all the tools you need and I'll be with you every minute of the time. Just as I promised. I owe a debt to Josiah and I mean to repay it."

"How noble of you."

"No." His voice was hard, his eyes burning into hers. "Not noble. A matter of honor."

Whatever else he might have said was lost as the speaker in the cabin buzzed to life. "Mr. Cantrell? We'll be landing in fifteen minutes."

Noah depressed the Speaker button. "Thanks. Would you let Carlos know?"

"Yes, sir."

Carlos moved silently through the cabin, putting it to rights. Then he disappeared again to wherever he went. Taylor retreated to the bathroom to repair whatever damage the little interlude had created. When she returned, she and Noah belted themselves in. Moments later, the plane bumped gently onto the ground and they sped down the runway toward the terminals.

* * * *

Taylor's watch, reset for Central time, read eleven o'clock when the plane rolled to a stop and the engines were switched off. Carlos came into the cabin, opened the door and flipped down the stairs.

Noah studied her face. "I have people waiting for us. Are you ready?"

Taylor swallowed hard. Did what she and Noah had been doing show in her expression? Would people guess? Would that be their first impression of her? She looked at Noah, his face lacking any expression at all. Well, she could be as composed as he could. She was Taylor Scott, after all. Daughter of Josiah Gaines. She took a deep breath and nodded. "As much as I'll ever be."

"Good. Here we go."

Warm night air, moved by a soft breeze, washed over her as she followed Noah Cantrell off the plane. Floodlights cut into the darkness, lighting up a row of private planes in their tie-downs and the steel building that housed the offices for private aviation.

Two black Expeditions, twins of those in Tampa, stood waiting on the tarmac with three tall, lean and lethal-looking men leaning against them. Noah's hand was at her elbow as they descended from the plane and he steered her toward the waiting vehicles. One of the men broke from the waiting group and came forward, nodding to Noah.

Do they all come out of the same mold? Taylor wondered. *Is there a place that manufactures men like this and you just call up and order them? I'll take twelve, please. Black suits, not gray.* Hysterical giggles threatened to bubble from her lips.

The man and Noah shook hands. "Everything okay, *amigo*?"

Noah nodded. "Not bad, under the circumstances. Tomas, say hello to Taylor Scott, your new boss. Taylor, meet Tomas Sandoval. He'll head your personal security detail."

He dipped his head once. "Miss Scott."

"Security detail?' With a shake of her head, she turned to look at Cantrell.

"He's one of four men assigned to you. Handpicked by me."

Tomas nodded. "We don't want to alarm you, Miss Scott, but since Mr. Gaines' murder we're ramping things up. Noah — Mr. Cantrell — felt that since you're a wild card being introduced into the equation, so to speak, he didn't want to leave anything to chance."

She looked up at Noah, stunned. "I'm in danger? You brought me out here so someone could kill me?"

The muscles in his face tightened. "Not if I can help it."

Tomas looked from one of them to the other, a flash of something in his eyes. Then he opened the tailgate of one of the Expeditions. "I'll get Miss Scott's things stowed. Then we'd better get going. Charlie and I will be the trail car."

Behind him on the tarmac, two black Expeditions stood

with open doors. Tomas retrieved her luggage and placed it in the first vehicle, then handed the keys to Noah, nodded and walked toward the other SUV.

Then they were off.

Noah wound his way expertly along Interstate 10 leading out of San Antonio. It seemed to take forever to leave the city behind, but then she realized it wasn't much farther than driving from downtown Tampa to its northern suburbs.

"You have a busy morning tomorrow, so I hope you sleep fast."

Taylor looked at her watch and realized her whole life had changed in less than six hours. "I'll do my best." Her voice held an edge of sarcasm that Noah ignored.

"Open that folder I gave you. The personal shopper comes at eight-thirty. Then you and I meet for an hour to go over details of the corporation. We'll have a conference call with the attorney who drew up the will so you have all the details straight. There's a copy of it in there. I suggest you look at it before you go to bed."

"While I'm sleeping fast." She grinned.

He slid a glance at her. "This is serious business, Taylor."

She wiped the smile from her face. "You don't need to lecture me, Noah. I never doubted that for one minute. Especially since I've just become target number two." She blew out a breath. "What else?"

"Your office at corporate headquarters and a review with Carmen. The executive staff. We'll break for lunch, which will give you a breather. Then the board of directors."

"What am I supposed to say to them?"

"That's part of what we'll discuss in the morning. And watch out for Kate Belden and Paul Hunter. They'll want a one-on-one with you right away. Hold them off until you've got your sea legs under you. At least twenty-four hours."

Oh, God. Could she handle this? *Yes. The new Taylor Scott can handle anything.* If only her bones would stop shaking.

"I'm curious," she told him. "What would you have done

if I'd said no? If I'd turned you down?"

"I told you. I wasn't coming back to Texas without you. That was a given."

A given. For a minute, Taylor had the feeling she was swimming in deep water — the tide had carried her far from shore and no one had given her a life jacket. Any minute now, she might drown.

"Heads-up." Noah's voice intruded on her thoughts as he turned left. "We're at the ranch. Your role as queen of the empire is about to start."

Taylor hadn't been able to see much in the darkness except a vastness space rolling away from her. Now they pulled up to a massive stone entrance with an iron gate, the initials RA twined in the center. Noah reached out to punch codes into an electronic box and the gates swung wide.

The ranch stood at the end of a long, curving driveway, a massive, sprawling one-story building that was lit up like a ball park. Lights shone everywhere.

She looked at Noah. "Is something going on here?"

"No. Just Jocelyn's idea of a proper welcome."

As Noah pulled up in front of the house, the heavy wooden door opened and a man and woman walked out to the edge of the open porch. Taylor opened the passenger door and climbed out of the vehicle, her eyes on the woman.

Five-foot-six at a guess, her slim body as erect as a soldier's and not a strand of her short blonde hair out of place. Her linen slacks had a crease sharp enough to cut paper and her short-sleeved sweater looked as if it had been custom-knitted for her.

The man was a head taller, lean and wiry, with thick dark hair and heavy eyebrows. In a blue chambray shirt and Levi's, shod in boots Taylor was sure were custom made, he looked every inch the ramrod for a ranch. All that was missing was the ubiquitous Stetson.

Taylor was doubly conscious of her own rumpled appearance and wondered if on top of that, she reeked of sex. She forced herself not to pat her hair or smooth her clothes, nervous gestures that would give away her shaking knees. *I'm in charge,* she repeated to herself. Lifting her chin, she strode forward and held out her hand.

"You must be the Harts. I'm Taylor. Thank you for getting things ready on such short notice and waiting up for me. I apologize for the late arrival."

The fine tremor in Jocelyn's body communicated itself in a nervous smile. Her hand, when she clasped Taylor's, shook slightly.

"Welcome to Rancho Arroyo, Miss Scott. I hope you find everything to your satisfaction."

"I'm sure it will be. Mr. Cantrell tells me my…Josiah depended on both of you heavily to run things here. I hope you'll do the same for me."

Both Harts relaxed visibly, as if to say, *'Good. You're not here to fire us or tell us how to do our jobs.'*

Tony curled his lips in a slight smile. "Noah would certainly know." His voice was low and pleasant. "We had the pleasure of working with Josiah for fifteen years. Rancho Arroyo is our home."

"And I hope it will be for a long time. I'm sure you can understand what a shock this has all been to me. Thank you for accommodating the situation."

Taylor could sense Noah's silent approval as he urged her forward.

Jocelyn gestured toward the doors. "Please let me show you to your rooms. You must be very tired and I know you have a long day ahead of you tomorrow."

Taylor smiled at her. "Thank you."

The first hurdle had been crossed. Without giving voice to it, she and Jocelyn had silently taken each other's measure and exchanged mutual approval.

Noah stopped to exchange a few words with Tony as Taylor followed Jocelyn through a massive foyer and down a wide hallway off to the right.

Taylor was used to guest suites in her grandparents' house and others she'd visited, but this one went beyond all of them. The living room was big enough to hold a party, with a fireplace and an office setup. A bay window curved out of one wall and a small round table and chairs had been placed there, making a cozy nook to eat. Off to the left, she saw the bedroom and, she was sure, a bathroom beyond description.

"If there's anything you'd like changed, please tell me." Jocelyn's voice was tentative again. "I wasn't sure you'd be comfortable in Josiah's suite, but I'll be happy to make the switch if you'd rather."

Taylor shook her head. "I'm having enough trouble taking all this in as it is. I don't think I'm quite ready to sleep in Josiah's bed."

Jocelyn smiled and warmth darkened her blue eyes. "I understand." She looked at Noah, who'd come into the room, then back at Taylor. "Noah has informed me you and he will be meeting in the study in the morning and requested I have breakfast served in there. But first you'll have to deal with Audrey and the wardrobe business. Would you like coffee first thing?"

That brought a real smile to Taylor's mouth. Her system didn't start without an initial intake of caffeine. "Thank you. I'd love it. That's very kind of you."

"I tried to tell Noah you could wait on the clothes for a day or two, but he insisted we had to do it now."

"She has to project a certain image the minute she sets foot in that den of vipers." His voice was strangely harsh. "You only get one chance to make a first impression."

"I don't think you'll have to worry about the kind of impression I make." Taylor waved her hand. "But it's fine. I'll deal with it. No problem."

"Would you like anything now?" Jocelyn asked. "Lupe's gone to bed, but I could probably scare something up."

"Lupe?" Taylor raised an eyebrow.

"Our wonderful, wonderful cook. She feeds us all. Whatever you'd like, just tell her and she'll fix it."

"I hate to ask, but is it possible to get some tea now?"

"No problem. I'll get it myself."

"Oh! Please don't go to any trouble."

Jocelyn's smile was warm and reassuring. "It's really not a problem at all. And it's my pleasure. I know this has been quite a night for you."

"She likes you," Noah commented. "You handled things just right. The Harts' loyalty can't be bought and their friendship is a treasured thing. Josiah considered them like family."

"That's good to know." Taylor kicked off her shoes and stretched out on the couch. "If Jocelyn and Tony are running a smooth operation here, it's not to my advantage to change anything. They have to know I'm in charge, but I'm not here to disrupt things."

He eyed her with speculation. "Think you're up to what's waiting for you tomorrow? Except for Carmen, they'll all be looking to slit your throat."

"How comforting. Let me tell you something, Mr. Cantrell." She got up from the couch and went to stand by the bay window, hands shoved into the pockets of her slacks. "No one was harder to please than my grandparents, two people who made their displeasure with me known every minute of every day. Until I read my grandmother's letter, I didn't know why. But I promise you, there isn't a person I'll meet tomorrow who'll be any harder to deal with than they were. You pulled me into this situation, but I didn't come here to be bullied. By you or anyone else."

A knock sounded at the door, interrupting her monologue. Noah opened it and Jocelyn came in carrying a tray with tea and a plate of cookies, which she placed on the round table by the window. "Noah, your suite is ready for you. I assumed you'd be staying here tonight."

He nodded. "Thanks. For everything. I know how last minute all the arrangements have been."

"My pleasure." She turned to Taylor. "If there's nothing else, I'll turn in. We'll be having an early start tomorrow."

Taylor gave her a weary smile. "Thank you, Jocelyn. I'll

see you in the morning."

"Yes. I'll have your coffee here at eight. Will that give you enough time to be ready?"

Taylor nodded. "More than. Thanks again."

"Fine. Good night, then." She was at the door when she turned back toward the room. "I know you have a full schedule, but Tony and I want you to know whenever you're ready, we'd like to sit down and explain the ranch operation to you."

"As soon as I figure out what I'm doing." She unclipped her hair and ran her fingers through it. Fatigue and the hours of tension had caught up with her. "In the meantime, if you just keep things running as they are, I'd be very grateful."

"Of course." And she was gone.

"Your suite?" Taylor looked at Noah with curiosity. "Do you live here at the ranch?"

"No. I have a home in San Antonio. But there were many nights I needed to stay here. Right now, I'll be here for as long as it takes to get you settled in."

Taylor's senses went on full alert. *Nights.* Would those nights include more of the addictive sex that gripped them? *How the hell am I supposed to handle this and find my equilibrium in this situation at the same time? Especially with a man who could easily consume me if I let him?*

"All the sleeping areas are suites," he went on. "In case you wondered. Josiah designed it that way."

"Oh." Taylor poured tea into one of the delicate china cups then gestured with the teapot. "Well, I'm sure he had his reasons. Just as he did for everything else." She stirred sweetener into the hot liquid and squeezed a wedge of lemon, collecting her thoughts. "About tomorrow."

"I think…" he began, but Taylor held up her hand to stop him.

"When I discovered what my grandparents had done, they were both dead and there was nothing I could do to make them pay. Josiah's rejection didn't help. When you showed up at my office, my first inclination was to tell you to take the will and stuff it. But then I thought maybe by doing this, I can achieve some kind of retribution for my mother." She paused, weighing her words. "Once you've learned to live in a situation where any variation provokes the worst kind of emotional abuse, and not shatter under it, you can do anything." She closed her eyes then snapped them open. "Anything."

Noah looked at her with a strange light in his eyes. If she hadn't known better, she'd have thought it was respect.

"There is far more of Josiah in you than you can even begin to know."

She gave a short laugh. "A compliment? Am I hearing right?"

"Just consider it a quick assessment. This won't be a cake walk, Taylor, but I'm beginning to think you can do it."

"We're in for a fight on all fronts, aren't we?" Her smile was rueful.

"More than you know." He came to stand beside her, took the cup from her hands and put it down on the table. He rested his big hands on her shoulders. "You're nothing like either Josiah or I expected. You have a sharp mind, a wicked tongue and a fearlessness that you'll need starting tomorrow. I had my doubts but he made the right decision."

More compliments. She had to remind herself not to take them too seriously. She wasn't foolish enough to think it put her on any kind of equal footing with this man, but she was grateful for the praise just the same.

"God, I hope so." She desperately wanted to lean her head on his chest and draw from his strength, but that would show a weakness she couldn't afford. He might assume command when they were naked with each other, but, fully clothed, she gave up no control to anyone. She'd made that clear and she couldn't afford to ease back in any way.

Then he threw her a curveball. He bent his head and kissed her. A light brush of his lips against her, a breeze that dissipated so quickly she wasn't even sure she'd been touched at all. Its very gentleness surprised her and unsettled her, an unexpected gesture from a man with a constant undercurrent of anger and a healthy dose of arrogance.

"Get some rest," he called over his shoulder as he headed for the door. "You'll need it." Then he stopped to look at her, the supreme confidence back on his face. "And starting tomorrow night, don't lock your door."

Taylor just stared after him. Dealing with the corporate complexities of Arroyo would be a snap compared to handling this man. She was suddenly sure that Noah Cantrell would be her biggest danger of all.

* * * *

Even the sanctuary of his rooms didn't ease the strain that had gripped Noah all day. He stripped off his clothes and turned his shower on full blast. Under the pounding of the hot water, the tension began to ease from his muscles.

Damn Josiah, anyway!

Noah had argued with him until he was hoarse, trying to get out of this obligation, but the old man would have none of it.

'I don't trust anyone but you with this. Just do it for me. It's the only favor I've ever asked of you.'

That was true enough. For ten years, Josiah Gaines had been both his mentor and surrogate father, saving him when he would have destroyed himself. How could he have refused this?

But being with Taylor Scott was like standing too close to a fire. It required a lot of dissembling to control the heat she ignited in his body whenever he got within five feet of her. He had a constant erection and all he ever thought about was fucking her. Damn him for letting himself get involved with her in the first place. He should have walked out of that hotel room a month ago. Taylor Scott was trouble, just like all women, a lesson he'd learned in the most painful way possible.

Well, too late for that. Now he had to figure out how to put out this fire that threatened to consume him. Compounding everything was the sickening sensation that what he felt for Taylor was far more than lust. Cursing under his breath, he leaned against the shower wall, wishing he'd never heard of Taylor Scott. Wishing his heart didn't show signs of coming to life again.

Ten bitter years had passed since a woman had nearly destroyed his life. His soul was permanently scarred, his emotions shackled. What would Miss Taylor Scott think if she knew his black secrets? He was sure the knowledge would change everything.

He turned the shower on to full cold, hoping the icy water would cool down his body and get his brain working. Otherwise he was cooked, because even in the midst of all this chaos, the thing uppermost in his mind was taking Taylor Scott to bed.

Chapter Seven

Taylor felt as if she'd just closed her eyes when she heard a knock on her bedroom door.

"Miss Scott?"

"Yes?" Taylor struggled into a robe and opened the door.

Jocelyn entered, carrying a tray with coffee and toast, which she placed on the table by the window. "Here's your coffee, as promised. Audrey Campbell will be here in thirty minutes with your wardrobe."

Taylor stifled a yawn. "Thank you. That will give me time to shower and get ready. And thank you for the tray." She tried to make her voice as friendly as possible. "The coffee will be a big help."

Jocelyn stood where she was, eying Taylor with curiosity. "I hope you won't think I'm rude, but I have to say you're not at all what we expected."

Taylor laughed. "Were you looking for the wicked witch?"

Jocelyn actually blushed. "Noah gave us a one-page bio. To tell you the truth, we expected a money-hungry know-it-all who'd come in here and throw her weight around."

"Well, I've been known to do that on occasion, but not until I know which way to throw it."

Jocelyn gave her an answering smile. "I'll leave you alone to get ready. I'll be back when Audrey gets here."

Taylor gulped the coffee as if it were life-giving fluid. The day had barely started and a dull ache already throbbed at the back of her head. She found her bottle of aspirin in her suitcase and washed two down with the coffee.

A quick shower helped, along with the aspirin and coffee kicking in. Dressed in lingerie and robe, she examined her face in the mirror. She decided the occasion called for something a little more dramatic than her usual hint of blush and lipstick. *Better rummage in my cosmetic bag.* She added deep eye shadow, a warmer blush and swiped on a new lipstick she hadn't previously used. Her hair she gathered smoothly at the nape of her neck and pulled into place with a dull gold barrette. Finally, she fastened her mother's gold and diamond studs in her ears and took one last look at herself in the mirror.

"Go get 'em," she told her reflection. "Show these people they can't lead you around by the nose." Shoulders back, chin up and she was ready.

Audrey Campbell arrived with a list and an attitude, making Taylor grateful for Jocelyn's presence in the room. At the end of an hour, however, the woman showed grudging admiration for Taylor's taste as well as her ability to wear clothes well. The pile of new clothing covered the bed and Audrey was putting the finishing touches to Taylor's current outfit — a navy silk suit, no blouse but a silk scarf of blues and purples knotted loosely at her neck.

"Very nice. Isn't that what they call a power suit?"

She hadn't seen Noah arrive. He leaned against the doorjamb, cradling a coffee mug in his hands, his gaze glued to her as if he could see through her. For a moment, Taylor felt as if every bit of material had been stripped away and she stood naked before him.

"Good morning, Mr. Cantrell," Audrey trilled at him.

He dipped his head. "Audrey."

"Miss Scott wears clothes very well. Everything looks good on her."

"I expected no less." Although he kept a careful distance, the look he gave Taylor was smoldering.

"So what now?" She gestured toward the other room.

"Take them all. You'll need them. Audrey can send the bill to the office and Carmen will take care of it." He crossed the room to take her arm. "We need to get to the study. Jocelyn, can you call the kitchen and have our breakfast delivered?"

"No problem. I'll get these clothes hung up, too."

"Thank you both." Taylor smiled at the two women. "Thank you so much for everything."

"Our pleasure," Jocelyn said while Audrey nodded.

"This way." Noah guided Taylor out of the suite, through the large foyer and down another hallway.

"Do I get a GPS locator to find my way around?" she asked.

"When we get a minute, I'll give you a guided tour. Everything runs off the central foyer, so that makes it easier."

Noah unlocked a carved oak door and stood aside to let Taylor precede him into the room.

Taylor caught her breath as she walked into the private sanctum of the man whose genes she carried. Would she find anything in here to give her a clue to his personality? She inhaled deeply, as if the essence of the man still lingered and she could capture his scent.

The room was very masculine. She trailed her fingers along the edge of the massive desk. Eyed the vast array of telephones and other electronic equipment on a table set at right angles. Silently admired the woven Native American rug that partially covered a gleaming hardwood floor. Through a wide picture window, she saw a corral holding several horses and beyond that a row of barns with immaculate coats of paint and a smattering of cattle.

"The rest of the stock is pastured farther out." Noah had come up quietly behind her. "We rotate them, depending on the season and the calendar. When we sit down with Tony, we'll go over the details of the cattle operation."

"Good. I'd like to see the books before I do that."

"I'll arrange it."

A row of framed photographs sat on the long credenza behind the desk. They were all of the same man—astride a horse, in a pickup, standing beside a plane with two other men, sport fishing. She picked one up, curious.

"Josiah?"

Noah nodded once.

"The newspaper photo barely did him justice."

Josiah Gaines, like Noah, had been tall and both his erect carriage and the look on his ruddy face bespoke a go-to-hell attitude. His thick head of salt-and-pepper hair was cropped close to his head, almost military-style. Even at his age, he had been a very good-looking man.

"I can see why my mother fell in love with him," she said softly.

"As did many other women."

She frowned. "But he never remarried."

"No." And in that one word was a wealth of meaning to be explored at another time.

"I wish I had known him." Her voice was sad. All these years, she'd had a father she'd known nothing about. What kind of impact would he have had on her life?

Noah wound an arm around her waist and held his hand against her stomach, pulling her back against him. The hard length of his cock pressed into the cleft of her buttocks.

"You'll be the topic of conversation if you don't get rid of that bulge in your trousers before we reach Arroyo headquarters," she pointed out.

He slid the other hand inside the jacket of her suit and into her bra, cupping her breast. His mouth was next to her ear. "I'd love to, little girl, but the damned business is interfering with everything." He nipped the lobe of her ear. "You drive me nuts. I get hard just watching you walk into a room. Have you cast a spell on me, Taylor? Is that it?"

"I must be under the same spell." Her breathing quickened as he moved his hand lower until it rested on her mound. When he rubbed his swollen cock in the crease of her ass, moisture dampened her panties. This wasn't a spell — it was a drug and there didn't seem to be any cure for it. Whatever happened, there was no place to go in a relationship with Noah Cantrell besides the sex, so why didn't she just stop it right now?

Noah pinched her nipple and grazed his teeth lightly on her ear lobe. "If this wasn't Josiah's office, I'd lay you across that desk and fuck your brains out." His voice was thick with want. He moved his hands to slide her skirt up to her waist, grunting at the obstruction of pantyhose but managing to slip his hand inside and find her wet cunt. "You want it too. Damn it, Taylor. Danger's out there waiting and all I can think of is how many times I can stick my cock inside you."

She moaned as he skimmed his fingertips across her clit, but a knock at the door made him pull back and smooth down her skirt. She kept her face turned toward the window, sure that if anyone looked at her right then, they'd see a face marked by passion.

"*Señor* Cantrell. My mother hopes this is to your liking. And the *señorita*'s."

"Taylor?" Noah touched her shoulder. "This is Rey Pedrosa, Lupe's son. Lupe does all the cooking for the ranch."

Taylor hoped her face was composed as she turned and held out her hand to the good-looking twenty-something man. "Hello, Rey. Thank you for bringing our food."

"My pleasure, *señorita*." He arranged their trays on the desk. "*Señor* Cantrell will show you the house phone. Please call if you need anything else."

"I'm sure we'll be fine." Deliberately, she moved away from him and sat at the desk. "Shall we get started?'

Noah took a stack of file folders out of a drawer, pulled a chair close to hers and sat. "We'll eat while we work, if you don't mind." He handed her the top folder which contained what appeared to be a summary of Arroyo's structure. "Arroyo started out in natural gas and oil exploration. Now, it's a conglomerate covering everything imaginable. You'll find divisions in electronics, media outlets, farm equipment—even arms manufacture."

Taylor raised her eyebrows as she flipped one-handed through the sheets of paper. "Arms manufacture? Doesn't that get a little…tricky?"

Noah shook his head. "We have a number of government contracts and we're monitored very carefully. I can make arrangements for you to visit each division and meet with the people there."

"Yes. Later. That would be a good idea." She looked at him.

"I drew a corporate diagram for you." Noah pulled out the sheet and slid it in front of her. "This should simplify things."

Their hands brushed and heat flared at once between them. A muscle jumped in his cheek and he moved an inch or so away. For the next hour, he reviewed information with her on each of Arroyo's divisions and gave her a thumbnail assessment of each member of the executive staff. When they were finished, he locked the files in the drawer and handed a set of keys to her.

"Is this office locked when no one's here?"

"Yes. Always."

She nodded. "Good. I'd like to come in here by myself and go over these things again. I can make notes and come up with some questions to ask you." She drained the last of her coffee.

"Tomorrow, I'll brief you on Josiah's community and social activities. You'll be expected to take up the slack in a lot of them."

"That'll certainly be interesting," she said, her tone dry.

"We'll be leaving for the office in twenty minutes," Noah told her as Rey removed the dishes. "Do you need more time than that?"

"I'll be ready in ten. Where shall I met you?"

"I'll come get you." He opened a cupboard in the wall and took out a slim briefcase. "For you."

She held up the briefcase she was carrying. "You bought me a new briefcase? Why? I already have a perfectly good one."

"You might want to make a switch. I wasn't the one who bought this. Josiah did. Before he was killed, he planned to go to Tampa, make amends with you and bring you back here." His hand came up and brushed her cheek in a curiously tender gesture. "I think you'll do him proud."

For the first time since the beginning of the entire nightmare, Taylor was overcome with a desire to cry.

* * * *

Noah slammed papers into his briefcase and snapped it shut with enough vehemence to break the locks. He'd told Taylor there was danger hiding out there, awaiting them, but for him the greatest danger was just down the hall. Touching her was like putting his hand to a hot flame. Only this one burned him everywhere.

Damn it all to hell, anyway. How had he gotten himself in this situation? And what the fuck could he do about it?

This couldn't go anywhere, for reasons far beyond the fact she was Josiah's daughter and heir. There were things he could never tell her — the same things that made a long-term relationship impossible with anyone. He'd learned that very painfully.

He had to find a way to resolve things before the situation got really out of hand. He'd given her a taste of sex that was mild compared to how he really liked it. If he pulled out all the stops, she'd run screaming into the night.

But maybe that was the answer. Let her see the full scope of his needs and desires, the games he liked to play, and that would be the end of it. A wave of pain and bitterness reminded him just how efficiently it had worked once before.

Then, of course, he'd have to leave. No way could he stay around her when it was all out in the open, everything about him, and still he'd want her beyond all rational thought. From the minute he'd taken her to bed he'd known this was more than sex, more than a tangle in the sheets. More than he wanted or could handle. And he desperately needed to find a way to kill it.

Because there was no place to take this.

Ever.

Okay, time to get this show on the road.

They caravanned into San Antonio in the same manner they'd used the night before — Taylor and Noah in the lead vehicle, Tomas and Charlie trailing.

"I feel like I'm in a movie." Taylor smoothed imaginary wrinkles from her skirt, trying to keep the nervousness from her voice.

"Too bad it isn't." Noah's voice was tight. "We'd already have all the answers. Just so you know, we also have men on the two country roads that cut into this one, checking traffic. When they know we're rolling, they'll make sure no one's setting up an ambush as we go by."

Taylor shivered. "Somehow, when we talked about all this, it didn't seem quite real. Now, it does."

"Oh, it's real enough all right. That's the hell of it."

Silence stretched thickly between them, the air charged with the sexual energy that was so combustible it shimmered. Then Noah cleared his throat.

"You'll be under a microscope today. I want to assure you I'll make sure nothing about our relationship is obvious to anyone."

"Our relationship?" She turned her head to look at him. "Do we have a *relationship*?"

Fuck. He clenched the steering wheel. "To tell you the truth, I don't know what we have. Or where we can go with it. I'm… There are things… Damn."

Taylor looked straight ahead through the windshield, then turned to look out of the passenger window. Anywhere but at Noah. Her pulse was beating hard enough at her throat to leap through that tender covering of skin and the butterflies had come to life in her stomach. This was a terrible time for her to wonder if he wanted more from her than just sex. To hope for it. She had to focus, keep it together to deal with what awaited her.

She swallowed, forcing saliva past her dry throat.

"I have no idea what you're talking about. Unless you're referring to the fact that from the minute we fell into bed together we haven't been able to keep our hands off each other. I accept as much responsibility as you do. We both agree there's nothing beyond that, so what difference could anything you're keeping bottled up possibly make? And why would I even care?" She hoped her voice sounded cooler than she felt.

"Listen, little girl. You're a novice at this. A neophyte. And I'm not talking about the corporate quicksand waiting for you. There are things about me you don't know…"

From day one Noah Cantrell had unerringly found her weakness — an unexplored passion that yearned to burst into full flower — and taken control of her with it. The control she'd been determined not to give him. She had to find a way to unravel the invisible ropes he'd bound her with. In this strange world of international finance and intrigue she'd been thrust into, she had to admit that Noah's support and guidance were critical. There could be no hint of the flames they danced in at night. Certainly nothing that could give the waiting vultures any sign of weakness on her part. And his presence had to be defined as her choice, not his.

But just when she began to almost like the man, he turned into an asshole again.

"I think we'd better drop this for now." She fought to control her anger. "Let's discuss what's waiting for us at Arroyo headquarters."

As if he'd donned a second skin, the man next to her became someone else — cold, aloof and all business. They might never have shared an intimate moment or be fighting the sexual pull that kept drawing ever tighter. For the rest of their trip, he went over again the people waiting for her, the meetings he'd set up and what she could probably expect.

Then they were pulling into the Arroyo Corporation campus in northwest San Antonio. Taylor still remembered it from that one visit a month before. The three-story building was skillfully landscaped with gravel and colorful plants requiring little water. The two Expeditions drove into the attached parking garage and pulled in to two slots where a security guard waited for them. He came forward as Noah got out of the vehicle.

"All set, Mr. Cantrell. I've checked everything myself. Nothing looks out of place. And I've had the elevator locked on this floor."

"Thanks." He shook hands with the guard, then led Taylor to the elevator.

Tomas got in with them. "Charlie takes the first shift. I'll check out the building."

Taylor looked from one man to the other. "Are we expecting an attack?"

"Yes."

The one word chilled her and made her remember why she was here in the first place. She gripped her briefcase, trying not to show the trembling in her hands.

When the elevator doors opened again, the group walked out into an area of thickly carpeted floors and oak-paneled walls, with wide hallways leading away from a circular reception desk. Sound was muted, almost hushed, people moving quietly about their business. Several of them glanced at Taylor, unable to conceal their curiosity. The king was dead, the queen had arrived, conjured up out of thin air and they all wanted to know what it meant for them.

Noah guided her past them, an air of command and inbred arrogance firmly in place. The ultimate alpha male. Taylor sensed him beside her, striding confidently down the hall. Here, in this building, he was the man with the power and the atmosphere told her that while people might not too happy about it, they couldn't deny his position.

She had to discover the reason for his relationship with Josiah. With the situation as volatile as it was, there was no room for secrets. She needed every edge she could get.

"I feel as if I have a target painted on my back," Taylor whispered to Noah as he walked her down the wide corridor.

"Hopefully with us around, people won't be hitting it," Tomas told her as he moved noiselessly down the hall at her other side.

Through partially open doors, she saw more people sitting at their desks, glancing up in what they so obviously hoped was a casual manner as they watched her progress. Still others moved out to cluster around the reception desk she'd just left, pretending to gather their messages.

"Make no mistake." Noah's voice was still harsh. "You do. It's my job to find out who's aiming it at you."

"Now there's a comforting thought."

She would have said more, but he ushered her into a suite of offices with a legend on the door that read simply *Arroyo Corporation*.

"Josiah wasn't much for putting his name on doors," he explained. "He figured if whoever came through them didn't know who he was, they had no business being there."

A striking woman with wavy black hair and bright eyes, about Taylor's height, was waiting for them at her desk. She held out her hand, a welcoming smile on her face. "I'm Carmen Obradors, Miss Scott. It's an honor to meet you."

"Thank you. I've looked forward to meeting you too."

"I haven't touched anything in here," she said quickly, leading the way to Josiah's private office. "You said to leave everything as it was, Mr. Cantrell, and I did." She bit her lip, then blurted out, "Mr. Hunter wanted to go through the files, but I told him he'd have to clear it with you and Miss Scott."

"Good for you." Noah nodded his agreement. "I haven't even studied them myself."

"Perhaps the three of us could do it together," Taylor suggested.

Noah nodded, his face implacable. "After the staff meeting."

"Orders?" she asked quietly.

"Recommendations." His voice was just as quiet and a

grin flirted with the straight lines of his mouth.

Taylor swallowed her own smile and looked around at her surroundings. This office, like the den at the ranch, carried the imprint of Josiah Gaines. Heavy oak furniture, soft leather and another dazzling array of electronics. On the walls hung artwork that Taylor recognized as the work of Texas artists. Bookshelves with volumes on Texana, oil and glass and international business.

But it was the single framed photo on his desk that made her gasp. The woman was much younger, the picture obviously years old, but Taylor recognized her right away. Her mother. Laura Scott. She looked at Noah, eyebrows raised.

"He must have had it all these years. After he found out you were really his, he took it out, framed it and kept it there."

"It gave him sadness," Carmen interjected, the unhappiness touching her own face.

"Sadness?"

"Yes. The only thing that ever made him depressed." She twisted her hands. "I think he loved her very much."

"As she loved him." Taylor shook her head. "My grandparents ruined everything for them both. And for me." She sighed and turned back to Noah. "Somehow, occupying this chair will feel strange, as if Josiah's still in it."

"This is the office of Arroyo's CEO." His voice was uninflected but firm. "Right now, that's you. So this is where you sit."

A folder with her name written on it sat on the desk. Taylor opened it to find a list of the executive staff and division heads on one sheet, a list of the board of directors on another and several newspaper stories clipped together.

"I thought you might like to read all the stories about Mr. Gaines...your father..." Carmen looked at Taylor with a helpless expression.

"Calling him Josiah is fine. I've only known he was my

father for a month, so I can't even get used to calling him that myself. And thank you for getting these things together for me."

Carmen nodded and handed her a set of keys. "These are for both office doors as well as the desk drawers and the cupboards in the wall. Mr. Gaines kept everything well-secured."

Taylor put them in her briefcase. "Mr. Cantrell can help me check them over later."

Noah moved next to her. "Carmen, is everyone here?"

She flashed a grin at him. "They sure are. Buffed and polished, you might say."

"Good. Thank you." He took Taylor's arm again. "Best to get this over with first."

The executive staff. Hope their knives are sheathed.

Carved wooden doors opened to expose the largest conference room Taylor had ever seen. At their entrance, everyone in the room turned and blatantly stared at Taylor. The expressions on their faces were very clear.

Who is this interloper? What the hell is she doing here?

"Let's see some of that fire, little girl," Noah whispered, bending to her ear.

The name galvanized her as she was sure he knew it would. Taylor moved forward to the empty seat at the head of the table, placing her briefcase next to the chair.

Noah stood beside her. "I think we're ready to begin."

No one was smiling. Taylor thought she'd never faced a more hostile collection of faces that somehow reminded her of her grandparents. Their expressions were curious, defensive, even antagonistic, but none of them were the least bit welcoming. She was the interloper, the stranger who held their fortunes in her unfamiliar hands. And for at least two of them, the possibility of an uncertain future. They wanted to take her measure and decide whether she was in control or they were.

This not going to be fun. Noah had suggested introducing her, but she wanted them to know she was in charge from the get-go. Despite his alpha pride, she had to establish that he was the fallback, not the primary.

My, how things have changed in a little more than a month.

She swept her gaze over the table, her client smile firm on her lips. "Thank you all for coming today. I know I must be a shock to all of you. The recent turn of events has been a surprise to me also." She drew in a steadying breath, let it out. "I was not fortunate enough to know my father, Josiah Gaines, in life, but he has placed a great deal of trust in me in his death and I don't intend to disappoint him."

Taylor didn't think the silence in the room could get any thicker, but it did. Then someone began to clap politely and the others joined in, although with a noted lack of enthusiasm. She cleared her throat and plunged ahead. "I want you to know this is as much of a shock to me as it is to you. I'm only sorry that my father and I were not able to establish a relationship before his death."

A dark-haired man in an impeccable blue suit straightened in his chair. "What are your plans for Arroyo, Miss Scott?"

"I think it's a little premature for me to discuss that right now. I plan to review everything about the corporation, including the subsidiaries, and meet with key executives before coming to any decisions at all. I'll be doing that over the next couple of weeks."

A heavyset man at the far end of the table leaned forward. "You think two weeks will give you enough information to make decisions for a corporation as large and diverse as Arroyo? What qualifies you for this, anyway?"

"I assure you, I have the credentials, but since you ask, an MBA degree, a major in accounting and several years as an associate in a major investment firm have given me the background I need. I'm not a novice coming to the table." She gestured toward Noah. "And Mr. Cantrell will be helping to bring me up to speed."

"You sure ran yourself up the flagpole, Cantrell," another man at the same end of the table said bitterly. "Got yourself a nice cushy place next to the new boss, right? Anything going on there we should know about?"

"I think you—" Noah began.

Taylor put her hand on his arm. "That is a completely inappropriate remark and one I won't tolerate. Mr. Cantrell's position was dictated by my father, whose judgment I'm sure you all admired. We will be putting things in place together. If any of you have a problem with that, or with our relationship, I'd like you to let me know now. I'll be happy to provide references and a severance package."

Shock waves rocketed through the room. Beside her, Noah tensed, then relaxed. *'Always show them you've got your hands on the controls,'* Paul Clemens had drilled into her. *'The good ones will hang with you. The others, you don't want.'*

"Well?" She looked around the table, stopping for a brief moment at each person seated there. "Anyone else? This is your opportunity. Today is just supposed to be show and tell, but if anyone's unhappy, I won't stand in the way of their leaving."

A man two seats down from her, medium height with gray hair almost the color of his suit, broke the silence. "I don't think anyone is running out of the door, Miss Scott. We're all a little stunned but more than happy to abide by Josiah's wishes."

Yeah, right. In a pig's eye.

Noah's thigh moved against hers and she forced herself to relax. "And you are?"

"Sorry. Paul Hunter. Corporate counsel."

The weasel.

The woman next to him leaned forward. "Kate Belden. Executive Vice President."

Taylor took a moment to imprint the woman on her mind. Blonde, with a fashionably short haircut that framed a smooth, pale complexion. Her ocean-blue eyes had the hardness of diamonds. The long slender hands resting in front of her were steady as a rock. The erect line of her body had a touch of arrogance. Her red power suit said it all.

The ice-queen bitch.

Taylor inclined her head. "Nice to meet you."

"I've been the de facto head of Arroyo for the past four weeks." The woman's voice sounded like honed steel. "I hope you'll arrange an opportunity for us to meet as quickly as possible."

"Of course. I'll have Carmen call you with a time."

Kate Belden's eyes narrowed and the muscles of her face tightened, barely perceptible signs that she'd expected a better response than that.

Did she really think I'd just let her go on running the company?

Taylor nodded her acknowledgment and focused on the next person. As they went around the table, she mentally cataloged everyone. Her inborn ability to remember names and faces had been a valuable tool in many IPO negotiations and would stand her in good stead now, when so many were thrown at her at once.

Introductions over with, someone tossed out a question and suddenly she was hit with a barrage. Everyone seemed to speak at the same time, no one leaving any breathing room. They all seemed to have a question they wanted answered right now.

Noah's hand rested on her shoulder and squeezed once, gently. An unaccustomed sign of reassurance. Taking her cue from him, she was as noncommittal in her answers as possible. To each person, she said she was looking forward to one-on-one time with them and Carmen would be calling to schedule appointments.

Finally Noah cleared his throat. "I think that will do it for the day. Miss Scott will be in the office tomorrow and we'll begin the process of letting her know what we do here. Thank you for welcoming her into the company."

Welcoming! What a laugh.

"I appreciate your time," she told them.

They were nearly to the door when Kate Belden rose from her chair. "Miss Scott."

Taylor turned. "Yes?"

Kate gestured at those still seated at the table. "I think everyone here will agree with me that Josiah depended on me a great deal. I functioned as his second in command. I hope to have the privilege of doing the same thing for you."

Taylor had to swallow a laugh. Could the woman be more obvious? Noah's hand pressed on her arm, a silent signal not to rise to the bait as she gave Kate back stare for stare.

"As I said before, I'm not ready to make commitments to anyone until I have a complete picture here. I'll be meeting with each of you individually and making my own assessments. That will be plenty of time to discuss future roles with Arroyo."

Kate pressed her lips together, biting back anything that might be inappropriate.

But Taylor felt the invisible knife sliding in between her ribs and forced herself not to shudder. She'd taken another step toward the door when a hand closed over her arm. She jerked, startled.

Paul Hunter had disengaged himself from the group rising from the table and moved quietly to her side.

Instantly, Tomas, a silent presence watching everything, was beside her at once. "You might want to remove your hand, Mr. Hunter." He spoke in a low voice that managed to be both polite and menacing at the same time.

Hunter pulled his hand away. "Sorry, but I needed to let Miss Scott know it's imperative that I meet with her as quickly as possible." He glanced at Noah. "Privately."

Taylor looked at the man with a mixture of disdain and apprehension. She didn't need a sign to tell her that Josiah had stopped trusting this man. Maybe he believed in the old saying, 'Keep your friends close but your enemies closer'.

"I'll pass your request along to Carmen as she puts together my schedule. But Mr. Cantrell will be participating in all of the meetings. I'm sure you won't have a problem with that."

You bitch, his eyes seem to say, but he kept his face bland. "You may want to reconsider. There are things that I'm sure

Noah isn't privy to that mandate we discuss them alone."

"Mr. Hunter." She wanted to smack his supercilious face. "If there are things Mr. Cantrell doesn't know, it's time to bring him in on them. Carmen will be in touch. Now, please excuse me. I have a busy day."

I can do this. I can do this. I can do this.

Carmen opened the doors to the hallway and Taylor swept out, Noah right behind her. To every eye scrutinizing her in her new power outfit that she was sure cost more than she used to make in a week, she was in charge — sure, confident, in command. Inside she was quaking, drained by the control she'd exerted. But she was proud of her performance. The new Taylor wouldn't let anyone kick her to the curb. Or bend her to their will.

Except in bed.

She stamped out the thought as soon as it intruded. *Not now,* she told herself.

Tomas looked at her with a new respect in his eyes. He dropped in behind her as they moved down the hall.

Taylor stared straight ahead as she followed Carmen through the outer office and into her private one, posture erect, steps sure, aware that many eyes were tracking her progress. When the door was closed, she placed her briefcase on the desk, dropped into the chair and let out a long breath.

"Well, that was fun." She looked at her watch and realized almost two hours had passed. "I could almost see the vultures circling and feel the swords of the gladiators."

Carmen grinned at her. "I think you're not quite what they expected, Miss Scott."

Noah studied her with a strange expression on his face. "Josiah would have applauded."

Carmen laughed. "At least they won't have to wonder what they'll be dealing with."

"Set your meetings with Kate and Paul right now," Noah advised her. "You'll get a better sense of them one-on-one, and maybe a hint as to what drove Josiah that last day or two. And the sooner the better."

"But if either of them is involved, won't they be trying to hide it?"

Noah actually smiled. "Yes. And it'll be damned entertaining to watch you catch all the nuances of the conversations."

"I told everyone you'd be sitting in. Was that too presumptuous of me?"

"Is that a question or an order?"

For a moment her temper flared, until she realized he was trying to lighten the atmosphere with subtle humor.

She relaxed the tiniest bit. "Oh, a question, by all means."

"Wouldn't miss it for the world."

Chapter Eight

"Good." She turned to the woman beside her. "Carmen, can you make that happen? Late tomorrow morning, I think. Let them stew a little."

Carmen nodded and handed her a pile of message slips. "Calls to return. I arranged for lunch to be brought in for you and Mr. Cantrell. Perhaps after that, before the board meeting, we can go over some of the files Josiah left."

Taylor flipped through the message slips, her face dropping, then handed the pile back to Carmen. "Please call everyone back and let them know I'll be returning their calls as soon as possible."

"Clip notes to the ones that need immediate attention," Noah added. "Miss Scott will get to them as quickly as she can."

Taylor worried her bottom lip. "I keep going over in my mind what you told me about Josiah's trip and the shooting on the way home from the airport. I still think we need to take a closer look at his last day here. Occam's Razor, you know."

"When there are many answers to a question, the simplest is always the best," Noah recited.

Taylor's eyes widened a fraction.

"I'm not a completely uneducated savage," he pointed out, his irritation at her surprise evident in his tone.

"I never thought for a moment you were," she snapped back. "Carmen, do you have time this afternoon to double-check everything Josiah did those last two days? And call the pilot and get the log for the flight, too."

"Yes. No problem."

"Start with Mr. Rivas. Something could have happened at lunch." The mind that had been trained through six years of college and an equal amount of time at Clemens Jacobs to analyze detail was clicking into operating mode, much as the gears of a car clicked into place when the clutch was engaged. Discipline had taught her analysis. Paul Clemens had marveled at how she dissected stocks and market trends with the clinical precision of a surgeon performing a delicate heart transplant. With nothing else to fasten on in this situation, her mind grasped Josiah's last day and his activities as the only place to begin a search. Regardless of the fact that nothing had turned up so far, they still needed a starting place and Howard Rivas was it.

"Of course. What shall I ask him?"

"If there's anything that stands out from his lunch with Josiah. Anything at all that might seem the least bit out of the ordinary."

"The police checked with him," Noah interjected, "and got nothing."

Taylor narrowed her eyes. "Forgive me, but they may not even have known what to look for. Not to pat myself on the back, but I've been trained to evaluate the most minute pieces of information and process them. So let's just see where Josiah was headed and what, if anything, Howard can give us, okay?"

Noah shrugged but his eyes were shrewd, calculating. "Then let's go for it."

"I'll get right on it." Carmen hurried from the room.

Noah took Taylor's arm. "By the way, I meant to tell you I had Tomas sweep your room for bugs."

"Bugs?" Her jaw dropped. "You've got to be kidding."

"Not for a second. So at least there's one place besides this office, which we check regularly, that I know is secure." He led her to the wall behind the desk. "Come on. Lunch is waiting."

"Where are we going?"

"My office. My very private one. No one will bother us

there."

"What about Tomas?" She realized he'd left the office when Carmen did.

"He can get his own lunch. Besides, he has work to do. He'll be back when we need him. Let's go."

He pressed a button in the wall. A panel slid open and they stepped into a hidden elevator. Seconds later, they were in a large room that looked more like a den than an office and which seemed to have no doors to it.

"Hidden." Noah anticipated her question. "Just like the elevator. My real office is through another door that slides into that wall." He gestured with his hand. "Shall we?"

In the center of the room, a round table had been set with a white linen cloth, china and crystal. A rolling table at the side held covered dishes. Taylor inhaled the mouthwatering aroma and started forward, but Noah's hand on her shoulder held her in place.

"No."

She looked up at him and frowned. "No?"

"No. Not yet."

He turned her to face him and bent until his lips touched hers. She was frozen in place, held captive by the sensual touch of his mouth, the caress of his tongue against the seam of her lips, the heat of his body pressed against hers. Where almost every other kiss had been brutal and demanding, this one was tender and teasing. Seductive. He nibbled at each lip in turn, licking their softness in the wake of his teeth before insinuating his tongue inside.

This is crazy! Not here, not now. But somehow, the moment he touched her, she gave up control to him without a whimper. *So much for being in charge.*

They were taking a terrible chance, succumbing to their need here in this place where every stranger was a potential enemy. If anyone at all discovered this, her newly acquired position would be compromised. Noah had to realize that even more than she did.

So why does this keep happening? Why can't I just tell him to go to hell and keep his hands to himself?

The threads of sexual desire tightened around them more and more each time they were alone. She felt as if she'd suddenly stepped into quicksand. Noah was right. This thing between them was a wildfire, burning out of control. All they had to do was look at each other and they ignited. Greedy tentacles of flame wrapped around them whenever they were alone, burning them alive. If they couldn't control it — or extinguish it altogether — they'd be reduced to ashes. But instead of extinguishing the flame with an excess of activity, they were only building it higher. Resisting him just didn't seem to be an option. The feel of his hard-muscled body against hers, the grip of his fingers, the scent and taste of him made her head swim.

"I know I said the next time I planned to go slow," he breathed into her mouth. "But I hadn't planned on being so hard just from watching you work that I can hardly walk." He lifted his head. "Take off your clothes."

She blinked. "What?"

"Your clothes. Take them off." He brushed his lips against hers again, a gentle touch, but his voice was firm. Commanding. In his mind, there was no choice. "Don't want to wrinkle them before the board meeting." His hands were already reaching for the fabric of her jacket. "Want me to do it?"

"Noah, we can't keep doing this." It was a token protest and they both knew it.

"You're right. We have a board meeting we should be focusing on. And I don't like quickies with you. I told you that." He rubbed his thumbs across her cheeks, staring intently into her eyes. "But if I don't get rid of this hard-on you give me all the time, I won't be able to go anywhere. Certainly not to a board meeting."

He unwound the scarf from her throat and carefully undid the buttons on her jacket. She stood like a child as he removed first one item of clothing, then another, including the lacy bra. When she was down to her pantyhose, he picked her up and carried her to the couch, then rolled the hose down her legs with great care.

"You need to start wearing the ones that only come to the top of the thigh." His voice wasn't quite steady, an unusual indication of his frayed control. "Makes life a lot easier."

"I don't... I can't..." She struggled to find words that wouldn't come, but the sheer power of the sexual pull between them left her tongue-tied and rattled her brain.

Propping her against the pillows, Noah spread her legs and just stared at her cunt. Lust flared in his eyes and he lazily ran one fingertip down along the seam of her sex and back up again, a movement that was becoming a habit with him.

Taylor lay there as if drugged and perhaps, in a way, she was. In the middle of her debut at Arroyo Corporation, with the wolves nipping at her heels, she let this man she still didn't understand strip her naked and made no protest.

She had one startled moment when he removed his jacket and she saw the gun tucked into his waist at the small of his back.

He looked over at her. "I want you to be protected at all times. We're not playing with amateurs here."

The thought that whoever was doing this could get at her even in the Arroyo headquarters almost killed the desire rippling through her. But then Noah shed the rest of his clothes and was kneeling before her and a jolt of electricity speared through her again.

"You make me lose my mind," he ground out. "I can only keep my hands off you for so long." He moved her thighs farther apart and with his thumbs spread the lips of her sex as wide as he could. "You have the most gorgeous cunt I have ever seen. Pink, soft. And slick." A self-satisfied look rolled across his face. "Oh, yes. Very wet. You're as hot as I am, aren't you?"

"Yes." She could hardly get the word out. *Touch me. Fuck me. Do something.* She was sure every nerve in her body was screaming. *Hurry, hurry,* she wanted to scream. *Don't just sit there doing nothing.*

He touched her clit and she jumped. "If only we had more time today." He brought his face close to hers, capturing her eyes, his own filled with shifting light. "You're so new to this, little girl. You have no idea the things I'd like to do to you. You'd run back to Tampa as fast as your legs could carry you."

She thrust her chin up at him, fighting for some kind of control. "Are you so sure? How do you know what I'd do?"

He shook his head. "A woman who's never pleasured herself with her own hand? Never used a vibrator? I didn't think there was one left in today's society."

"Some of us have to keep too tight an emotional rein on ourselves." She wet her lips, then blurted out, "That doesn't mean I wouldn't want to. I've...thought about it."

Noah narrowed his eyes. "Thinking about it and doing it are two different things."

She studied his face, a slight blush heating her cheeks. "Do the other women you... I mean, do they...?"

"Use a vibrator?" The heat in his eyes was almost palpable. "Yes. Many types. They use them to pleasure themselves and me."

"You?" Her eyes popped open. "But how..."

He bent closer to her. "They know I love to watch them build their desire, see what happens to their bodies. Watch their pussy lips glisten as their juices flow. See them writhe in the throes of an orgasm, made greater because they know I'm watching them. Would you like to do that for me, Taylor? For us?"

Her breath was trapped in her throat by the images his words created. "I don't... I haven't..."

"No. You haven't. What we did in that hotel room? That's just a taste of what I like. You don't know how I really like my sex, Taylor. I promise you this isn't the kind of stuff you imagined in your little-girl dreams."

Taylor managed to reach her hands out to cup his face. It took her two deep breaths before her voice had a semblance of normality.

"I wouldn't be afraid with you."

Much. But I want to do that. Whatever 'that' is. With him. Because something burns inside me to explore everything with this man who turns me inside out sexually, enticing me to follow forbidden paths.

"Don't be so sure. And don't mistake this for anything but sex. There can't ever be anything else for us. Ever. I've lost my fucking mind to go this far."

His jaw tightened and his eyes lost all their fire for a moment. Then he bent his head to her pussy and caressed every inch of it with his tongue, licking it inside and out. He nibbled at her sensitive clit and stabbed his tongue in and out of her throbbing sex. When he teased at the flesh between her entrance and her asshole, she shivered all over and tried to thrust her pelvis at him.

Need gripped her, a desperate desire for him to put something inside her — his fingers or his cock. *Oh, please, his cock.* He hadn't even touched her breasts or her nipples, yet they throbbed and ached, demanding an attention they hadn't received. In desperation, she lifted her hands and began to pinch her nipples herself. Noah raised his head, a look of satisfaction on his face.

"God." The word escaped on a long-held breath. "The things I want to do to you."

He held her in a vise-like grip while exploring every inch of her cunt inside and out with his mouth and tongue. She was trembling with need, begging him in a low voice to give her release. He slid two fingers into her sopping sheath, teasing the sensitive flesh. Then, without warning, he withdrew them and pressed one against her anus.

She jerked.

"Do you want this, little girl?" His voice was thick and hoarse. "If you want my cock in here, take my finger first."

He waited and, when she nodded, long past the ability to speak, he pushed one finger inside her dark heat one inch at a time. He sucked in his breath when the finger was in to the last knuckle, but she couldn't hear anything else. She was too lost in a fog of erotic sensation and the roaring of her blood in her ears. Every inch of her skin felt inflamed, her ass the hottest of all. Noah's finger felt enormous, yet her muscles relaxed and accepted it. He stroked his finger in and out in a slow, teasing rhythm, the proof of her arousal pouring from her pussy.

The orgasm built low in her belly, tightening the muscles in her thighs, racing along her spine. Just as the tight coil of need began to unwind, he pulled away from her and she wanted to weep.

"No," she cried. "Please, no."

She felt empty, bereft, her body screaming for fulfillment. She wanted his hands and his mouth on her, bringing her toward that leap into space. She kneaded her breasts hard enough to leave marks, but the pain only increased her arousal.

Then he was back, latex-sheathed and poised at the entrance to her throbbing sex. Drawing in a deep breath, he entered with one long thrust to the hilt.

She climaxed at once, hips thrusting, legs locking around his waist, fingers rolling and pinching her nipples, her head thrown back and her neck arched. He rode her through it then began the drive to his own release. He stroked her steadily, in and out, slow then fast. Sweat dripped from his body and his breathing turned ragged. Taylor met him thrust for thrust, using her ankles as levers to pull him into her tighter and tighter. Finally, as his balls tightened and his ass clenched, she exploded around him again and his cock spurted into the condom. His body shuddered above hers, his lips drawn taut in a grimace, before he collapsed on top of her, dragging air into his lungs.

Long minutes later, he pulled himself off her body and looked down at her.

"What's happening with us?" she whispered, not even sure she wanted to know the answer. She had to believe it was just sex. He wasn't offering her anything else. But in the secret places of her mind, she was afraid of what was really growing between them.

Noah reached out a hand to help her rise. Something she couldn't quite understand shifted in his gaze.

"Too much. Way too much. But, damn it, I can't seem to stop it. Look at us. Do you think I make a habit of fucking people in my office in the middle of a business day? Or any other time?"

"I don't know," she answered softly. "Do you?"

Anger flared in his eyes. "I'll pretend you didn't say that. Taylor, if we go on with this, you'll be putting yourself in my control. You said you didn't want that, remember?" His voice was taut with tension. "And I didn't lie to you. There can't ever be anything between us but this. And even this is too much."

"Why? What is it you won't tell me? What is so damn terrible that you keep it hidden away where nobody can find it?"

A look of the most intense pain shone in his eyes just briefly. Then it was gone.

He pulled her close to him skin to skin, his big hands gentle as he stroked her spine. "Just be warned you may be biting off more than you want to chew." He sighed. "Damn my soul, anyway. This can't have a good ending."

She wrapped her arms around him and pressed her face to his chest, loving the feel of his chest hair against her cheek. "I don't know what's wrong, Noah. I don't even know how we got to this point. But it's like you said before. I can't turn away from you any more than you can from me. If I have control everywhere else in my life, maybe giving it to you in the bedroom is what I'm supposed to do. So maybe we'll both be damned."

"You may regret saying that." He kissed the top of her head. "We'd better get dressed. Give me a minute in the bathroom then it's all yours."

Fifteen minutes later they were seated at the table, eating stuffed chicken breasts and Caesar salad as if they hadn't just fucked themselves blind. Taylor had an urge to laugh hysterically. If she didn't know better, she'd think she was an actor in a bad movie.

She looked at the man sitting across from her, moisture seeping from her just at the sight of his bronzed body, his very masculine face, his bottomless black eyes.

What is his secret? What troubles him so much? And what did Josiah Gaines do that Noah pledged such loyalty?

"You're thinking again." His voice interrupted her thoughts.

"Just remembering what you said a few minutes ago." She put down her fork and took a swallow of her wine. "Noah, I've lived my entire life in the equivalent of a cold cell with an unyielding warden. In less than twenty-four hours, I've stepped into a life so different from anything I've ever known I might as well be on another planet. And I've learned a lot of things about myself."

His face was unreadable. "Oh? And those things are?"

"The main thing is I can pretty much handle whatever comes at me and not turn tail and run. So whatever you think is going to scare me off…" She paused, keeping her eyes on him. "Whatever it is, I don't think it will."

"Don't be so sure."

She gave him a trembling look, aroused just by the stimulation to her imagination. "You keep saying that, but I have no idea what you mean."

"And when you do…" He shook his head.

"Why don't you tell me?" Moisture soaked her panties just from the conversation. *God almighty.*

His silence indicated that avenue of conversation was closed. At least for now.

Okay, fine. For now.

"I'm curious about something." Her tone was businesslike. Unemotional. "You've stressed the importance of image as far as Arroyo is concerned, yet you seem to be willing to take personal risks with us. What if someone had come in just now?"

"Won't happen. Tomas and I have the only codes. He knows not to use them unless I tell him it's an emergency." He crumpled his napkin onto the table. "I wouldn't be down here with you, fucking our brains out, if I thought someone would walk in. Trust me. I'm not that big a risk-taker."

"Don't you worry that people will find out about us? You told me yourself you wouldn't do anything to put me at a disadvantage."

A muscle jumped in his cheek. "All you have to do is tell me no." When she didn't reply, he said, "I thought so."

Heat crept over her face. She filled her coffee cup from the carafe on the table, taking time to compose herself. "Let's talk business a minute."

"Afraid of discussing sex with me?" Noah's voice was low and deep, filled with unmistakable meaning. "Didn't seem like it a few minutes ago."

"No. Yes." She flapped a hand in the air. "I just want to get a handle on things."

"You don't trust me to get you through this?"

That wasn't true. She studied his face, wondering what he'd say if she told him she trusted him everywhere but in bed, the place where she was the most vulnerable. "I do, but I have some questions, okay? If Josiah hadn't gotten the proxies from the board, what would have happened?"

Noah pushed his plate away and leaned toward her. "This is still Josiah's show and no matter what, you hold sixty percent of the stock. It doesn't matter how they vote. He still held all the cards. Now you do."

"I should have asked this before, but there was so much to absorb. What if he didn't have an heir?"

"The stock was to be used to establish a foundation. Whoever was chosen as director, just like the new CEO, would end up controlling the lion's share of the stock."

Taylor stared at him. *A foundation? A Director? Would that have been him?* That would be a lot of money and power for someone to control. Lesser men than he was had been tempted by that. Could she really trust him? Another minefield to navigate.

"That could make for a tricky situation." *Especially if he has control.*

He shook his head. "But it's a moot point now that you're here."

And how does he view that situation? Maybe he thinks fucking my brains out would gain him entry to all that money.

Cool it, Taylor. He doesn't give off that vibe.

Still, the thought tucked itself away in her mind.

As soon as they stepped off the elevator, Noah buzzed for Carmen, who hurried in with her notebook and folders that held Josiah's personal files on his executive staff. A schedule of appointments was attached to the top one.

"I called Mr. Rivas," she reported, "but he was out of the office, so I left a message for him to return the call." She gave Taylor a hesitant look. "I left both your cell numbers in case the call comes in after-hours."

"That's fine," Taylor said. A secure Arroyo cell phone had been included with the goodies Noah had given her.

"Maybe Howard can point us in some direction," Noah said.

"Let's hope so. At the moment he's our best starting point."

"The board is here," Carmen reminded them. "I told them you'd be right there, but they don't look like a patient lot today."

Taylor dug into her purse and repaired her makeup. Snapping her compact shut, she smiled at Noah. "I believe I'm ready."

She was conscious of him watching her during the board meeting, surprised at the mixture of pride, surprise and admiration that swept briefly across his face. *What did he expected, an idiot? He knows better than that.*

He and Carmen had prepped her on each member and now, as she went through her paces, she realized these were people no different from the clients she'd handled at Clemens Jacobs. Having lived with money all her life — although a miniscule amount compared to Josiah's — and handled millions of dollars on a daily basis, the people sitting around the table didn't faze her. She was composed, controlled and knowledgeable.

However, she carefully avoided looking at Noah except when necessary and kept her voice even and controlled. She made sure that nothing in her manner gave away the nature of their relationship — whatever that was. She was a consummate actress. All her life, she'd had to be.

She tried to channel Josiah, even though they had never met. If anyone asked a question she didn't know the answer to, she made a note on the pad in front of her and promised to get the information. She gracefully avoided answering personal questions, focusing instead on her professional credentials.

At last the meeting was over. She stood at the door shaking hands with each person as they departed. Noah stationed himself at her side, ready to run interference if some question came out of the woodwork.

"I'm impressed," he told her when they were back in her office.

Taylor raised her eyebrows. "Another compliment from the silent sentinel? I'll have to mark it on my calendar." Then she smiled, to ease her words. "Thank you. I'm just glad to have gotten through it."

They spent the afternoon with Carmen, checking the files Josiah had left on his desk, discussing the phone messages and going over the last annual statement the company had issued. It was a lot to take in, but she was used to doing research and analysis.

Finally, at five-thirty, she tossed her pen onto the desk, loosened the tight twist she'd wound her hair into and raked its length back from her face. "I think I'm ready to get out of here."

Noah rose and held out a hand to her. "Come on. Let's head back to the ranch."

Chapter Nine

Taylor was more than ready to leave. Calling over her shoulder to Carmen that she'd have instructions for her in the morning, she let Noah lead her to the elevator down to the garage.

Throughout the day, Tomas had been a quiet presence wherever she'd been. Now he and her other security detail were waiting by both cars.

"Anything to report?" Noah asked.

Tomas shook his head. "Quiet as a church."

Everyone climbed into their respective vehicles and the little caravan pulled out onto Stone Oak Parkway.

"All right," she said, when they were on the Interstate. "Tell me about Jocelyn and Tony. I barely got to see either of them." The Harts were the last thing she wanted to discuss at the moment, but she needed to fill the space with conversation. Anything to counteract the sexual tension that surrounded them like steam heat whenever they were alone.

"When Josiah built Rancho Arroyo fifteen years ago and needed people to run things for him, he asked around and someone referred Jocelyn and Tony to him."

"Where did they come from?"

"Tony had been working on a ranch in South Texas and Jocelyn was managing a small hotel in the same town. They were looking to move up in the world and a member of Arroyo's board owed them a favor. I never found out what. Josiah interviewed them and hired them."

"And? I know there's more."

"They're very good at their jobs." He tapped his thumb on

the steering wheel. "When Josiah hired me, they somehow got the idea I was usurping their place at the throne. Fortunately, we managed to put that to rest fairly quickly. We've had a strong working relationship since then."

"Excellent. After today, I realize I'm going to need all the friends I can get."

They had left the Interstate behind now and were on the two-lane highway leading out to the ranch. Very little traffic passed them, the area being populated mostly by large ranches. Last night it had been dark when they'd made the journey. Today Taylor was able to take in the hills on both sides, dotted with mountain cedar and oak and separated by acres of pasture. The road dipped and rose as it cut through the hills.

As she sat digesting the information Noah had given her, the two-way radio on the seat crackled. Noah picked it up and keyed the Talk button.

"Tomas?"

"Pickup coming up fast behind me. I don't like the looks."

Noah glanced into the rearview mirror.

"I thought you had the side roads blocked until after we passed here."

"Me too. I can't raise either Gus or Hector and that worries me."

"The truck looks pretty beat-up to me."

"Maybe, but the engine isn't and the windows are tinted. Too much money for a junker."

"Okay. See if you and Charlie can slow him down."

Noah put the radio down and stepped harder on the accelerator. Suddenly another truck pulled out of a side road and headed right into their lane.

"Damn." He picked up the radio again. "Trouble. Let's do it."

He waited until the pickup was almost on them, then swerved sharply to the left and increased his speed even more. The pickup backed off slightly, but then there it was again. Noah zigzagged on the road and the pickup did the same.

Taylor clenched her hands in her lap, doing her best to hold it together.

Who are they? What do they want? Are they the same ones who killed Josiah?

She swallowed the metallic taste of fear clogging her throat and forced herself to breathe evenly. It wouldn't help anyone if she had a panic attack, but holy shit!

The two vehicles played cat and mouse, with Tomas coming up behind the pickup and trying to pass it. But whoever was driving that truck was an expert at what he was doing.

The radio crackled. "Rifle!"

"Get down and stay there." Noah pushed Taylor's head down until she was bent double. "Don't move."

She wasn't sure she could, anyway. *Rifle?* God, she hoped she didn't throw up.

A *crack!* split the air.

"Fucking damn," Noah swore. "That was close. Tomas? You got him in your sights?"

"Coming up on him again," the answer came back.

"Shit," Noah swore, just as the other vehicle bumped the SUV. "They must have some souped-up engine in that damn thing."

Oh, God!

Taylor wrapped her arms around herself to keep from shaking and bent over even more.

Noah jerked the vehicle right just as Tomas's voice came through the radio again.

"Watch yourself. He's doubling back to get between us. I think I can get a bead on him. I already called for the helo. Oh, fuck!"

"What?" Noah shouted.

"There's two of them now. Where did the other one come from? God damn it. Watch it, Noah."

Taylor jerked at the sound of two shots in rapid succession. Then their SUV swerved.

"Hell and damnation. I think they hit one of our tires."

"Ten-four on that," Tomas said. "And that fucker they're driving has those bulletproof tires on it. My bullets didn't even penetrate."

"Tomorrow we're getting these vehicles to Texas Armoring to make them bulletproof inside and out. Why the hell didn't we do it before?"

Taylor swallowed her fear and risked sitting up to take a look behind her. Tomas was in front of the pickup now, swerving back and forth across the road, trying to slow it down. Charlie leaned out of the passenger window, firing his gun, but the bullets rebounded harmlessly.

"I said get down." Noah pushed her head into her lap again. "And don't look up."

Another shot split the air and the side view mirror shattered.

"What's happening?" Taylor was proud of how steady her voice was.

"They're shooting out the tires on both vehicles to stop us. Then they'll have us at their mercy."

She glanced sideways just as Noah reached inside his jacket and pulled a gun from the holster she'd seen earlier. Strain etched deep lines in his face and there was no mistaking the rigidity of his body.

"No matter what happens, just remember to stay down," he ordered.

She bent over as far as she could again, trying to make herself invisible. Then she heard a different noise, a *whap! whap! whap! whap!* Taylor lifted her head just slightly, peeked up through the windshield and saw a black object approaching them in the sky.

"Helicopter," Noah told her. "Let's hope it's ours that Tomas called for and not theirs."

The helicopter drew closer and swept past them once. Even from her bent-over position, she spotted the Arroyo logo painted on the side and let out her breath in relief. The cabin door was open and a man holding one of the biggest guns she'd ever seen was leaning out, aiming toward the nearest pickup. In seconds, she heard the sounds of a rapid-fire gun, bullets hitting the ground as he pulled the trigger. The two trucks suddenly slowed down, spun around and headed in the opposite direction.

Noah keyed the Talk button on the radio again. "Greg, that you?"

"Sure thing, boss."

"Make some noise until those trucks are gone, then get down here. We need to get Miss Scott back to the ranch in case they decide to come back."

"Got it."

"Who's riding shotgun in the bird?"

"L. Q. He's our best shooter."

"Thought so. Tell him good work."

To Taylor, it seemed like only seconds before the helicopter landed on the road and Noah hustled her out of the Expedition and toward the waiting whirlybird. She ducked down as she ran, trying to make herself as small a target as possible. A husky light-haired man crouched in the open door and held out his hands to her.

"Help her in," Noah shouted over the sound of the rotors. Then he lifted her and thrust her into the man's waiting hands.

The blond pulled her into the helo even as people were yelling all around her.

"You'll be safe with these men. They'll get you to the ranch and into your suite. Okay?"

Taylor let the blond man help her into a seat and strap her in.

"Rey and Danny should be here in a minute in one of the trucks," Greg told Noah.

"Good."

"Noah, I gotta lift off," Greg hollered.

"You're good to go." Noah slapped a hand against the cockpit door. "Get the hell out of here."

As they lifted off, Taylor gripped the edge of her seat and

looked down through the window. Behind her she heard the blond man on a satellite phone.

"Headquarters, this is the bird. We are in full security alert. Repeat. Full security alert."

In no time at all, they'd landed at the ranch on the lawn in front of the house. Jocelyn had the front door open and L. Q. hustled Taylor right into the house. By the time she was in the suite, she had stopped shaking, her fear replaced by a raging anger.

"Would you like some tea, Miss Scott?" Jocelyn was standing in the doorway.

"Actually, I'd like a drink. You know what happened, right?"

Jocelyn nodded.

"If I see them again, I might kill them with my bare hands."

Jocelyn laughed. "I'll say this. You're no shrinking violet. Your...father...would be proud of you."

"You can refer to him as my father. It's okay. In fact, I'd really like it if you would." She sighed. "I'll take whatever connection to him I can get."

"Good for you." Jocelyn paused. "You know he was making plans to see you and bring you back to the ranch?"

"That's what Noah said. So I'm going to do the next best thing—find out who killed him and who's behind all of this."

"Let me get you that drink. Any preference?"

"Jack Daniel's Black. Two ice cubes."

Jocelyn gave her a strange look. "I should have guessed. That was Josiah's favorite drink."

Taylor swallowed a smile. One more thing to connect her to the father she'd never known.

* * * *

Noah drove the second Expedition back, leaving the men in the chase car to deal with the shredded tires on the other one. Then he leaned back in toward Tomas.

"More men. ASAP. And you'd better get with Tony and tell him what we need the hands to do on the ranch."

Tomas nodded, Noah slammed the door and the SUV roared off toward the barn area.

Noah took the three steps to the wide front terrace in one stride and shoved the front door open. He'd been cursing steadily for the past five minutes, as angry at himself as he was at the shooters. Some protector he was, nearly getting his charge blown away. He was so sure he'd covered every angle, blocking the side roads to provide safe passage. His men were damn good. The shooters, whoever they were, had been better and that had scared the hell out of him.

The other thing terrifying him was the growing connection between himself and Taylor Scott.

Thank God his reflexes had kicked in when the shooting had started, because his fear for her was a living thing. The very last thing he needed in his life was to feel anything for any woman except lust, easily called up, easily sated. Anything else was a sure path to destruction for him, a lesson learned long ago.

Yet tonight his first reaction had been to pick her up in his arms and carry her far away, to someplace safe and stroke and pet her until the nightmare of the incident faded. Emotions that vaulted from the heart, not the brain. He needed to compose himself before he gave any hint of it to her. It was already bad enough that he couldn't control his desire around her.

Christ, what am I going to do?

From the moment he'd met her—the first time he'd touched the smooth satin of her skin, felt the tight fist of her cunt grasping his cock—he'd had the feeling he was swimming against a tide that was threatening to drown him. He'd tried using anger as a shield, but all that did was make the waters roil in a more dizzying motion. It didn't make him want her less or push her away, as he'd intended. If she'd resisted him, rejected him, it would have made life a lot easier, but she was drawn into the relationship as much as he was.

What if…?

Don't go there, asshole. She's not for you and you know it. Guide her through the canyons of Arroyo during the day, fuck her brains out at night and walk away when this is over. Just go.

Get his act together, that was what. And try to keep her from being killed.

He paused at the door to her suite, centered himself with a deep breath and knocked on the door.

Jocelyn opened it and gestured him inside.

Taylor had changed into jeans and tailored silk shirt and, even in the intensity of the situation, Noah couldn't keep himself from noticing how the supple denim hugged her body and the soft fabric of the shirt outlined her breasts. She'd left her hair loose and it fell to her shoulders in shimmering waves, like a thick curtain. His cock hardened automatically. He had to fist his hands to keep from reaching for her and running his fingers through that heavy fall of silken hair.

She looked up and came to a halt in front of him.

"Good. You're here." Her eyes were fiery but there was no mistaking the sheen of unshed tears or the slight tremor in her hands as she folded her arms across her chest. The abstract had met reality for Taylor Scott and she was doing her best not to fall apart. She lashed out at him with temper that was equal parts of anger and panic. "What happened to the roadblocks you set up out there? How did those men get through? We could all have been killed."

He knew she was right, which didn't make things any easier. He'd fucked up by underestimating their enemy and had no one to blame but himself. He swallowed back any retort, because the news he had to deliver was unpleasant and another load of guilt on his conscience. "You're right and I accept full responsibility. My men were blindsided and badly beaten. Two of them were sent to the hospital and one of them is dead."

The color drained from her face.

"Oh, Noah, I'm so sorry." She was instantly contrite, pushing her hair back and tucking it behind her ears. "I hope the injured men will be all right."

He nodded once, a sharp motion of his head. "They will, but it doesn't lessen in any way how badly I misjudged the situation. What concerns me now is how good these people are, because the men I had out there are among the best."

Fear flashed in her eyes as she took in what he'd said.

He opened his mouth to try to reassure her when Tomas appeared in the open doorway.

"We should fly her in and out after this," he told Noah. "If someone goes after her in the air, at least we'll know we aren't dealing with anyone penny ante."

"Agreed."

"Stakes are heating up since she got here," Tomas commented. "I think this is a lot more than she expected."

"Hell, it's certainly more than *I* expected."

"*She* is right here, gentlemen. Please don't discuss me as if I'm thin air."

Charlie let out a laugh.

"She's sure no shrinking violet, boss." Tomas grinned.

"I just don't want her to be a dead one," Noah told him.

"I'll drink to that." Taylor lifted her glass and took a sip.

Noah turned to her. "Here's my assessment. At first I thought this was personal. That someone was just after Josiah and we could smoke them out. But it looks like Arroyo's the big target, along with anyone in the Gaines family that controls it. Tomas, we'd better do some rethinking."

"No kidding. Okay. Give me a holler after dinner and we'll have a sit down to plan." He nodded at Taylor and was gone.

Jocelyn cleared her throat, reminding them she was still there. "Noah, what instructions do you have for the house?"

"Tomas will get with you and Tony when he comes back later. We'll definitely beef up the security in the immediate vicinity. Meanwhile tell your husband his hands should ride with weapons for the next week or so, just in case."

Jocelyn's face tightened at the mention of guns, but she just nodded. "I'll let him know." She turned back to Taylor. "I'm sure dinner is the last thing on your mind right now, but you should eat something. What would you like me to tell Lupe?"

"Oh." Taylor was startled, obviously not used to leaving dinner instructions for anyone. "I-I don't know. Anything will do, I guess." She looked at Noah, a question in her eyes.

"Can you ask Lupe just to fix us something simple and bring it in here? That way we can work while we eat."

A corner of Jocelyn's mouth turned up in a smile. "Of course, although Lupe's champing at the bit to roll out one of her famous dinners. But I'll get her to do sandwiches for tonight. Is that all right?"

"That's fine," Taylor assured her.

"I'll have Rey bring a tray as soon as it's ready, Miss Scott."

"I think I'd feel a lot better if you called me Taylor. If you'd feel comfortable, that is."

Another tiny smile. "Thank you." Then she was gone.

Taylor turned back to Noah. "This is getting really nasty, isn't it?"

He nodded. "We need to find answers quickly so we're not just running around blindly in circles. Maybe we'll be lucky and catch a break."

"What do you mean?"

"Howard Rivas reached me on my cell right after the 'copter took off with you."

"And?" she demanded. "What did he say?"

She vibrated with nervous tension. Noah was reminded of a climber who was full of confidence that he could reach the top, then looked down and realized how far he had to fall.

He wanted badly to pull her against his body, infuse her with his strength and promise her everything would be all right. But he couldn't do that and touching her right now would be his undoing. Instead, he leaned a hip against the couch and crossed his legs at the ankles, hands jammed into his pockets.

"Howard does an annual review of all the Arroyo insurance for all the divisions. The last few years Josiah's had Kate doing it, one more responsibility he was backing away from. But Kate was in an auto accident and unconscious for four days. No one was sure what was going to happen."

Taylor frowned. "She seems fine now."

"Yeah. And that was a little strange, too. She came out of the coma and in two days was nearly back to herself. She had a lot of bumps and bruises, but fortunately for her no broken bones. And no lasting effects from the head injury."

Taylor's eyes widened. "You don't think someone put Kate out of commission because of some insurance policy, do you? That sounds completely idiotic."

"No." Noah shook his head. "That I did check out. The car that hit her came out of left field and was driven by some soccer mom with rowdy kids. Besides, I can feel Kate's fingerprints all over whatever this is."

"And?" Her face was taut with impatience. Back went the thumbnail between even white teeth.

Strange habit, he thought, for a woman who gave off such a strong vibe of self-possession.

"Apparently, Howard called Josiah to see who else he wanted to assign, or did he want to wait until Kate was better. Josiah said no, he'd go ahead and do it himself. The two of them hadn't had lunch in quite a while so they decided to combine business with pleasure."

Taylor raised an eyebrow. "And that was it?"

"Except for one thing. There was a little aberration that could mean nothing or something. He said Josiah was concerned because someone else seemed to be handling the insurance for one of the farm equipment plants, a facility Howard knew nothing about and had no policies for. Never had. He thought maybe Kate had decided to use a local agent."

Taylor frowned. "Well, on the outside that doesn't look too suspicious. But I'll tell you, when you're analyzing stocks, you train your mind to look for those aberrations, any tiny thing out of the ordinary. That's what this is. We need to see those policies."

"Already taken care of. I asked Howard to fax the cover pages for each one to the house." He glanced at his watch. "They should be filling the fax machine in the study as we speak."

"I can't imagine insurance being the motive for anyone's murder, unless it's life insurance."

"Neither can I." He rubbed his hand over his face. "Howard said the rest of the meeting went well, but when they were finished, Josiah seemed in a hurry to leave."

Taylor paced, worrying her lower lip. "We need to get a look at the financial reports from that division, too. If something's out of whack, it will carry over to everything. Can we do that from here?"

"Got your keys to the study?" When she reached into her purse and pulled them out, he said, "Then let's go down there and boot up the computer. I gave you the password. We can pick up the insurance fax at the same time."

Taylor looked at him directly. "I'm the unexpected wild card, aren't I? No one knew about me except you. Until yesterday. Hence the attempt today." She dropped her gaze and threaded her fingers together.

"Yes, but I'm hoping we can put ourselves in the dealer's seat soon with our own deck of cards." He unfolded himself from the couch and opened the door. "Let's go down to the den and get what we need. We can bring it back here and go over everything while we eat."

The meal was consumed and both the pitcher of iced tea and the carafe of coffee empty by the time they'd waded through every one of the faxes and computer printouts. All of them had notes in the margins and many items had been highlighted in yellow. Taylor and Noah stared at each other across the table.

"Well," Taylor said at last, "I have a lot of questions but not many answers. There's a reason why the Idaho plant is the only one not on the policy, but I can't find anything in the division reports to tell me why. There are payments for the insurance, but the company has no relationship to any other Arroyo policy."

"We could always make calls beginning with the division head. Or Kate herself." He shook his head. "No, not Kate. Not yet. I don't want to tip our hand to anyone that we're checking things."

"You're right," Taylor agreed. "Whatever we're looking for is in there somewhere. We just have to find it."

Noah narrowed his eyes. "But you don't even know what you're looking for."

"That's true. But I know someone who can help us. Do you know what a forensic accountant is?"

For a moment familiar resentment raced through him, memories of unintended — or intended — slights — and he forcibly tamped it down. "I actually have a college degree, in case you're interested."

A flush of embarrassment stained Taylor's skin. "I'm sorry. I-I didn't mean — "

"Don't worry. I'm used to people assuming I'm an uneducated hired gun."

"Look, Noah — "

"Forget it. Let's get back to what you were saying."

Her hands shook slightly as she stacked the papers into piles. The day had been one assault after another and he wasn't helping. She was still unsettled and he wanted nothing more than to pick her up and cradle her on his lap.

Well, that would be stupid. Having sex with her every five minutes is bad enough, but emotions get you into trouble. Remember?

What he really wanted to do was slip his hand beneath her shirt and cup those warm breasts with their plump nipples. Unfasten her jeans and slide his hand under her lace panties to the welcoming wetness he knew he'd find there. Touch the skin that was so much like satin beneath his fingertips, open her like a flower and inhale the delicate scent of her arousal.

In less than five minutes, he could have her begging him to fuck her. His cock hardened at the wayward thoughts and fire streaked through his groin. He shifted position to conceal his growing erection.

Jesus Christ.

Would he ever get past this raging desire for her? And what would little Miss Taylor Scott, so recently the product of a starched upbringing, say to the things he'd really like to do to her? With her? He'd given her enough hints and she hadn't backed away. Yet. He'd watched her change from the angry, unsettled woman he'd met in the hotel to someone taking charge of her own life. Making her own decisions. Pushing the boundaries she'd lived within all those years. But was she ready to make the leap to sexual experiences beyond anything he was sure she could even imagine?

She turned to him and fire blazed in her eyes. Maybe he could take her on a sexual adventure after all. Or maybe not.

What would she expect when the Arroyo business was settled and she was faced with the rest of her life? Would she want to continue holding the reins Josiah had handed to her? Choose another path? And what would she want of him? Something he was damned sure he wouldn't be able or willing to give.

Maybe he could just shoot himself and not have to worry about anything.

Taylor bent forward over the table, shifting papers around. Anything to distract herself from Noah's nearness. The scene in his private room at Arroyo was still vivid in her mind. Not even almost being killed seemed to dull the need for him that throbbed constantly in her sex and kept her nipples tight and hard. Even now, just being in the same room with him, her panties were soaked and a quivering began deep in her cunt.

This whole thing was insane. She was trying to find her footing on the slippery slope of the world into which she'd been thrust. Noah was her designated guide, the alpha male who automatically assumed command. Under any other circumstances, she would feel completely secure. But these circumstances were far from ordinary, where beneath the steel veneer of business thrumming in her body was the almost addictive need to feel his cock inside her, his hands and mouth on her.

Succumbing to the passion that roared constantly between them was a dangerous move. It could compromise her situation and send the wrong message to anyone who learned their secret. And it was very clear they had no future beyond Arroyo. She hadn't been looking for one and he'd said as much. Over and over. So what did she do about her constant readiness for the intense sex that bound them together?

He'd hinted more than once of sexual activities that might chase her away. Her sexually untutored mind couldn't begin to imagine what he meant, but her newly awakened body craved the dark eroticism he was tempting her with. The lure of the forbidden unknown lay coiled deep inside her, ready to unwind and spring.

Two days and I'm in so deep I can't find a way out.

"There are lots of questions here that we have no answers for. We can do some of the digging, but I don't want to trip anyone's sensor. Or trigger a warning to whoever's behind all this."

Noah fiddled with his empty cup, watching her. "I agree. So what do you have in mind?"

Taylor cleared her throat. "John Martino is probably the best forensic accountant in the country. Maybe anywhere. He'll be able to tell us what's going on and not give out any clues while he's conducting the search. Plus, he can give us some guidelines on how to pursue some of it on our own."

Noah frowned. "I know who he is. Josiah tried to hire him once, but he indicated he didn't have any free time. If Josiah Gaines couldn't get him here, what makes you think you can?"

"He was a client at Clemens Jacobs. I made a lot of money for him and we became good friends."

Noah's face tightened and his body stiffened. "Exactly how good?"

Taylor threw up her hands. "For God's sake, Noah. He's twenty years older than I am and we had a client relationship. Maybe *you* have sex with everyone you know, but I certainly don't."

He was beside her before she could blink, hands tight on her arms, his face inches from hers. "Just with strangers, right?"

She tried to pull away from him, her head jerking as if he'd slapped her. "You can be sure that won't happen again."

"Oh, it'll happen all right. But only with me." His voice was hard and seductive at the same time. "Not with anyone else."

She twisted in his grasp. "What is it with you, anyway? You've made no bones about telling me you wish this… whatever it is hadn't happened. That we certainly don't have a relationship beyond business. Which, just so you know, is fine with me. But you don't own me, Noah Cantrell. So don't make those kinds of decisions for me."

They were so close she could count his eyelashes. His spicy scent wrapped itself around her and her pulse skittered as he bent his head toward her.

"Don't push me, little girl." He pressed his mouth to hers, hard, while using one hand to cup a breast. He kneaded the soft flesh, rasping his thumb over the swelling nipple pushing at him through the thin fabric of her blouse and bra.

She couldn't help the moan that escaped her lips or stop her back from arching into his touch. His tongue was hot in her mouth, scorching her. Automatically, she reached her arms around his neck to pull him close, pressing her body against his.

Noah broke away first, a subtle move that reminded her that as always in this situation, he was in control. Taylor pressed her hands against the hard wall of his chest and pushed herself away from him. She stood, smoothing her hands down the fabric of her jeans.

"It's adrenaline," she told him, still a little breathless. "That's all. Just a reaction to what happened out there. And all the tension today."

He was silent for a long moment, his face betraying nothing. "If that's what you want to believe." He turned away from her, forcing his own breathing to slow down. "Why don't you call John Martino and see if he's willing to do this? And plan to put him up here at the ranch where he's away from everyone's prying eyes."

Noah stood just inches away, his eyes twin lasers focusing on her as she took up the phone.

I have to pull myself together to make this call with some semblance of intelligence.

The few minutes she spent talking to John seemed longer under that scrutiny. "He'll do it," she told Noah when she hung up. "He'll be here tomorrow. I said we'd send the plane for him, so you'll have to tell me how to do that. And we'll have to pick him up at the airport here, of course."

Noah took the phone she was still holding and punched in some numbers. "There's a sheet in the first folder I gave you that has the numbers for the pilot and also the private terminal. I'll get him on the phone for you this first time and you can give him instructions." He spoke rapidly to the voice on the other end then handed her over.

"All set," she told Noah after she completed the phone call.

"We'll be ferrying you to work in the helicopter tomorrow," Noah told her.

"Because of what happened today," she guessed.

"Yes. I don't think they'll try to shoot us out of the air, but

L. Q. will still ride shotgun, just in case. But that way we can also leave Arroyo, pick John up at the airport and come straight back here to the ranch."

The adrenaline rush was wearing off now and tendrils of fear crept through her again. She had to face the stark truth that someone—maybe more than one—wanted her dead. When she'd said she wanted to change her life, this wasn't quite what she had in mind—inheriting a vast empire, running a billion-dollar conglomerate, being shot at by unknown killers.

Being ravished—the only word for it—by a stoic warrior who made her blood boil.

Be careful what you wish for, Taylor.

Taylor finished making notes and stood. "Tomorrow you'll have to help me access the reports I need for John. He'll want to compare the division that owns the facility that the stray insurance policy is for with the others. He'll look for any red flags in the record-keeping. Can we put everything on flash drives for him?"

"Better yet, we'll set him up in his room with a secure computer and give him a password to access whatever he needs for himself. I can make those arrangements. At the same time, I'll show you how it's done for the future."

"Thank you."

"No problem."

"Well, then." She blew out a breath. "What time should I be ready to leave?"

"Nine-thirty. I'll let Greg and Tomas know. And we'll take L. Q. with us also."

"Fine." She opened the door to the hallway. "I'll see you then." Was that firm enough?

Get out and give me some peace. I don't need you getting in my head tonight.

He stared at her for a long moment, nodded then walked out of the room.

Taylor leaned against the door, gathering her wits that had been scattered so easily by Noah's presence. Arroyo

Corporation presented far less of a challenge to her than Noah Cantrell did with his simmering anger, blatant sexuality and dark secrets. Taming the panther might take far more than she was capable of giving.

Deliberately pushing it out of her mind for the moment, she set up her meeting with the Harts for eight-thirty, then headed for the bathroom. She turned on the shower full force, dropped her clothes on the floor then stepped under the spray, welcoming its needle-sharp feeling on her skin.

She had soaped her body and was letting the multiple shower heads do their thing when she saw a shadow through the frosted glass. The door slid open and a very naked Noah Cantrell stepped under the water with her.

Chapter Ten

Taylor froze, the bar of soap still in her hand. Her heart tripped over itself and her breath caught in her throat.

His powerful warrior's body towered over her and surrounded her. He was magnificent, his well-defined musculature gleaming in the shower light as the water pelted him. His cock rose proudly from its cushion of dark curls. Droplets clung to the fine hair on his chest. Fire in his eyes, his intent very clear.

Instinctively, Taylor backed up until the shower wall left her no place to go. "I-I thought I locked my door," she stammered.

"You did." His voice was low and thick with desire. "I've never let a little thing like that stop me."

"But what…? Did anyone…? People will see…"

"Give me a little credit for common sense." He crowded her, resting his hands on her shoulders, caressing the indentation at her collarbone with his thumbs. "There's a short back corridor that connects our hallways. Josiah had it built that way."

"So he could visit his lady friends?" She couldn't help the bitterness in her voice.

"So he could conduct business conversations out of view of others in the house. No more talking."

"B-But we already did this today—"

His kiss cut off the rest of her words and stole what little breath she had left. His tongue danced across the sensitive tissues of her mouth while his lips, soft and pliant, pressed into hers. Taylor clutched at the hard muscles of his biceps for support as sensations rippled through her body. Her poor befuddled brain tried to tell her she should push him away and run as fast as she could to whatever sanctuary she could find. But her body kept her riveted to the spot, begging for more. No—demanding more.

When he lifted his head at last and looked at her, she was shocked to see a sadness in his eyes that made her heart trip. Where was this coming from? What did Noah Cantrell keep hidden behind that solid granite mask that shielded him from the world?

But then he was touching her everywhere and thought fled like a thief in the night.

"Let me bathe you." His voice was soft, not hard and demanding as it usually was.

"A-all right." She closed her eyes and leaned against the shower wall.

He began with her neck, his fingers sensuous weapons calling to every one of her nerve endings. With unexpected tenderness, he massaged the muscles that had grown tight and corded with the day's anxieties, loosening the hard knots of tension. He worked expertly to relieve the tightness, forcing the stiffness from each muscle. As her neck muscles relaxed she rolled her head back and gave herself over to the sensuous massage.

He moved outward to her shoulders, back to her collarbone and the hollows that defined it. Every stroke of his fingers aroused her as much as it eased her, her body stirred by the familiar touch. The water was a gentle sluice running down her body and mingling with her own fluids sliding from her cunt and down her thighs. The pulse at her throat was hammering so hard she thought it would burst from her skin. Noah pressed a gentle fingertip against it, the knowledge of its cause blatant in his gaze.

He lifted each of her arms, continuing the sensuous massage. She'd never known the crook of her arm, the inside of her wrist, her elbow could be such erogenous zones, but each stroke and caress turned her body to liquid and heated the fire burning inside her. Deep in her womb, she felt the now familiar flutters growing and spreading.

Using a slow, circular motion, he rubbed lather into her breasts which already felt swollen, the skin stretched and tight. When he touched them, those flutters increased their tempo. He teased at nipples already hard and engorged, pinching each one lightly. Heat arrowed straight to her already quaking sex and tiny spasms rocketing through those inner muscles. Each stroke of her breast, each tease of her nipples sent that heat higher.

She looked down at his dark hands as he moved them in a hypnotic pattern against her paler skin and the image itself was so erotic she nearly came just from the sight of them. Her breasts felt heated, her nipples near to bursting and still he worked them with a tender rhythm that was at once pleasurable and torturous. *Squeeze them,* she wanted to shout. *Bite them.* But all her words were trapped in her throat behind her breath.

Just when she would have used her own hands to press his more firmly against her, he slid his fingers down her ribcage and began the same stroking motion on her abdomen. With the tip of a finger, he traced the indentation of her navel, over and over, the touch so light she wasn't even sure it was there, before moving lower across the sweep of her belly.

She widened her stance and tried to push herself against his hard, muscular thigh, to straddle it, wanting the abrasive feel of the rough hair against her now demanding cunt, but he backed off an infinitesimal amount and shifted his thighs to an inaccessible position.

"Patience," he whispered in her ear. "You've had a very long, very hard, very frightening day. You handled everything with an incredible amount of strength. But now you need to let me help you relax, because tomorrow will be here before we know it. So don't rush me."

"You're always saying that." She was surprised she could even move her lips move.

"You are a treat to be savored, little girl. I haven't had many in my life and I want to enjoy this one while I can."

While I can.

His words almost—but not quite—catapulted her out of the trance she was sinking into. But then he rested his fingers on her hips and slid his thumbs up and down the creases between her thighs and her mound. Reality fell away again.

Touch me there, she wanted to scream, as he slipped his hands down again. Instead he crouched and began the same mesmerizing massage on her feet, her ankles, her calves. Rubbing the lather into her skin. Rubbing. Pressing. Again she tried to shift her legs apart, but he turned her away from him. He was so unbelievably gentle when he lifted her arms and placed each of her hands flat against the shower wall. Then he resumed the slow, erotic massage, beginning at her shoulders and working his way down her back.

Her body was humming like a finely tuned instrument, a need building inside her and growing with each sweep of his hands, each magic touch of his fingers. She wanted him inside her, stretching her. His fingers or his cock—it didn't matter. Her body remembered him even in such a short time and it screamed for him to fill her. She rocked back at him, trying to urge him, to indicate her need.

His soft chuckle resonated in her ear. "And to think not long ago you were so green at all this. Afraid of it. But wanting it, right?" When she didn't answer, he tightened his grip on her waist. "Right, little girl?"

"Yes." The word hissed from her mouth. Oh, he was so right. She knew she was such a novice. A neophyte. But the more pleasures he showed her, the more she wanted. She had no idea what plane he'd take her to next. What terrified her was that she wanted it. *Craved* it.

But this, tonight, was torment. Where before everything had been wild and devouring, tonight his attentions were soft and teasing, coaxing her body to relax even as he teased it to intense arousal. Her clit, still sensitized from the wild session at lunch, begged for his touch and the walls of her slick channel were quaking with tiny tremors. Sensations assaulted her over and over, now tormenting her, now soothing her. When he stroked lather up the insides of her thighs, she wanted to squeeze her legs together and force his fingers inside her.

The hot water did nothing to cool her desperate need and when two soap-slicked fingers slid into the cleft of her ass, liquid seeped from her opening. She wanted his fingers in there again, in that tight little ring of muscles at the entrance to her rear, pushing inside her. Those muscles still remembered the feel of his intrusion and screamed for it. Resting his big hand at the base of her spine, he held her firmly in place. All she could do was try to push back at him, wiggling her rear end in silent invitation.

"You want it, don't you." A statement, not a question. His voice was hoarse and deep as he moved his fingers back and forth, touching the pucker but not opening it. "You're still a virgin in so many ways, but you love wild sex, don't you, little girl? I wonder just how wild you're willing to be."

She moaned as he traced the shell of her ear with the tip of his tongue as all the while he continued stroking, stroking, stroking.

"You're in my blood, little girl, a drug I can't wash out." He bit down lightly on her shoulder. "I'm in yours too, aren't I? Ever since that first night."

"Yes." She forced the word out, the only word she seemed able to manage, unwilling to give voice to it but unable to lie to him.

"Would you like me to tell you what I really want to do to you?"

Her tongue was so thick she could only nod, all powers of speech having fled.

He eased one of his big hands around in front of her and moved it in lazy circles at the top of her mound, a deliberate whisper away from her clit. "Would you let me tie you up? Use a vibrator on you? Spank you? Keep you on the edge of orgasm for so long you'd beg me to let you come? Is that more than you bargained for, Miss Taylor Scott?"

Oh, God. The walls of her sex vibrated with hunger as dark images of his whispered demands flooded her mind. Things she'd never done, never thought of. Forbidden things. And she wanted to do them all with him, her jungle warrior, the panther whose lightest touch made her lose all sense of herself.

"Would you?" he prompted, demanding an answer.

Taylor swallowed and nodded.

"No, say it. I want to hear the words." He teased at her anus again, setting off a riot of sensations. "Say it and I'll make you come."

Oh, God, please. Yes. "Yes."

"Yes, what?"

"Yes, I want you to tie me up. Spank me." The words came out in a rush. "Do whatever you want with me."

Oh, God, what am I getting myself into?

"You aren't scared? I like a lot of things that could send you screaming back to Tampa." In a low voice, he told her in explicit terms exactly what he wanted to do with her. "Those aren't the nice, neat kind of things you know about. You'd run like mad."

She shook her head. "No. I won't. Oh, please." The words burst from her mouth.

He kissed her cheek. "You're such a wildcat underneath that repressive upbringing. You were a wildcat today, shredding those people and they didn't even know it." He licked her ear again. "You got me so hot watching you I wanted to rip your clothes off right then and shove my cock into you until you begged for mercy." He backed off a little. "But not tonight. Tomorrow you'll be thrown to the wolves again. Tonight is to make you feel good and sleep well. And dream about me."

As he finished speaking, he slid one soapy finger into her ass, pushing past the tight sphincter muscle with a force that had her gasping.

Oh, yes, she'd dream about him tonight.

In and out he stroked, the initial burn receding to a pleasurable pain that suddenly became not enough. She pushed back against his finger and he laughed, a low, throaty sound.

"Soon, little girl. Not tonight but soon."

She was melting inside, her legs threatening to fold beneath her. When he moved the hand resting against her soft belly and pinched her clit, she nearly screamed. Instead, she clenched her teeth and it came out as a strangled moan. She felt his thick, magnificent cock brushing against the side of her thigh. His dark chest hairs tickled her arm. The jungle sense of him — the panther — surrounded her.

Taylor moaned again and rocked her pelvis into his hand, then back into the finger still stimulating the hot, dark tunnel of her ass. Forward and the friction against her clit increased. Back and she was impaled on the probing finger. Forward. Back. Forward. Back.

He put his mouth next to her ear. "Come for me, little girl. Let me feel that cunt ripple around my fingers and your juices spill into my hand."

He shoved two fingers into her pussy, both of her channels now manipulated by his wicked fingers. She came with a gasping cry, shudders racking her body, a scream at the intensity of it ripped from her throat. Her inner walls gripped his fingers, pulsing around them, lubricating him with her juices. She couldn't stop rocking, her body demanding that his fingers never leave her, never stop their erotic dance.

If his body hadn't been pressing her into the wall, she'd have melted into a pile of nothing on the floor. At last the spasms subsided. When every quiver had disappeared, he withdrew his fingers and leaned her against the wall while he soaped himself and rinsed.

As gently as if he was carrying a baby, he lifted her out and dried them both. She was grateful for his hold on her. A bowl of gelatin would have had more control than she had. Every muscle was loose and lax, her body nerveless. When he carried her into the bedroom, she leaned into the hard wall of his chest, her arms loosely around his neck, face pressed into his shoulder. She could have stayed there forever and never been unhappy.

The bed felt soft when he placed her in it, the sheets cool and smooth against skin still flushed from the shower and her orgasm. Fingers that had moments ago made her shatter now caressed her cheek with a gentle touch. With whatever part of her brain still worked, she wondered at his gentleness tonight and where it had come from in this hard, unyielding man.

He rolled her onto her back, spread her legs and leaned down to plant a soft kiss on her sex. After settling her on the pillows, he pulled on the clothes which he'd left on a chair. Then he bent and kissed her cheek. "Sleep well, Taylor." His voice had a strained quality to it.

Something pricked at her brain. "We didn't… You didn't… I mean…" She was confused. Why had he not satisfied himself? He'd been hard as a rock. Still was.

He shook his head. "This wasn't about me."

Then he was gone.

Her eyelids were so heavy she could hardly keep them open. As she drifted off into a deep sleep, her bronze warrior floated across the edge of wakefulness, naked and proud, a look of hunger on his face.

* * * *

Noah closed the door to his suite softly so as not to disturb anyone, but he really wanted to slam it as hard as he could.

God damn it.

He was out of his fucking mind. In such big trouble he couldn't figure a way out. Bad enough that he'd taken Josiah's daughter to bed when he was supposed to be checking her out for the old man. Bad enough that he'd fucked her blind. Himself, too. Bad enough that he hadn't been able to keep his hands off her since he'd walked into her office. But to lose all common sense now where she was concerned was unthinkable. Yet that was exactly what he'd done.

This was a lot more than his cock leading him around. That he could deal with. This woman was in his blood and devouring him, reaching places he'd guarded for years and breaching them without even realizing it.

Since the night Josiah had found him and helped him put his life back together, he'd exerted the most rigid discipline over his mind and body. No more emotional loose ends. No more cracks in the armor to crumble his hard-won foundation. He'd set about creating the man Josiah encouraged him to be. No one did corporate security better than him, his private life little more than a footnote in his existence. Then Taylor Scott had stumbled into his life. Literally. And nothing had been the same since then.

He couldn't open himself up to that kind of damage again. He had no resources left to deal with it. Yet here he was, smashing his own good intentions again.

Fuck!

He stripped off his shirt and pants and tossed them onto a chair. Then he sat on the edge of the bed and dropped his head into his hands. He had a responsibility here. To Josiah, to Arroyo and to Taylor Scott. They were surrounded by assassins, literally and figuratively, and he'd bet his last nickel tonight was only the first of many attempts to get rid of Taylor, much as they had her father. The two of them were tiptoeing through treacherous waters and all he could think about was that enticing body, that hot mouth and delicious cunt.

If it was just her body tempting him, he might be able to handle that. Find someone else and satisfy the raging lust consuming him. But, damn it, she was smart too, and full of wildfire. Just like the old man. She'd walked into the lion's den today — only she'd been the one with claws. The beauty of it was that the people wouldn't even know they'd been clawed until they started bleeding.

He allowed himself a brief smile as he thought of ice-cold Kate Belden, who'd thought she had Josiah tied around her finger. And Paul Hunter, who Noah was sure had used his position as corporate counsel to hide things from Josiah.

Only Josiah had been too smart for them. Someone had made a slip somewhere and he'd begun to look for answers. So they'd taken him out, hoping to wrest control of the company away from the board and continue whatever games they were playing.

He was sure it was Paul and Kate, although as yet he had no proof. Probably others, too, but those two were in it ass-deep. Now that they'd weathered the shock of Taylor's appearance, they'd regroup and paint a target on her back, just as they had today. Noah had good men on his team but Taylor's safety was his responsibility alone. He'd turned over the running of the Security Division to Mark Jensen, his assistant director, so he could devote himself to this one hundred percent. He just hadn't thought he'd be devoting so much of it in bed.

He pushed himself off the bed and began pacing the room. Letting his emotions get involved would be the end of everything. He knew what a trap that was. Taylor Scott wasn't someone who could look at his past, at what he was and shrug it off. And he didn't need another tragedy in his life.

For ten years he'd kept a tight control on himself. Now this woman had moved in under the radar and was destroying all the walls he'd erected. He'd walk away from this if he could. Pack a suitcase and disappear. But that wasn't an option. He had a debt to pay and he planned on paying it in full.

For once he was faced with a problem that he had no answers for, no solutions. Only an impending sense of disaster.

* * * *

Taylor woke early, filled with a strange mixture of lassitude and energy. Lying in bed, she wondered if the whole scene with Noah last night had been a dream. No, not a dream but an incredible experience. She stretched, feeling the wonderful softness in her muscles and recalling the tender care with which Noah had bathed her and massaged her.

Last night had been strange. On the one hand, he had been demanding, flaunting his sexual power over her, leaving her with wild fantasies. On the other, he'd been gentle and tender, two things she had trouble ascribing to him. He'd soothed her and caressed her until her muscles were as limp as yesterday's lettuce. Then he'd given her an orgasm that had taken her breath away and left her even more undone.

Words popped into her brain as she remembered his dare to her. His graphic description of what he wanted to do with her. To her. She blushed as the explicit nature of his words echoed in her head, but at the same time that lure of dark, forbidden pleasure beckoned her. Moisture gathered in the folds of her sex and she squeezed her legs together, trying to still the tremors that undulated through her.

Before her arrival in San Antonio, her sexual experiences had been limited to a few very inept lovers. Then Noah Cantrell had exploded into her life and she was off on an erotic rollercoaster that showed no signs of slowing down. Was the ever-present sense of danger what ramped up all her senses?

Sighing, she pushed herself out of bed and headed toward the bathroom. No time to fantasize this morning. She had a long To-Do list.

The first thing she did was ring the kitchen for her coffee. She had just finished showering when a tap at the door announced its arrival. She raised her eyebrows in an unspoken question as Jocelyn herself carried the tray in.

"I didn't mean for you to fetch and carry for me," Taylor protested. "I don't expect that at all."

Jocelyn gave her a tentative smile. "I don't mind. I thought this would give us a minute each morning to see what you needed from me during the day."

Will I ever get used to this?

Taylor cleared her throat. "As a matter of fact, I do have something I need to go over with you. I have a guest arriving today. A client of mine from Tampa. I'll be picking him up at the airport after I leave the office. Do we have a place to put him?"

Jocelyn actually laughed. "Taylor, we could probably put up a battalion of Marines if we had to. Do you want him near you?"

"It doesn't matter one way or the other. He needs a quiet place to work on a project and I offered him my hospitality. But I'll need you to make sure he gets fed and watered properly."

"No problem. Would you like to do something special for dinner?"

"Mmmm, maybe some special food that Lupe's itching to make. But we'll eat in here. Noah will be joining us."

Jocelyn couldn't hide the curiosity that Taylor saw flash in her eyes, but she just nodded.

Noah was standing in the foyer, waiting, when Taylor emerged from her suite. She searched his face as discreetly as possible for some sign of what last night had been all about, but his face was its usual mask.

"Ready?" His voice was equally unemotional.

"All set."

Greg was already set in the pilot's seat and both Tomas and L. Q. climbed in after her.

She'd never flown in a helicopter before last night and that trip had been so short and her adrenaline pumping so hard she remembered little of it. At first, when they lifted off, her stomach did the tango, but then her body settled down after a few minutes and she tried to enjoy the scenery below.

Noah, sitting in front of her next to the pilot, gave her

headphones so they could talk during the trip. He pointed out the more well-known sites — the Alamo, the Riverwalk, Hemisfair Park, the zoo.

"When we get things under control," he told her, "you'll probably want to do some sightseeing."

"Yes. I'd like to. All I've seen of San Antonio so far is… rooms."

She started to say 'hotel rooms and offices' but instead bit her lip. She was very aware of Noah in the small cabin. Even though they weren't touching, ignoring his powerful presence and the sexual energy radiating from him was impossible.

When he shifted position, his muscles moved like those of the sleek panther he reminded her of, rippling smoothly beneath the civilized fabric of his suit. His face wore its usual taut expression but his black eyes smoldered behind the cover of thick lashes. His spicy scent drifted past her nostrils. He might try to hide it, but she was sure last night still lingered with him too. She wondered if he felt the sparks arcing between them right now as sharply as she did.

Again she reminded herself how crazy this was. Danger was everywhere, Josiah had been murdered, one attempt had already been made on her life and she couldn't make her body behave where this arrogant man was concerned.

She needed a distraction. "I didn't see Charlie at the helipad."

Noah nodded once. "He's driving the Expedition into town so he can scout the roads. He's got one of the hands riding with him today, just in case."

She sucked in her breath and tiny fingers of fear skittered over her spine. "You think someone's keeping track of us?"

"Of course." His gaze narrowed. "Last night's episode was hastily planned. That's why it didn't come off more smoothly. As it was, they almost had us. But you can bet they're watching and tracking every move you make."

Once again, Taylor realized just how high the stakes were

in this game.

"I don't think we should be putting any of the hands in that kind of danger."

L. Q., sitting next to her with his shotgun held loosely in his hands, grinned at her. "Don't you worry. Clay Morgan was an Army Ranger. No one gets one over him."

"And he's ranching?" Taylor lifted her eyebrows.

"What can I say? The man loves cattle." L. Q. shrugged. "Clay worked on the ranch before he went to Afghanistan. Josiah kept a spot for him. He's one of Tony's lead wranglers."

"Thank you. That makes me feel better."

"We're landing." Noah's voice in her headphones broke into her scattered thoughts.

In a matter of seconds, Greg had set down the helicopter on a helipad next to the Arroyo building.

Noah leaned over to speak to him then jumped down and helped Taylor out.

They might have been any two people on their way to a business meeting, if not for the fact that Noah reached inside his jacket and adjusted the gun in his shoulder holster. Glancing behind her, Taylor saw Tomas do the same. And today L. Q. joined them as they entered the building. Once again, her stomach clenched and she looked around to see where danger might be hiding.

In minutes, they were in the building and riding the elevator up to her suite of offices, one man on either side of her. Carmen rose from her desk and greeted them with a smile. She picked up a stack of messages from her desk and followed Taylor and the men into Taylor's office.

"Everyone in the world apparently wants to talk to you, Miss Scott." She grinned. "A lot of them are call-backs from yesterday. You're the newest celebrity around here."

Taylor grimaced. "I could do with a little less of that, you know." She flipped through the message slips in her hand and looked at Noah, standing next to her desk like a block of granite. "I have no idea who any of these people are. Can

I just have Carmen keep putting them off?"

He held out his hand. "Would you like me to look through them? I can advise you on the ones I know. The others Carmen can fill you in on and we can decide how to proceed."

"Yes. I think that's a good idea." When she slid them into his hand and their skin touched, Taylor thought hers had caught fire. Her nipples hardened at once and moisture flooded her panties. She hoped her dark suit and silk blouse would effectively camouflage her body, but what would people see in her eyes?

"We can discuss these at lunch." His eyes were smoldering when he looked at her. "Carmen, why don't you order lunch for the three of us and we can eat and work here in the office?"

The three of them. Good. She relaxed a fraction. Another lunch like yesterday would have killed her composure altogether. Especially after last night, which they hadn't even addressed yet. What a complex man Noah Cantrell was. She wasn't sure she'd ever find the key to unlock that mystery, but she damn sure planned to try.

"That's sounds good." She turned back to Carmen. "Kate Belden's first this morning, right?"

Carmen nodded.

"Then I'd better get ready for her." She looked at Noah. "Tell me about the ice queen. Not what's in her folder, either."

Noah dropped into one of the chairs in front of the desk. "Forty-four years old. Graduate of the University of Texas and Wharton School of Finance. Ten years with an overseas corporation in the Middle East and Mexico. Josiah hired her nine years ago and gave her an unbelievable amount of authority. All the division heads report to her."

"She must have something. Is she married? Have a lover? Partner? Significant other?"

"Not married and her love life is a blank page, although I suspect she keeps Paul Hunter in line by gracing him with her body now and then. No one knows anything about her personal life." He paused. "Yet."

She looked up at him. "Yet?"

He shifted in his chair and crossed his legs, one ankle resting on the opposite knee. "I think it's time to do a deeper background check on our Miss Belden."

"I agree. How soon can you get on it?"

"Now." Noah pulled his cell phone from his pocket and punched in some numbers. "Yeah. Me. Restart on Kate Belden. Don't leave me hanging on the updates." He disconnected the call. "The man I have on this doesn't work for Arroyo. I didn't want any leaks or accidental discoveries. But I've known him a long time and he does a lot of work off the books for me."

"That's good." She chewed on her lower lip, wondering if she should bring up last night, when the intercom buzzed. "Yes, Carmen?"

"Miss Belden is here."

"Okay. Send her in."

Taylor couldn't miss Kate Belden's displeasure at finding Noah in the room. When she entered, he rose from the chair he was in and moved to the couch against the wall, leaning back in a deliberately relaxed pose, the ankle of one leg on the knee of the opposite one, as he'd been sitting before.

"Don't you think we'll get much more done with just the two of us?" Her tone of ice could have chilled water.

The look she gave Noah made Taylor look to see if he was bleeding. It only made her more determined than ever to keep Noah in the room.

"Mr. Cantrell will be sitting in on all my meetings. With everyone." She smiled politely. "Is that a problem?"

Kate looked at Noah then back at Taylor. "All right. I'll be very frank here. Josiah had a great deal of confidence in me. He turned over supervision of all the division heads to me. But for the last few years, Noah has worked to erode that confidence and probably to get rid of me."

Taylor put her elbows on the desk and leaned her chin on

her folded hands. "And what makes you think that?"

"You can't be that naïve. He moved in on the...your father. Wanted the power for himself. And I can't imagine why, since he's hardly qualified."

Taylor opened her mouth to say something, but Noah's voice interrupted her. "Kate. Taylor may look like she's green, but I assure you she's not. Don't try to create scenarios for her. She'll see right through them."

Kate's face reddened slightly and she turned in her chair so her back was to Noah. "Fine. Then let's get on with it. I guess you'll have to find out things for yourself."

Taylor studied the woman as they talked. Kate was well-kept for forty-four, with her makeup, hair style and clothing calculated to take five years off her age. She wore a simple sheath that Taylor recognized as part of a high-priced designer's collection and no jewelry except diamond studs at her ears and a Cartier watch. Her hands were still in her lap and she didn't change positions frequently.

She's used to being in the power seat. She knows self-control. Noah better kick that investigation into high gear.

An hour later, nothing had been accomplished except for the two women sizing each other up and Kate Belden hopefully understanding she wasn't going to run roughshod over the new kid on the block. She'd answered all of Taylor's questions on exactly what she did and how she did it politely but without giving out any real information.

As soon as she was out of the door, Taylor looked at Noah.

"I know. I'll goose the investigation. I get the same feeling you do."

"She spent ten years on foreign soil. Who knows what contacts she still has or who she could be working with? I wish you hadn't let things drop when Josiah was killed."

Noah stood and paced the office. "Yeah, well, me too. But we were a little busy with a lot of other things. Like trying to keep this whole ship afloat until you decided to talk to me."

Taylor bit back her reply. "Just get it done."

Chapter Eleven

Paul Hunter was no more or less than she'd expected. She'd dealt with men like him at Clemens James, the older investment counselors who had an inflated assumption of their image and worth. He was gray from head to foot— hair, suit, shirt, ties, socks. Only the black shoes and the tiny black stripe in the tie provided any relief.

Like Kate, he stated his preference that Noah not be included in the meeting. And again like Kate, he was unhappy with Taylor's rejection of his request, but there the similarity ended. Where Kate had been all ice and arrogance, Paul tried every approach from avuncular uncle to experienced executive. He, too, was unprepared for Taylor's firm hand and reluctance to accord him special status.

"Your father and I were friends for many years," he protested, when she mentioned bringing in another attorney. His gaze skittered, and a thin layer of sweat appeared on his forehead.

"I've learned in this business there isn't room for friendships," she told him.

"I think you'll make a huge mistake if you listen to Noah Cantrell in all of this." His words sounded as if he'd bitten off each one. "He's looking out for himself."

"Isn't everyone?" She gave him a humorless smile. "I've been thrust into a situation with a steep learning curve and not much time to climb it. It's my decision who I choose to help me with this." She dropped her gaze to the folder open on her desk. "And frankly, Paul, I can't see exactly what it is you do that necessitates a place on the executive staff.

Filing papers and checking points of law can be done by any young attorney."

Dark red suffused his face. "I helped Josiah keep this ship on the right course, dotting all the Is and crossing all the Ts. Don't make hasty decisions, young lady."

Taylor tamped down on her anger. "Mr. Hunter. Paul. I am the CEO of this leviathan. And your boss. And Noah Cantrell, not you, is the one chosen by Josiah as my connection. Let's keep this in mind, shall we?"

By the time she'd finished with him, she'd added him to Noah's list for further investigation.

Noah studied her with great care as soon as Paul walked out. "Well done. More spine than they expected."

These were the first words he'd spoken to her all day, except to give orders or ask questions. She felt an unreasoning thrill of satisfaction and immediately tried to suppress it.

"I think there's a lot about me they don't know." She looked directly at him. "You, too, for that matter."

"You may surprise all of us, little girl." His gaze scorched her. "Maybe the things I want wouldn't shock you so much after all."

Her nipples felt as if they would burst through the fabric of her clothes. The idea of exploring new sexual boundaries with Noah Cantrell made her so aroused she was sure if he merely touched her, she'd come right there.

For her own sake, she deliberately ignored his implication.

"I want you to do the same kind of investigation on Paul Hunter you're doing on Kate Belden. Let's see if, in addition to everything else, we can tie them together personally. And I want to know what he really does here, what his job consists of."

"He wasn't high on Josiah's list," Noah told her. "Kate was in a much better position to put the screws to him."

"But Paul's the corporate counsel."

Noah shrugged. "You had him pegged. Basically, he's just a paper pusher. Gets paid far too much money for filing forms and making sure the tax returns get in on time."

"Still, if there's funny business going on, he's in a position to help make it happen."

Noah's smile was sardonic. "He thought I should report to him, you know."

Taylor couldn't help laughing. "That would have been a disaster. All the way around."

"Didn't matter. Never would have happened."

She stared at him. He was still in his position on the couch, the caged panther lying in wait. "Are you ever going to tell me about you and Josiah? And why you seem to have a relationship no one else even comes close to?"

"No." He rose from the couch. "I'll go tell Carmen to have lunch brought in."

Taylor fidgeted at her desk, opening and closing folders without really seeing what was in them. She'd had an unsettled feeling since that morning and she knew she could trace it right back to Noah's attitude. When she'd reminded him it was important to keep their sexual activities hidden from the world, she hadn't meant for him to treat her like a leper.

And she was having a hard time reconciling all the many faces of this man. But whatever he was doing, beneath it all he was the same, the jungle animal surviving in a civilized world, ready to attack at any moment if the situation called for it. She suspected he could be a formidable enemy, that people who crossed him regretted it badly. He was as good as his word, shepherding her through the Arroyo minefield. And he was a challenging lover, driving her across boundaries, demanding things of her she didn't know she had to give. Her body had been his to do with as he wished since that first night. That was a given.

If she could only figure out what was going on now.

"Here's something you need to put on your calendar." Noah walked back in with yet another handful of messages. "There's a combination fundraiser and birthday party for one of your board members tomorrow night at the Alamo

Country Club. You'll have to go."

Taylor gaped at him. "Go? To some party? But…"

"He's right." Carmen was right behind him. "Sherry LaForte's birthday is always used to raise money for her foundation and Josiah was a big supporter. You'll be expected to attend, host a table and bid outrageous prices for the auction items."

"Host a table? I don't even know anyone."

Carmen smiled. "Not a problem. We made the reservation and sent in the check for the table before Josiah was…before his death. Sherry selects the people for the table and faxes us a list, so that's already done. You just have to show up with an escort."

"An escort."

Carmen laughed. "Josiah had a number of women happy enough to accompany him to something like this, but I don't think you'd want any of them as your date for the evening."

"I'll be taking Miss Scott." Noah's voice was firm. "She can tell people I'm her security."

Carmen frowned. "But you don't like to—"

He cut her off. "This isn't about liking. It's about what has to be done."

Taylor looked at him. "I'm not sure about all this. Facing San Antonio society in one large gulp isn't something on my list of pleasurable expectations."

"You don't have to stay all evening," Carmen told her. "Sometimes Josiah just stayed for part of dinner, gave Sherry a large check and left before the auction and dancing."

Taylor blew out a breath of relief. "Then that's what I'll do. But I don't know any of these people, or what else is expected of me."

"I can go over the list when it gets here," Carmen assured her.

Noah shook his head. "Just give her the basic details and I'll brief her. Where's lunch?"

"Right here." Carmen stepped aside.

The waiter from the company dining room wheeled in a table with covered dishes on it. Behind him came another waiter, pushing a cart with a coffee urn and a tray of pastries. Tomas, who had again been her shadow, ate his lunch in Carmen's office then quietly patrolled the halls and checked the surveillance cameras. She had no idea where L. Q. was but then she figured she didn't need to now. He'd be there if needed.

As she, Noah and Carmen ate, they began the wearisome task of sorting messages and reviewing the afternoon's schedule. As far as she could tell, it was a parade of the balance of the executive staff. And they were exactly what she expected. Some were pleasant, some obsequious, some outright hostile. She was conscious every moment of Noah in the room watching her, studying her, analyzing her. Her skin prickled under the constant scrutiny. Each time she raised her eyes to him and met his gaze, she felt as if every piece of clothing had been stripped from her and she sat before him naked. She had to drag her eyes back to the work before her or the person sitting in front of her.

By the time she was ready to leave for the day, she had all her notes arranged for clarity and easy reference, her head was throbbing and she was more than ready to get out of the office.

Noah was silent as he handed her into the helicopter, speaking only to tell Greg they were heading to the airport and where to land. The previous night still lingered in her mind. He'd been a strange combination of tenderness and lust, one minute caring for her, the next murmuring the way he'd really like to fuck her, the things he wanted to do. Today he'd watched her with the smoldering look that said he wanted to consume her in whatever fire raged within him. The complexity of his actions gave her the first tiny feeling of uncertainty. She was glad for the distraction John Martino provided when they landed to pick him up.

The good-looking blond-haired man, elegant as always, was waiting at the private terminal with one of Noah's men standing beside him.

"I didn't realize you'd be sending a bodyguard, Taylor." He grinned as he climbed in next to her.

She glanced at Noah, who inclined his head a fraction of an inch.

"Just taking extra precautions," she told him. "We've had some...challenges lately. In any event, it's very good to see you again, John. Thank you so much for coming. You can't know how I appreciate it."

He laughed. "I may write a book about this. What happened to my conservative investment counselor? How did you get mixed up with bodyguards and shotguns and cloak and dagger?" He looked at L. Q., poised in the outside seat. "And what's with the guy and the rifle?"

"I'll tell you all about it when we get to the ranch."

She noticed the men constantly scanning the skies as they flew, L. Q. never relaxing his grip on the rifle even for a moment. Taylor focused entirely on John throughout the ride, mentally putting as much space as possible between herself and Noah. Something had shifted between them and she wasn't sure if it was a good thing or not.

Yet when they landed, it was to him she whispered, "No mishaps tonight."

"Don't let your guard down. They're just regrouping."

"Nice digs, Taylor," John said when she showed him to his suite. "Let me guess. A rich relative died and left you a bundle."

She made a face. "Not so far from the truth. A few months ago, I discovered Josiah Gaines was my father. You can imagine the shock for both of us, even more for him, I think. We can get into details later, but he changed his will and made me his sole heir." She felt a momentary stab for the father she never knew. "When he was murdered, everything came to me."

John whistled. "Gaines is legendary in the world of international corporations. That's some responsibility to have handed to you."

"No kidding."

He squeezed her shoulder. "My money's on you, though. With your mind, you can handle anything."

"Thanks. I think."

Rey brought in a tray with a pitcher of sangria and hot tortilla chips. "Lupe says save room for dinner." He smiled and left as quietly as he'd come.

Silently asking her approval, John dispensed with his jacket and tie and rolled up his shirtsleeves.

"You can take time to change, if you'd like," Taylor told him. "Informality's the key here at the end of the day."

"Later. Let's talk first."

Taylor was just happy to have something to concentrate on, a subject that would divert her mind from Noah. Just being in the same room with him now rattled her senses.

Stop it! This is why you shouldn't have gone to bed with him in the first place. Get over it.

When they were settled with their drinks, Taylor and Noah laid everything out for John, from Josiah's suspicions and murder to the insurance policies and financial reports. They had nearly finished the explanation when Tomas and Greg brought in a computer and began setting it up.

"We're hooking you into a secure satellite line, since out here broadband is practically nonexistent," Noah told him. "Josiah's link was separate from the rest of the house, so we'll use that one. I didn't want to do it before you got here, so you could supervise and also set your password."

John nodded. "Good. It's dangerous to be on a shared connection with sensitive information."

"After we eat, I'll show you how to access each division. Start first with the farm equipment. Those are the plants Josiah visited on his last trip. They've pretty much flown under the radar until now. Look for anything that seems the least bit out of sync that could have prompted that trip." He paused, looking from John to Taylor and back. "Let me add my thanks to Miss Scott's. Josiah was a very good friend. I'd like to catch whoever's behind all this."

"If the clues are there, I'll find them."

Taylor rose from her chair. "I'm going to change. Do whatever you need to with your computer and get out of your suit." She hugged John again. "Noah will come get you in a little bit and we'll have dinner in my suite." Impulsively she hugged him. "Oh, John, I'm really counting on you."

"We'll do it, Taylor. Don't worry."

Noah walked back down the corridor with Taylor, lost in thought. John Martino was a lot younger than he'd expected. His mind had conjured up the image of a paunchy, middle-aged man, so the real thing was an unpleasant surprise to him. For reasons he didn't want to acknowledge, watching Taylor hug the man made his gut twist, a feeling that irritated him.

In fact, all the feelings she stirred up in him irritated him. Last night he'd exposed more of himself to her than he should have. Okay, so she'd had a tough day. What perverse emotion had prompted him to care for her like a lover, at the same time testing her to see just how far he could take her? He couldn't afford to feel anything, not where Taylor Scott was concerned. And Josiah and the outside world had nothing to do with it. Noah's black secrets made any relationship with her impossible.

He wanted to pull back today, determined to place distance between them and try to regain some control over the situation, but fate conspired to thwart him at every turn.

"You and John are pretty cozy." *You asshole. Keep your mouth shut.*

Taylor looked up at him, surprised. "Why, Noah, you sound almost jealous." Her voice had a teasing tone to it, but underneath was the edge of irritation due, he knew, to his attitude.

"Just curious." *Yeah, right.*

"I told you, John was a client. I built a very nice portfolio for him and he's been very pleased with the way I handled it."

"I'm surprised a good-looking man like him isn't married."

Taylor huffed a breath. "He's divorced, but I don't see what that has to do with anything. We hired his skills, not his personal life. John and I are friends, nothing more."

"You looked more like old lovers to me," Noah snapped then wished he hadn't said anything.

She stopped in mid-stride, her eyebrows drawn together, irritation in every line of her body. "What's wrong with you, Noah? I don't feel I have to explain any of my relationships to you."

"Nothing." His voice was as flat as glass. "Nothing's wrong."

Anger flared in her eyes. "I'd think after impressing on me the fact we had nothing but sex and saving Arroyo between us, it wouldn't make much difference to you. And what if John and I are lovers? What business is it of yours? We can stop this thing between us any time. Just say the word."

He gripped her shoulders with painful intensity. "If John Martino is your lover, he's done a piss-poor job of teaching you about sex. And you can bet your sweet adorable little ass we're not stopping *anything*. We haven't even started."

"Oh, damn you," she shouted and raced down the hallway, seemingly anxious to put space between them.

Noah stared after the slim figure running headlong away from him. Disaster was written all over this. This was no ordinary situation and Taylor Scott was no ordinary person. He'd already made his share of mistakes with her and feared the worst was yet to come.

He was in big trouble and he knew it.

Watching her at work had given him an unreasonable sense of pleasure. It wasn't just her body but the movement of it, the gestures she made that had become so familiar to him in such a short time. The tiny straightening of her spine that indicated displeasure. The upward thrust of her chin that was like a sword heralding battle. Her razor-sharp mind that could cut a person to ribbons and walk away while they were bleeding. She called to him with a song that evoked every one of his senses. Her very presence was a visceral punch that socked at him hard.

Seeing another man's hands on her tonight, even in an innocent gesture, made his blood boil and fed an unreasoning surge of jealousy.

He wanted to possess her. To own the body that gave him a raging hard-on just by proximity. To have that golden fire in those emerald eyes blaze for no one but him. To know that he was the only one who could put that look of wanton pleasure on her face.

That was his problem and had been from the very beginning. But what was he to do? No amount of effort on his part kept him away from her, or killed that sensation deep in his gut that a jungle animal got when it sensed it'd found his mate. And that simply was not going to happen. Not now. Not ever.

The situation was impossible. He had a debt to discharge to Josiah, which meant he couldn't take the easy escape and run away from this. Yet being with her every day was close to torture. He'd tried to make it just about sex, but in his hidden places he knew that was a lie. Despite what his brain told him, he'd never be able to stay away from her.

Damn it.

* * * *

Taylor slammed her door and leaned against it, her breathing as harsh as if she'd just climbed a mountain. The light, outdoor scent of Noah's cologne still clung to her nostrils and the heat of his body wrapped itself around her as if he was still beside her. Her breasts throbbed and moisture dampened her panties.

Ridiculous! Insane!

She slid to the floor, bending her knees and touching her forehead to them. How could he affect her this way? Today she'd been outrageously aware of him watching her the entire time she worked. And wondering why his attitude had taken such a drastic turn overnight.

She had to pull herself together. She'd been thrust unexpectedly into an atmosphere of turmoil. How was it possible she'd become so obsessed with a man whose feelings for her seemed as chaotic as hers did for him? If he showed up in her room tonight, despite everything, she'd welcome him. Open her body to him, let him do whatever he wanted with her. To her.

Damn it!

Josiah, what have you done to me? Is he my reward or my punishment?

Finally, she pulled herself to her feet and headed for the bathroom. Before long, dinner would arrive and with it the realization again of the danger she was in. She needed a clear head for tonight's discussion. She only hoped Noah would feel the same way.

* * * *

"I took a quick look at the insurance information you left me," John told them as they met for dinner. "Just a brief glance."

They'd finished the incredible food Lupe had prepared for them and Taylor had refilled everyone's wineglasses. John lounged at one end of the couch, Noah at the other.

Like twin gladiators sizing up the arena.

"I knew you wouldn't have much time to study anything until tonight," she said, "but did anything catch your eye?"

"One thing stands out. There aren't any policies for the plant in Idaho. That makes no sense, unless it's a small plant and the division head wanted to throw a little business to the locals."

Noah shook his head. "Kate would have made that decision. She handled all the insurance, she and Paul Hunter. She would have handled the annual review this year if she hadn't been in that car accident."

"I want to check out the coverage for all the other divisions before I make any snap judgment. It's possible we'll find the same thing in other areas. Sometimes business like that goes a long way to buying local good will." He took a swallow of his coffee. "I want to look at the summaries of the division reports tonight, then tomorrow start going through everything line by line."

"I can't really tell you anything, either," Taylor told him. "Just what I've learned from Noah. But something spooked Josiah and I think the rumblings about a takeover when he...died are part of it."

"I agree." John leaned forward. "And taking over Arroyo would be the easiest way to keep the status quo. Taylor, what would have happened if you hadn't popped up? Who'd be running the company?"

"That would be up to the board of directors, but if I hadn't shown up, Josiah's stock would have gone to set up a foundation, with the director having voting privileges. My guess is they would have probably picked Kate Belden. She'd be a logical choice because of her position."

Even as she said the words, she glanced at Noah to see his reaction. Was this a little something he'd had tucked in his pocket? Hoping to take the position and everything that went with it? Would he fight Kate Belden for it or had Josiah already promised it to him? She wished she could get that niggling little thought out of her head.

"I've reopened the investigation into the background on both her and Paul Hunter, by the way," Noah told him. "After someone took a shot at Taylor it seemed like a good idea."

"Absolutely," John agreed. "Well, if it's there to be found, I'll find it. That's what I get the big bucks for." He smiled and winked at Taylor.

Noah frowned and Taylor hid her smile. "Thanks, John."

John finished his coffee and rose. "Pleasant as this is, it doesn't get my work done. Noah, if you can access those files for me, I'll get started tonight."

As if sensing the undercurrent in the room, he leaned over and kissed Taylor lightly, an amused smile teasing the corners of his mouth.

Taylor grinned. "How about if we meet here for breakfast at eight? I'd love to eat out on the patio, but I don't want to take a chance on eavesdroppers."

"Sounds good to me."

Noah also stood, looking like a thundercloud. "I'll walk you back to your rooms and pull up those files for you." His voice was like a bullwhip. He turned to Taylor. "Then I'll check back with you about what we're doing."

What we're doing. Translated – fucking our brains out.

"Of course." She could be as smooth as he could. "John, if you have any questions, no matter how late, just pick up the house phone in your room and dial five. That connects directly to me."

"I'll try not to wake you." With that amused smile still on his face, he planted another kiss on Taylor's cheek. "Okay, Noah, let's get it done."

Taylor thought about taking a shower while she waited, then decided she needed to be fully dressed for Noah. The quintessential alpha male would take any advantage she gave him and some she didn't. And his behavior tonight had irritated her. His possessive attitude was out of place when he was so careful to remind her that all they had between them was sex.

She was pouring herself a glass of wine when Noah walked in without knocking, a habit he'd gotten into very quickly. Just like locking the door behind him.

"Don't bother." She made her voice as cool as possible. "You won't be here that long."

He was beside her before she could lift the wine to her lips, eyes blazing into hers, muscles bunching at his jawline.

"What the hell is that supposed to mean?"

"Just exactly what I said." She turned away from him and walked to the other side of the room. Space. She needed space. Lots of space.

"Don't you walk away from me," he ordered, his voice tight with anger.

From several steps away, Taylor turned to look at him again. "Since when do you give me orders?"

His entire body vibrated with tension. He shoved his hands into his pockets and leaned his hip against the arm of the big leather chair. "I beg your pardon, Miss Scott." He was furious under the even tone of his voice. "I ask that you not walk away from me when we're talking."

Taylor sipped at her wine, taking time to collect her thoughts. Even with this distance between them, he put her off balance. *Damn the man, anyway.*

"I'm not walking away. Just staying at a safe distance."

In three strides, he'd closed the space between them and was gripping her arms. The wine sloshed over the rim of her glass onto her hand.

"Just exactly what the hell is going on?" he asked between clenched teeth.

Taylor had to fight to keep her mind focused. No matter how she tried to discipline herself, the minute she felt his power surrounding her, his male scent teasing at her nostrils, she turned into a blithering pile of hormones. *No!* He wasn't going to do this to her this time. She had questions she wanted answered.

She picked up a napkin and blotted her hand. "I'm the one who wants to know, as you say, what the hell is going on. Why you acted the way you did today. Last night. You spell it out for me that we have nothing but sex between us. Fine by me. Then last night you were almost like a lover and today John Martino pushes your jealousy button. So what is it, Noah? Tell me what's going on."

She had no sense of him moving until he was there again, the wineglass out of her hand, his mouth so hard on hers she was sure her lips would be bruised. The sweep of his tongue inside her mouth touched off every nerve in the sensitive flesh. Her heart stumbled then picked up the beat, her legs suddenly so weak she had to grasp his upper arms to steady herself. And still the kiss went on.

By the time Noah lifted his mouth from hers, she couldn't remember what it was she was so mad about or even what they'd been talking about. She was dazed and disoriented, her body a throbbing mass of need. Her panties were soaked, yet the simple act of the kiss released another flood of liquid. This was more than a need. It had become a craving as essential to her as food and water, a complication she hadn't expected to deal with.

When she raised her unfocused eyes to Noah's, she saw the same thing reflected in his face, felt the blood thrumming through his veins. He visibly struggled to control his breathing.

Finally, she found her voice. "Is that an answer or a question?"

He thrust her away from him and walked to the other side of the room. He was silent for so long she might have thought he'd left, except she didn't hear the door open or close. Then she heard him moving behind her, pouring ice water into a glass. When he spoke, his voice was like the splintering of wood, a log cracking into pieces.

"I wanted you to be like every other woman in my life. Disposable. Someone I could use and walk away from. But you're not. You're inside me. Your touch. Your scent. The feel of your skin. You're a punch to the gut that I least expected." Ice clinked in his glass. "Last night happened because I...deluded myself into thinking for one brief instant that maybe we could have something more. But that's impossible."

Disposable? He wants me to be a throwaway?

The passion he'd roused in her was wiped away by a surge of anger. She wanted to slap his face. To punch him. To tell him to get away from her, get out of her life. How dare he say these things to her? His arrogance was unbelievable.

"It did show me one thing," he went on, unaware of her reaction. "I can't stay here. Not this close to you and retain my sanity. I'll stay until the crisis has passed and you're out of danger. Then I think it's best if I leave."

What? Leave? He's planning to leave?

Taylor swallowed hard and turned away from him, unable to look at him while she spoke.

"I won't deny I'm as attracted to you as you are to me. You wouldn't believe me, anyway. And why should you? Whatever this…thing is between us, it seems to have a mind of its own. We're apparently unable to put the genie back in the bottle." She shoved her hands into her pockets to conceal their trembling. "And I won't accept your decision to leave. We'll discuss it when everything else is settled."

"My decision, not yours," he pointed out.

"And what happens in the meantime? Since we can't keep our hands off each other or maintain any distance, do we just take every opportunity to go at each other like rutting animals? Put on an act in public? Be reasonable."

"Sex is never reasonable." He moved closer to her. "Especially the kind I want with you." He was in front of her now, his eyes burning into hers. "We have a job we'll continue to do. But yes. I will take every opportunity to ravish you in ways you can't even begin to imagine. Are you willing to go there with me? To have what we can now, knowing that's all it can ever be? Not expect anything more?"

Was she? Knowing in the end he'd just walk away? Could she put herself in that kind of emotional jeopardy?

She knew she should be frightened. At the very least intimidated. Instead, a dark fist of thrill curled in her stomach and a throbbing spread from her womb to every part of her body. Noah Cantrell was more addictive than drugs and she was simply unable to kick the habit. She wanted more. As much as he could give her. Whatever it turned out to be.

She thought of all the reasons this was impossible. All the arguments why she should tell him they were finished now. But he had become as necessary to her as breathing, a fact she fought to conceal from him. Giving him complete control was out of the question, yet he took it without asking. She knew she would strip naked at the snap of his fingers, for the touch of his hands on her, the feel of his mouth, the rough caress of his tongue.

At last she nodded, unable to say anything, sure she was stepping off a cliff with no safety net. Wetting her lips, she met his gaze. "Fine. Okay. That's good with me."

"Just don't try to romanticize it, little girl." His voice was harsh. "When this is finished, so are we."

Maybe. We'll see about that when the time comes.

But even if that turned out to be so, she couldn't turn back now.

"As long as we're focused the rest of the time on the reason why I'm here at all—to find out who killed Josiah and keep Arroyo intact."

He studied her face for the space of two heartbeats. "All right, then. But not tonight." He turned back to the small table and refilled his water glass, drinking half of it in two smooth swallows.

And without another word, he was gone.

Taylor dropped into an armchair, eyes closed, and wondered how things would be now if that night at the hotel had never happened. Would she still have come to San Antonio? He was a big part of the reason she was here. Oh, she had no illusions that this was some happily ever after. He'd made that plain enough. But just as he couldn't stay away from her, neither could she turn away from him.

Josiah, is this a joke you're playing on me from the grave?

She wondered what had happened to her well-ordered life. Here she was in a strange place, with her own team of bodyguards protecting her from unnamed dangers. Playing the role of high-powered CEO with flair she didn't know she had while acutely conscious that every person in every meeting was a potential threat. And giving her body without reservation to a man who took her deeper and deeper into a sexual abyss with only the promise that when this was over, he'd be gone.

Yet nothing could make her get up and walk away from the responsibility Josiah had handed her, or from the man who was more dangerous than the threats against her life.

Right now she wanted a long, hot shower. Tomorrow night was the party at the country club. With Noah as her escort. She couldn't help the tiny shiver of excitement that raced through her.

She fell into bed wearing her old sleepshirt rather than one of her new designer nighties and was hovering just on the edge of sleep when she heard the soft click of the door in the sitting room. Her heartbeat picked up its tempo. *Noah!*

She lay there immobile, waiting for his approach, her body readying itself for him.

His footsteps were like whispers on the carpet then he was in the doorway, his big, solid figure outlined by the moonlight sifting in through the window above her head. His hair was loose about his shoulders, his chest bare and the moonlight limned the sculptured lines of his lean body. He had the look of a fierce warrior stalking his prey. In an instant, he was beside the bed shedding his jeans, the only garment he wore.

Taylor wet her lips. "I thought you said —"

"I did. More fool me. You destroy me, Taylor. I have no common sense where you're concerned." Silently, he lifted the covers to look at her, shaking his head at her sleeping apparel. "Well, it's obvious you weren't expecting company. Take it off." His voice was heavy with desire.

Taylor gave no thought to refusing him, simply sat up, pulled off the sleepshirt and tossed it to the floor. She lay back on the pillows, pulse racing, cunt throbbing, nipples aching, waiting. Just waiting. Just as he had no power to stay away from her, she had none to refuse him, whatever he wanted from her.

He clicked on the bedside lamp, the circle of pale yellow light bathing her body. She resisted her still automatic reaction to cover herself, forcing herself to lie still under his heated scrutiny. He used one hand to cup his shaft, which was aroused to enormous size, a tiny drop of fluid glistening at the tip of its broad purple head.

"Spread your legs for me and bend your knees," he commanded, eyes glittering, magnificent cock jutting from its sheltering nest of curls at the root.

She knew what he wanted. Breath hitching, she opened her legs as wide as she could, feet planted on the mattress, knees bent. The faint current from the air conditioning vent brushed softly against her skin.

"Open yourself for me." He stroked himself as he watched her. "Open yourself so I can see how wet your cunt is."

Her heart rate picked up again as it always did when he ordered her to display herself to him this way. There was something so deliciously wicked about it. Shyness and embarrassment had long since left her.

Noah leaned down and slid one long, lean finger along her wet flesh, causing shivers to run through her. When he lifted it, the skin was glistening with her juices. Slowly, he slid the finger into his mouth and sucked it clean.

"You taste like honey and spice. Better than the finest wine or the best aged cognac."

She couldn't help herself. She reached out and slid her fingertip over the head of his cock, to capture the moisture beaded there and licked her finger as he'd done with his.

"Salty," she told him. "And sweet." She ran the tip of her tongue over her lips and was rewarded with the flash of heat in his eyes and the tightening of the muscles in his face.

He kneeled on the bed in front of her, hooked his arms under her knees and pulled her tender, heated flesh to his mouth. He held her captive with his fingers as he plunged his tongue inside, licking her flesh with a steady sweep. When he massaged her clit with his thumbs, touches so light she wanted to beg for more, she bit her lip to keep from screaming in need and frustration.

She tried to move her hips toward him, force his mouth harder onto her, but he held her so tightly in his grasp she could barely move. He continued to torment her with his tongue and his talented thumbs. Her clit was so swollen from his attentions that the line between pleasure and pain was blurred.

The orgasm built inside her as it always did, low in her belly, radiating out, gripping her, shaking her. She tried desperately to close her legs together and squeeze against his tongue, but he would have none of it. He held her there, just on the knife edge, until she was sure she'd lose her mind, his tongue as much an instrument of torture as it was of arousal. Her body was in desperate need of release, every nerve strung tight.

"Please," she begged.

"Please what?" His eyes were like hot black coals.

"Please make me come. Please fuck me."

"Remember this," he told her, pulling his head back. "I decide when and how you come. And how often. Are we clear on that?"

She bobbed her head, willing to agree to anything if only he'd take her over the edge. "Yes." She continued to thrust her hips at him, seeking fulfillment.

"This is just the beginning." His voice was thick with his own need, rough with the need to control her. He spread her legs wider as he leaned toward her. "This is just the beginning, Taylor. Do you understand?"

"Yes. Yes, yes, yes. But please, I need you inside me." Her stomach and her thighs cramped with repressed release, her body straining to reach the precipice.

"I'll let you come. But my way." He sat back on his knees. "As much as I want my cock inside that hot, tight sheath, I want to watch that beautiful petal-smooth center convulse for me even more. See those glistening pink tissues and watch your cream flood into the crack of your ass."

His words were making her hotter and hotter.

"One of these times," he went on, "I'm going to watch you make yourself come for me. Watch those graceful fingers stimulate your clit. See you finger-fuck yourself for my pleasure. And giving me that pleasure will increase yours.

Do you understand?"

She nodded, by now barely coherent. All the while he talked to her in that low, deep voice, he continued to tease the tip of her clit, moving his thumb back and forth like the even sway of a pendulum. The fluttering began deep inside her, the spasms building, but he held her just at the edge. His eyes glittered as he watched her gasping and writhing.

"But tonight," he growled, "when I finally let you come, I'm going to hold that beautiful cunt wide open so I can see every spasm, every convulsion, every stream of fluid. Tonight is for me."

He pinched her clit hard between his thumbs and her orgasm broke over her like a wild thing. The more she spasmed, the more open he held her. She twisted and thrashed as she tried to find relief from a climax that was no relief at all. And all the time he watched her with the hungry look of a predator devouring its prey.

At last, he pulled a condom from the foil he'd dropped beside him on the bed, sheathed himself and plunged into her. He was enormous, so totally aroused by watching her that he stretched her to the utmost. Her aftershocks pulsed around his cock, milking it. He leaned forward on his forearms, his gaze still capturing hers, thrusting in and out of her pussy with hard, heavy strokes, the force of them driving her into another orgasm.

When the last spasm died away, she lay sweaty and quivering, her arms wrapped around his solid body, her breath coming in short gasps.

She had no idea how long they lay there entwined. He was heavy on her, his weight crushing her, but she wouldn't have moved for anything. The heat of his skin, the warmth of his breath, the touch of his long hair were erotic kisses against her flesh. She smoothed her hands over the muscles of his back, loving the feel of their strength beneath her fingers. What would she do when this was over and he was out of her life?

At length, he lifted himself from her body, his softened

cock sliding out of her wet pussy with a satisfied sound. He braced himself on his forearms and framed her face with his hands, studying her with that penetrating look that had become so familiar.

"Sometimes I wonder if Josiah would kill me or applaud." He leaned down and kissed each of her breasts before levering himself off the bed. "Either way, I'm not sure he'd be giving me any medals."

Taylor pushed herself back up on the pillows. "Noah…"

He shook his head. "Don't say anything. We have what we have. That's it." He pulled on his jeans. "Get some sleep. Tomorrow's a long day."

Then he was gone, leaving her feeling like nothing more than one of his disposable women.

Chapter Twelve

"Today, I'm going to take the reports of each section of that division apart item by item," John Martino told them the next morning. "Check suppliers and customers. Find a reason why it has an orphaned insurance policy."

They were eating breakfast in Taylor's sitting room, a place where they could speak freely without the danger of eavesdroppers. She would have loved the outdoor setting so they could enjoy the air of the clear Texas morning, but she was wary of being overheard. With everything that had happened, she trusted no one.

Noah raised an eyebrow. "You've found something already?"

"Not really, but my fingers are itching, my own personal indicator that something stinks."

"I'll want to go over everything with you after you've dug into it." Taylor refilled her coffee cup. "I did a basic study of the corporate structure and an overview of the divisions. I think I can be of some help to you."

"I agree. Let me get started and we'll take it from there."

"Will you be all right by yourself here, John? I have to go into the office and I'm told I have to put in an appearance at some sort of charity farce tonight." She made a grimace of distaste.

John laughed. "When have I ever needed handholding?" He leaned over and kissed her cheek. "You do what you have to, kitten, and I'll do my thing. Mrs. Hart already stopped by to tell me anything I wanted, just ask her and she'd get it for me."

"I want us to meet later," she told him. "I want to be

involved in this, John. Not to interfere in your work in any way, because God knows you're the best at this. But I'm very curious about the whole situation. I want to know what happened and why."

"I think that's a good idea."

Taylor didn't dare look at Noah, simmering silently beside her. She smothered a tiny smile. On some subliminal level, she was aware of the high level of testosterone in the air. Despite Noah's deliberate air of detachment, his insistence that what they had amounted to little more than two animals in heat, he gave every sign of the panther defending his area of the jungle. And John, with his peculiarly playful sense of humor, was yanking the panther's tail.

She began to slide folders into her briefcase. "All right. I need to be on my way. I'll be back briefly to change for tonight's shindig, so if you need to touch base with me then, you can."

"Don't worry. If I have something for you, I'll find you wherever you are."

He shook hands with Noah and left the room.

Taylor busied herself closing her briefcase and gathering her things, acutely aware of the thickness of the silence in the room. Finally she blew out a breath and looked up at Noah. "Is there a problem?"

"Problem?" Not a muscle moved on his face, but his eyes were black as coals. "Why would you think that?"

"Oh, I don't know. Maybe this macho silence you wear like a suit of armor, disseminating your displeasure to all within its circle. So if something's bothering you, spit it out."

A muscle twitched in his cheek. "Kitten?"

Taylor burst out laughing, probably the first real laugh she'd enjoyed in weeks.

"I see nothing funny about this," Noah said through gritted teeth.

Taylor swallowed the last of her laughing jag and patted her eyes with a tissue. "Surely you can't be jealous, Noah.

You've very diligent about reminding me that what we have is not personal."

"I'm just trying to get a handle on your relationship with John Martino." His voice was stiff. "People don't usually use terms of affection in a strictly business relationship."

Taylor almost laughed again, but she bit down hard on her lip. "John calls me kitten because we sat in a meeting with the CEO and CFO of a corporation he was thinking of investing in. I didn't like their attitude and afterward he told me they didn't even know they'd been raked with my claws. Kitten is kind of a joke between us." She tilted her head. "Are we going to have some kind of problem here, Noah?"

His jaw worked as he ground his teeth. "None at all," he said at last.

"Good. Because the relationship between John and me is strictly business." She slid a look at him. "Just like ours."

"Not quite," he said in a tight voice, grabbing her arm and leading her out of the door. "Not quite at all, little girl."

The helicopter deposited them at the Arroyo helipad and they went through the same routine as the previous day. Carmen was waiting for them with the information Taylor would need for the day as well as a fresh pot of coffee.

"Bless you," she told the woman, pouring herself a cup at once.

The day seemed endless. Taylor had decided to meet with Kate Belden and Paul Hunter again, this time pushing for additional information. How was the corporate structure set up? Who made decisions about what? How often did they each interact with Josiah? She was really poking and prodding to see what nuggets they might accidentally reveal, but they were sharp and close-mouthed. Whatever she found out would have to come from someplace else. Well, that was what John was there for.

Noah has been a looming presence on the couch against the wall, sitting with one ankle resting on the opposite leg, still as a marble statue. Again, she had the odd sensation that he was undressing her with his eyes, imagining her nude at her desk conducting corporate business. The vision made her instantly wet, her suddenly sensitized nipples pushing against the fabric of her blouse. She heard his words whispering across her mind as if he'd said them out loud.

Would you like to know how I really like my sex, Taylor? You might run screaming into the night.

That ribbon of dark temptation was uncurling within her again. It took every ounce of self-discipline to concentrate on the work at hand.

She barely tasted the sandwich Carmen ordered for her for lunch, trying to sort through myriad impressions in her mind. Then they addressed the telephone calls which couldn't be put off any longer.

Throughout the afternoon, as they worked, Noah paced, as if his body was rebelling against the morning of enforced stillness. Periodically he would stop and although she forced herself not to look up at him, Taylor was acutely aware of his eyes on her like twin lasers, burning his brand into her.

What do you want from me? she cried silently. *You take my body and shut out my soul. You guide me through a maze filled with dragons then retreat behind those invisible walls. Is emotion so dangerous for you?*

If Carmen sensed any of the drama silently playing out in the room, she gave no indication. She was all business — taking notes, stacking papers, offering comments where appropriate.

By mid-afternoon, Taylor was nursing the mother of all headaches and wishing she had nothing to do but soak in a hot tub and crawl into bed. She'd been bombarded with questions from everyone she met with, questions she wasn't yet prepared to answer. The number of phone calls she'd had to return was staggering and her appointment calendar was rapidly filling with people she needed to be briefed on before she met them face to face. When they'd finished reviewing the key people she'd be meeting at the benefit, she held up her hand.

"Enough. I'm done for the day. Carmen, thank you very much. I could never do this without you." She raised her eyes to Noah's. "I think I'd like to go home, if that's all right. Maybe get a little rest before I'm put on display tonight."

He nodded. "You're the boss. I'll tell Tomas we're ready and have Greg fire up the 'copter."

"I can't think of anything I'd rather do less than be put on parade," she told him as they rode down in the elevator.

"You'll do fine." The doors opened and they exited into the garage where Tomas waited. "My tux is at my house, so I'll need to go home and change."

She frowned up at him, realizing this would be the first time since he'd walked into her office that they'd be separated. "What will be the transportation arrangements, then?"

"Greg will fly you to the ranch and back here. L. Q. and Charlie will be with you. Tomas will stay here to make sure we don't have any uninvited guests."

Tomas nodded. "I'm keeping the day shift guards over an extra two hours so we'll have a double squad. You'll be fine, Miss Scott. We're in wide-open land here, too, so there's really no place for anyone to hide."

Taylor inclined her head, determined not to show her nervousness. *Be in control. Stay in control.* "Thank you. I'm sure it will all work out. Noah, what time shall I meet you?"

"Seven-thirty." He helped her up into the helo's cabin. "Will that work for you?"

"Yes. I'll see you then."

"L. Q.?" Noah looked at the man cradling the rifle as if he were holding a baby.

The shooter looked at him. "Yeah, boss?"

"Take care of her. When in doubt, shoot first."

L. Q. nodded. "Not to worry."

"All right then. On your way."

Noah closed the door. Greg spun the rotors and they took

off.

The shower washed away much of the day's tension and John Martino's encouraging words that he was unraveling the mystery of the reports and the policies, albeit slowly, gave Taylor an extra measure of relief. Tonight, she was more than grateful for Audrey and the multitude of clothing. A simple black cocktail sheath wouldn't do it for this crowd. She'd chosen an ankle-length satin sheath slit to the thigh, the deep royal-blue enhancing the creaminess of her skin, the long sleeves and modest neckline somehow more enticing than if all her skin had been exposed, she felt. Her hair was pulled to one side and held in place with a gold and diamond clip, a legacy from her mother, and her mother's diamond studs glittered in her ears. Finishing the outfit were new stiletto heels in gold and blue which Audrey had paired with the dress, heels she'd spent twenty minutes practicing in, with Jocelyn's good-humored encouragement, before leaving the ranch. When she stepped off the helicopter she caught the flare of desire in Noah's eyes. She almost missed it, however, stunned as she was by the magnificent sight of him.

In his business suits or in jeans he was imposing, formidable, strong, appealing. A whole string of adjectives. But in formal attire he was a sensual god, his black hair reflecting the color of the tux, the white shirt accenting the darkness of his skin. He was magnificent, a man who women would throw elbows to reach, claw to claim ownership of. And again, beneath the layer of civility, the raw power of the ancient warrior, surrounding her and drugging her senses. She had to remind herself to move.

His eyes burned into her and captured every inch of her. "You are...exquisite." His voice was slightly unsteady.

"You're pretty magnificent yourself." She grinned, taking the hand he held out to her.

He helped her into the big black SUV as if she was a delicate piece of porcelain, then turned to Tomas. "Everything clear here?"

"No problems. Charlie and I will be right behind you."

Noah fastened his seat belt and cranked the ignition as the vehicle behind them also fired its engine.

Taylor smoothed imaginary wrinkles in her sleek satin skirt and picked at invisible threads. Somehow she was more intimidated meeting San Antonio society than she had been facing the sharks at Arroyo.

"You'll be fine." Noah flashed a quick glance at her and repeated what he'd said earlier in the day.

"Fine." She let out a breath. "Sure. Fine. I'm more nervous about meeting Josiah's friends than his employees and business associates. Talk about being under a microscope."

"Most of these people weren't his friends, Taylor. He socialized with them, but he wasn't close to many people."

She fiddled with the catch on her evening purse. "All the more reason for their curiosity to be at an all-time high."

"They're just people, Taylor." His voice was hard and flat. "They can only hurt you if you let them."

"Speaking from experience?" She bit her tongue, knowing her question was uncalled for.

"The society Josiah traveled in and you grew up in thinks people like me should be in the stable shoveling the horse shit."

The bitterness in his voice shocked her. She would have pushed for more, but the stiffness of his body and his tone of voice made it plain the subject was closed. They made the rest of the short trip in silence.

Alamo Country Club sat on forty acres of land on San Antonio's northwest side. Established long before the creeping residential encroachment, the founders had been wise enough to purchase enough surrounding real estate to maintain the natural environment. Consequently, the property was surrounded by untouched acreage and stands of oak and sycamore trees that provided an effective shield from the steadily advancing growth.

Enough daylight still existed for Taylor to catch a glimpse of the world-class golf course and the manicured landscaping as she and Noah moved slowly up the curving drive to the entrance of the graceful two-story stone building. The valet attendant helped Taylor alight from the Expedition and she slipped her hand into the crook of Noah's arm for support as they climbed the long flight of stairs.

"What will Tomas do?" she asked. She'd noticed the other SUV following them through the gate and pull ahead of them toward the parking area.

"He and Charlie will check out the area and keep an eye on things."

An attendant in a dinner jacket stood just inside the door, a polite but questioning look on his face. Noah reached into his inside beast pocket and slid out the heavy white linen envelope Taylor had handed him earlier, removed the engraved invitation inside and handed it to the man.

"Thank you." He bowed his head slightly. "Mrs. LaForte is greeting guests in the room to your right, where you will also find the bar."

"I think the doorman's tux cost more than mine," Noah muttered.

Taylor squeezed his arm. "Not so. I know an Armani when I see one. Come on. I can't wait to be fed to the vultures."

The evening was a mixture of experiences for Taylor. Sherry LaForte greeted her with an excessive dose of Texas hospitality, gushing effusively and offering her condolences on Josiah's death. Others Sherry introduced them to as they sipped their drinks were equally as cordial. There were just as many, however, who looked as if they wanted her to produce her birth certificate and DNA test.

Noah might have been a plastic mannequin for all the attention anyone paid to him. In their environment, he obviously didn't exist. Taylor took pride in the way he handled it all, ignoring everyone who ignored him, seeing to her needs, fetching drinks for her. She did her best to compensate. At dinner, as the other couples at the table tried to engage her in prying conversation, she directed most of her attention to Noah, introducing him as her guest despite his orders to identify him as her bodyguard.

She even insisted he dance with her.

"You're asking for trouble," he told her as they moved easily together on the dance floor. "These people will look at you fraternizing with the hired help and knock you down a few notches on their social scale."

"Like I care. I'm here to hold Arroyo together until we shake out the bad guys. That's all."

His arm tightened across her back. "Then what? Back to your comfort zone? Hiding out in Tampa? I thought you wanted to make major changes in your life."

I didn't know those changes would include you, Noah Cantrell, or addictive sex.

"I never really intended to make this permanent. Besides," she reminded him, "why would you care? You're leaving anyway, right? Isn't that what you want?"

He bent his head so his mouth was close to her ear. "I'll tell you what I want. I want to take you somewhere after this high-society shindig and fuck the breath out of you in more ways than you can imagine."

Heat coursed through her body. The growing thickness of his erection pressed against the softness of her belly and she wondered if the moisture seeping from her sex would show on her dress and embarrass her.

"What if I said yes? That's the last thing you expect, isn't it?"

He said nothing, only tightened his arm around her.

The music ended and Noah released her. Before the auction began and she changed her mind, Taylor sought out Sherry LaForte and handed her the substantial check Carmen had prepared for her.

"I'm sure you understand if I beg off early," she told the older woman. "It's been an exhausting few days and I'm just getting myself acclimated."

"Of course, honey." Sherry hugged her. "I'll give you a call next week and see if you're free for lunch. Josiah was a very old, important friend and I'd like to get to know his daughter better."

Then Noah was calling Tomas on the small walkie-talkie he pulled from his pocket and escorting Taylor down the wide stairway. She was grateful for his hand on her arm because the anticipation of the evening ahead made her slightly unsteady. So many images whirled in her head as she tried to imagine what Noah had in mind.

The two SUVs were lined up one behind the other at the top of the circle. Tomas opened the passenger door of the lead car for Taylor, Charlie standing right behind her as Noah moved around to the driver's side.

As Taylor gathered her skirt to step up into the vehicle, her tiny purse slipped from her hand and she bent to retrieve it. At the same moment, she heard a sound like a *thunk* and Charlie fell forward against her, pushing her into the open door.

Chapter Thirteen

"God damn it."

Noah's voice, angry and tense.

Taylor pushed away from the Expedition and turned, a small scream erupting from her mouth as she saw Charlie lying on the ground at her feet. A thick river of dark red seeped slowly from beneath him. Tomas bent down to turn him over, exposing the entire front of his jacket which was covered in blood.

"Down," Noah was shouting to people standing there. "Everyone get down."

People were yelling all around her, a cacophony of sounds like the screeching of chalk on a blackboard. More people rushed from the clubhouse at the sounds of the screams, not sure what was wrong and what to do.

Taylor stood rooted to the spot, frozen at the horrific sight at her feet.

"Damn it, we fucked up." Noah's harsh voice. "But who the fuck expected a sniper? Tomas, get her out of here. Drive until I call you. Go, go, go." He shoved Taylor into the vehicle and slammed the door.

"Going right now," Tomas acknowledged as he jumped into the driver's seat.

Noah banged twice on the roof of the vehicle and Tomas threw it into gear and roared down the driveway.

Taylor couldn't stop shaking. She clutched her purse as if it were a lifeline. "W-What just happened?"

Stupid question. Charlie got shot.

"Sniper, just like Noah said." Tomas' voice was as harsh as Noah's. "Damn, damn, damn. We should have had people checking out all those trees. My bad. And my very stupid. I just didn't think…"

"I don't think any of us did." *Sniper!*

"It's my job. Mine and Noah's. We fucked up big-time and Charlie paid for it."

"Is Charlie…?" She swallowed. "Is he dead?" She could barely get the words out.

Tomas shook his head. "No. And if Noah gets him to the ER in time, he won't be."

Taylor was shaking so hard she thought her body would break into pieces. She kept feeling the pressure of Charlie's body as he'd fallen forward against her. She was sure the memory would never go away.

Sniper!

The word echoed in her brain again.

"If I hadn't dropped my purse that would be me lying there. Right?" When he didn't answer, she repeated, "Right?"

"But it's not you and that's what's important."

"Are you kidding me?" She almost shrieked the words. "A man could die from a bullet meant for me and I'm supposed to say *good for me*?"

Tomas drew in a deep, controlling breath and blew it out. "Miss Scott —"

"Taylor." She gripped her purse harder, determined to stop shaking. "I think tonight's adventure qualifies as a condition for the use of first names, don't you?"

"All right, Taylor. It would be a disaster if these people were able to kill you as they did Josiah. Charlie will be all right. Noah will see to it. Right now, our priority is you."

She reached over her shoulder and tugged at her dress. Something sticky was gluing it to her skin. When her hand came away, it was stained red. *Blood!* She felt sick, nausea clawing its way up her throat. She stared at her hand and felt suddenly lightheaded.

"Oh my God," was all she could say.

Tomas was concentrating on weaving skillfully in and

out of the evening traffic, but he spared her a quick glance. "Put your head down between your knees," he ordered.

She couldn't do anything except focus on the blood staining her palm.

"Taylor," he snapped. "Miss Scott. Put your head down. Now." He reached over with one hand and shoved her head forward, holding it down in her lap. "Take deep breaths," he ordered. "Now. Do it."

In a moment, the dizziness receded. When she was sure she could sit up without vomiting, she lifted her head.

"I'm sorry. I'm very sorry."

"Don't be. Stronger people than you have fainted in situations like this. You've had some real shocks to your system." He spared her a glance again. "Better?"

She wet her lips. "Yes. A little. Thank you."

At that moment the cell phone in Tomas' pocket rang and he took it out to answer. "Go ahead." He listened for a minute or two, saying nothing. Then, "All right. Thirty minutes. Your lady's not in great shape, but she's a trooper. Fine. See you then."

"Was that Noah?" Taylor had finally figured out she wasn't going to pass out and embarrass herself.

"Yes. First off, Charlie's at the hospital. He's critical, but they think he'll pull through. The bullet hit him on the right side and splintered a rib."

"Thank God." The band constricting her chest loosened.

"Noah has taken care of things with the club and the police and now…"

"How? How can he handle it just like that?"

Tomas was silent for a moment. "When you mention Arroyo, it gets you a lot of perks."

"Oh." She was startled. "I don't think…"

"Right. Let Noah do the thinking for you in this situation. He's meeting us in thirty minutes."

Taylor dug a handkerchief from her purse and scrubbed at her palm, happy to see her fingers were barely trembling. "Tomas, I have to change clothes. I've got…I can't…"

194

They were on the Interstate now, Tomas constantly checking the rear and side view mirrors. "All in good time." His voice softened a little. "I know you want to get rid of that dress, but we've got to make sure you're safe first."

"Can't you just take me to the ranch?"

Yes. The ranch. Safety.

Tomas shook his head. "We need to give them a red herring. We have no idea where these people have eyes. They went to a lot of trouble to set up that sniper tonight. But I promise you they won't catch us with our pants down again."

Taylor stopped rubbing her hand and stared at him. "What do you mean?"

"You'll see. I'll let Noah explain."

Now they exited the Interstate into downtown San Antonio, Tomas zigzagging back and forth in the traffic lanes, sweeping around corners, rushing traffic lights. "Just checking to see if we have a tail," he said in answer to her unspoken question.

Taylor gritted her teeth to hold back the returning nausea and tried to forget that Charlie's blood was drying on her back. After a few minutes, they drove into the Rivercenter Garage next door to the Marriott Hotel and the Rivercenter Mall. Tomas carefully checked to see who followed them in. Then, apparently satisfied, he drove, up, up, up nearly to the top level. Finally, he pulled into an empty space next to a dark gray four-door pickup.

"Stay here," he cautioned as he climbed out.

A man as tall and dark as Tomas, also in a black suit, got out of the pickup and the two men shook hands. Taylor watched them chat for a few minutes, then Tomas leaned into the vehicle to exchange words with a woman sitting there. Finally, everyone nodded and the other SUV took off. Tomas climbed back into the driver's seat.

"What's going on?" Taylor asked, "Who are those people?"

"Decoys." Tomas glanced at his watch.

"Decoys?" She tried to keep her voice reasonable, but her tenuous hold on her nerves was fraying.

Tomas nodded. "They'll go to the corporate helipad and Greg will pick them up and fly them to the ranch. In case anyone's watching."

"But then why couldn't I just go?"

"Because you aren't armed and you're not a trained security guard." He started the engine and backed out of the space.

"Where are we going now?"

"To meet Noah. At my house."

And that was all he said for the rest of the ride. Taylor fought down the hysteria demanding release again and the screams bubbling up in her throat. The core of steel she'd finally discovered helped to push it all beneath the surface, at least for the moment.

Twenty minutes after they left the garage, Tomas turned into a quiet neighborhood and pulled into the driveway of a darkened adobe and limestone house. Noah was leaning against the side of a vehicle parked in the driveway. He uncrossed his arms and came forward to open Taylor's door, reaching out a hand to help her alight.

"Anything?" he asked Tomas.

The man shook his head. "The switch was smooth as glass. Greg should be lifting off with them right about now." He pointed at Taylor's back. "She's doing remarkably well, but she needs to get out of that dress."

Noah's eyes narrowed as he saw the blood covering the back of Taylor's dress. His eyes flashed to her white face and the death grip she had on her purse and he pulled her to his side.

"Can you hang on for just a little bit longer?" he asked in a soft voice. "I promise we'll get you out of this soon."

She swallowed hard and nodded. "How…how is Charlie?"

A shadow of pain crossed Noah's face. "He'll be fine. Rick Hidalgo's at the hospital with him. He's still in surgery, but the doctor sent a nurse out to report the progress."

"Thank God." A whoosh of breath left her lungs. "You'll have people there keeping an eye on him, right?"

"Already in place." Noah's tone was edged with barely restrained anger. "Bastards." And they all knew he didn't mean their own people.

"You going to Fredericksburg?" Tomas asked.

Noah nodded. "I'm taking the satellite phone with me. Will you go to the ranch and tell the Harts in person what's going on?"

"And John Martino," Taylor added, her voice shaky. "Tell him I need answers more than ever and I'll call him as soon as I can."

"All right." He shook hands with Noah. "Watch your back, *amigo*. And take care of our lady."

"Count on it." He settled Taylor in his Expedition as if she was a fragile piece of glass and pulled out of the driveway.

Taylor repeated the mantra over and over, concentrating on the road unwinding in front of them so she could block out the acute sense of what had happened.

"This trip will take a little over an hour," Noah told her. "Can you hang on that long?"

She clenched her fists in her lap, bunching the material of her dress. She was proud of the fact that, after the initial shock, she hadn't allowed herself to fall apart. "I can do whatever I have to."

"Good girl." And in a very uncharacteristic movement, he reached over and put one of his hands over both of hers. "I'm taking you where no one can find you until we get some answers."

"Oh?" She turned her head to look at him. "Where's that?"

"You'll see."

The usually taciturn man kept up running chatter as he drove, a move Taylor knew was meant to distract her. She was grateful for the distraction but it didn't erase the fact she wanted to rip off her clothes and stand under a shower for hours, although she wasn't sure she'd ever be able to wash away the feel of the blood.

She barely absorbed what little she could see of the landscape as they drove through the darkness on country roads. They passed through a couple of small towns, then they were out in the country again, vast open acres dotted with groves of trees. At last Noah turned off the narrow highway onto a gravel road nearly hidden by all the trees. They bumped along until they came to a stop in front of a small adobe house.

Taylor peered out through the windshield at it. "Where are we?"

"Someplace no one will find us. Come on." He helped her out of the vehicle, then unlocked the front door of the house.

Taylor saw that the inside wasn't much more than one large room. A tiny but efficient kitchen arrangement was tucked into one corner. A door at the far end led to what she supposed was the bathroom, a place she really needed to be.

"I'm sorry," she told Noah, gritting her teeth to keep from passing out, "but I have to get out of these clothes. Please."

He nodded. "I'm sorry you had to wait this long. Go on into the bathroom. It's not very fancy, but there are towels on a shelf in there and all the basic necessities."

"I-I don't have anything to change into," she stammered.

Noah strode to a chest against one wall, opened a drawer and pulled out a faded San Antonio Spurs T-shirt. "This ought to at least cover you up."

"Thank you."

Anything, as long as it's not covered in blood.

In the bathroom, she yanked her dress off, ripping the expensive material and tossing it aside. She knew she'd never wear it again anyway. Her bra and thong followed and her thigh-high hose, now a total mess. She dropped them all in a pile, which she would ask Noah to burn.

The shower felt like heaven, hot water washing away the traces of blood and dirt. Too bad it couldn't also wash away the memory of that instant when Charlie had fallen forward onto her back. The miasma of death clung to her like a sticky cloak. Even more than the shooting on the road — had that only been a couple of days ago? — she was now acutely aware of the danger she was in. And of everyone who was trying to protect her. As she leaned against the wall of the shower, she wondered if it wouldn't be better to just let these people — whoever they were — have what they wanted. She didn't think she could live with it if anyone else was killed.

Finally, when she was sure the hot water was about to run out, she shut off the shower and dried herself with one of the big towels she'd found. Noah's T-shirt came halfway down her thighs and slipped off one shoulder, but at least it covered her. If she was looking for warmth, this wasn't it, but at the moment she wasn't sure she'd ever be warm again.

When she opened the door, he was leaning against the short kitchen counter, talking on a satellite phone. He'd removed his jacket, tie and cummerbund and the studs from his dress shirt, leaving that hard-muscled chest and soft pelt of hair open to her eyes. He'd also kicked off his shoes.

She wondered what his reaction would be if she simply threw herself at him and told him to make love to her. No, *fuck* her. Noah Cantrell didn't make love, according to him. No matter. At the moment, what she needed more than anything was an affirmation of life. Something to wipe away the memory of all that blood and danger. Would he understand that?

Noah eyed her from top to bottom, assessing her, then he picked up a glass from the counter filled with ice cubes and amber liquid and held it out to her. "Better, but you still look shaky. Drink some of this." A tiny grin tickled one corner of his mouth. "And don't gulp it, all right?"

She took the glass with both hands and dropped onto the couch. The first sip stung the back of her throat, but the next one was a lot smoother. As the alcohol warmed her blood, the tremors that still shook her began to subside.

"Was that Tomas?"

"Yes. Charlie's going to be fine. He's got a long recovery, but he'll make it."

A breath whooshed out of her. "Thank God."

"Tomas has taken care of things at the ranch and doubled security everywhere. I told him not to call back unless it was urgent. You need to get some rest." He still had that watchful look in his eyes, studying her. "At least you've got a little color back in your face. How do you feel?"

She gave a shaky little laugh. "Like a man bled all over my back and almost died."

He grunted. "I am so damned sorry about this. I can't believe how stupid we've been. What kind of security are we to let this happen? We should have been looking at every angle then looking again." Every muscle in his body was taut with tension.

Taylor cleared her throat. "They just keep surprising us, that's all."

"Damn it, Taylor. I don't get paid to be surprised and neither do my men." He banged his fist on the counter, making her jump. "But it won't happen again. I promise you that. At least no one can find you here."

"Where is here, anyway?" She looked around the cabin, taking in more details.

The furnishings were simple—a huge bed with an old-fashioned iron headboard against one wall, a long couch and the chair she was sitting in facing a fireplace, a small table and two chairs near the kitchen area.

"A cabin just east of Fredericksburg. No one knows about it except for Tomas. You'll be safe here."

She took another sip of the strong liquor. "Whose is it?"

Noah hesitated a long moment before saying, "Mine."

Taylor's eyebrows shot up. "Yours?"

"Uh-huh." He straightened up from the counter and unfolded his arms, shoving his hands into his pockets. "It used to be Josiah's. This is where he lived when he was starting out."

Taylor laughed again, but there was no humor in it. "The place is great but—no offense—I can see why my grandparents dragged my mother out of here. They were snobs of the worst kind." Her voice softened. "I know she would have been happy here with…my father. She never got over him."

"Just as he never got over her." Noah took her face in his hands. "I'd like to shower and get out of this monkey suit. Will you be okay for a few minutes?"

"I'm not going to have a breakdown, if that's what you want to know. Yes, I'll be okay. I'll finish my drink."

His narrowed his eyes. "Maybe that's not such a good idea after all. I remember what happened the last time you drank."

She was trembling again, but this time not from shock. "So do I. And everything since then. Go shower, Noah. I won't pass out. I promise."

Chapter Fourteen

She only kept herself together by sheer force of will as she listened to the shower running in the bathroom and the sounds of him moving around. No matter what she did, she couldn't wipe away the feel of Charlie falling against her or the stickiness of his blood that had covered her. Or the sight of him lying on the ground looking all but dead.

And most of all, the knowledge that if she hadn't dropped her purse and bent down to retrieve it, she'd be the one with the bullet hole.

"Quit thinking about it."

She'd closed her eyes, but they flew open at the sound of Noah's voice. "I'm not—"

"Yes, you are." He was standing in front of her with only a towel slung around his waist, droplets of water still clinging to the matted hair on his chest, his long mane slicked back from his face. "It's a natural reaction. Maybe more of that whiskey would be good after all. Something to make you sleep."

"I don't want to sleep." She set her glass down on the little table next to her and stood. "I want you to make me forget. I want to know I'm still alive."

She reached for his towel and he grabbed her wrists with a bruising grip.

"Not a good idea, Taylor. You've had a bad shock tonight."

She stared up at him, wetting her lips with the tip of her tongue. "And what would be better medicine than to lose myself in some of that rough, wild sex you keep hinting at?"

He shook his head. "I will not take advantage of your

emotional state. I may be a bastard in a lot of ways, but that's too low even for me."

"You're not taking advantage. I know exactly what I'm doing."

His grip tightened even more. "No, you don't."

She might have given in a little if she hadn't noticed the erection tenting his towel that he was so obviously trying to ignore. "You said you were going to take me somewhere tonight and do things with me. Well, here we are and I want whatever you can dish out."

"You don't know what you're asking for." His voice was low, guttural.

"Yes, I do. And that's what I want." She forced the words past tears she refused to let him see. "Please. Don't make me beg, Noah. Help me lose myself tonight. I need it."

He stared at her for so long she was sure he was going to refuse. Finally, he nodded, stepped back and shoved his feet into his shoes, then grabbed his keys from the counter. "Don't move."

He was out of the door and back in seconds, a small satchel in his hand.

Taylor looked from it to him and back again. "What's that?"

"You want to play? I brought the toys."

A tiny ribbon of dark thrill curled in her stomach and her heart rate picked up. She swallowed the last of her drink and set the glass down.

Noah inclined his head toward it. "Another one?"

"No. I want to be fully aware of everything." She walked over to him and placed her hands on his chest. "Please, Noah. I need this tonight."

"All right then." He lifted her and carried her to the bed. In seconds, he'd yanked back the quilt and placed her carefully on the sheet.

"Stay right there," he ordered as he stripped off his T-shirt.

He picked up the small duffel bag, zipped it open and took out what looked like a handful of leather and silk. Before

Taylor realized what was happening, he had fleece-lined leather cuffs on her wrists, her arms stretched over her head and the cuffs tied to one of the rungs in the headboard. With an economy of motion, he did the same thing to her ankles, spreading her legs wide and fastening them to the corner posts. Then he got up and walked toward the bathroom.

"Where are you going?" She licked her lips nervously.

"Be right there," he called over his shoulder.

In the two minutes he was gone, Taylor lay there, totally exposed, her mind working furiously as she tried to imagine what was coming next. Then he was back carrying a bowl, towels, a razor and shaving cream. Her eyes flew open.

"What…"

"I'm going to shave this sweet cunt of yours so I can really see what it looks like." His eyes flashed heat at her. "I want to taste that flesh when it's bare naked, little girl. But let's decorate you a little first."

"D-Decorate?"

"Uh-huh. I have some jewelry here that will look outstanding on you."

He bent down and closed his lips over one of her nipples. She stared at him, her eyes full of questions she knew he wasn't about to answer. He flicked the tip of his tongue over the puffy bud, pressing it to the roof of his mouth then grazing it lightly with his teeth. His hand was warm on her breast, kneading the tip with his fingers until she thought for sure it was swollen to twice its size. Arrows of electric current shot straight to her depths, setting up a fluttering motion in her inner muscles. She shifted restlessly, trying to hold still for him.

Finished with one breast, he moved to the other, kneading, suckling, licking, grazing, until both nipples were equally swollen and wet from his mouth, throbbing in rhythm with her sex.

When he lifted his head and looked at her, the fire in his eyes almost burned her skin, sending arrows of thrill through her. He reached for a small box on the nightstand, removed something from it then he was pulling one nipple, elongating it and slipping a metallic circle over it. He turned a tiny screw at its side that tightened it and she jumped at the bite of pain. He gentled her with a soothing caress.

"Nipple clamps," he explained. "By the end of the night, you'll think your nipples are the most sensitive part of your body."

She looked down and saw the distended nipple poking through the loop with tiny gold chains dangling from it. The sight of it made juices flood from her damp sheath onto her thighs.

Noah fastened his gaze on it and her face flamed.

"Don't be embarrassed. I want these to make you hot and wet." He attached the second one with quick efficiency, then picked up the bit of silk, a scarf that he folded three times.

She wet her lower lip with her tongue, the edge of nervousness biting into her. "What are you doing?"

"I'm going to blindfold you, Taylor. The absence of sight enhances all the other senses and tonight I want you fully tuned in to the sense of touch." He placed the scarf over her eyes and tied it at the back of her head, then kissed her forehead. "Remember. Stay perfectly still."

She heard the scrape of a chair on the floor, then Noah's voice from the foot of the bed.

"Take a deep breath and let it out."

She did and as the air left her lungs, she left a warm cloth covering her mound, wetting the curls, then the hiss of aerosol and the light touch of the shaving cream. Noah spread it everywhere with his fingertips — across her mound, down her labia, on the inside of her lips over the line of downy hair.

"Here we go."

He talked to her as he worked, describing his actions in a quiet voice, but all she could think about was what he was doing and how arousing it was. She tried to hold herself as still as possible, but his touch was driving her crazy. Every time he tugged her flesh to give himself a better angle, the tip of his thumb or a knuckle brushed against her swollen nub and she had to bite down hard on her lower lip to hold herself steady. And with every touch her nipples throbbed within their tight confines. She was sure that just lying there she would come, flooding his hand.

She began to envision the process in her mind—warm cloth, shaving cream, efficient strokes, warm cloth again. Noah paid meticulous attention to each area, not rushing. Taking great care not to hurt her in any way.

When at last he was finished and had washed her thoroughly, he bent down and placed his lips over her clit, sucking it into his mouth. Taylor jerked at the touch, lifting her hips automatically and pushing herself against him.

"Delicious." She heard him lick his lips loudly, then chuckle. "Definitely better this way." The chair scraped back as he moved. "Let me get rid of these things."

In a moment he was back, releasing her from the bed, but before she could do anything, he had her retied facedown, arms stretched in front of her. But instead of tying her legs, he lifted her to her knees and placed the bed pillows beneath her. She had never felt quite so exposed in her life.

He stroked a hand down her spine, touching every indentation between the vertebrae. One lean finger slipped between the globes of her buttocks and teased at the entrance to her rectum, making her shiver.

Tonight. He's going to do it tonight.

She was effectively spread-eagled, wide open to whatever he wanted, completely at his mercy. She wasn't afraid. Instead a throbbing began deep in her body. She was sure her juices were seeping from her now naked pussy. She had never felt so helpless. Or so turned on.

Noah circled the opening of her sex with a fingertip. "You're wet already. Good."

Taylor was acutely aware of the cool sheet under her cheek, the touch of Noah's fingers, the scent of the soap he'd used when he showered and the clamps pinching and distending her nipples as they pressed into the bed. His fingers moved slowly, teasingly, along the insides of her thighs, up to the crease where they met her ass, again along that cleft of her buttocks. So lightly she thought she might be imagining it, his fingertips whispered along the sides of her breasts. But then he reached beneath her with both hands, found her aching nipples in their tiny circlets and gently pinched them. Her body twitched at the sensation and more cream dripped down her thighs.

"Magnificent," he said. "I'll bet by now I could make you come just by teasing your nipples."

I'll bet you could, too.

He lifted away from her and she heard movement of some kind. Then the bed dipped and she knew he was kneeling between her outstretched legs. A fingertip circled her opening, traced her now slick lips and drew the liquid back up into the cleft of her buttocks. With each touch, her body reacted, her pussy weeping with need, the throbbing heat inside her rising in intensity.

"You told me you'd never used a vibrator," he reminded her. "Remember?" He leaned over her and put his mouth close to her ear again. "You do remember, don't you, little girl?"

She nodded, not sure she could speak, need already building in her body. She just wanted to tell him to get on with it.

"I thought tonight I'd let you discover what it feels like." He moved back and she heard a buzzing sound. "I'll use this one first."

First? What does he mean, first?

Then she couldn't think, because he was pressing the vibrator against her and massaging every bit of her sex — her lips, her opening, her clit. Up, down, around, over and over. Nerves in her body were firing, her nipples felt as if they were on fire and within the deep channel of her sex, every muscle quivered with need. She tried to arch back against his hand, urging him to force it inside her, but he just gave a low laugh.

"Not yet, little girl. You're far from ready. But God, that naked cunt is so gorgeous. I could almost sit here forever watching it turn a dark pink and seeing those juices gushing from it."

I'm ready, I'm ready. Oh, God, I'm ready. Do it. Now.

He moved the little toy slightly higher and pressed it against the sensitive area between her channel and her rectum. If she hadn't been tied down, she was sure she'd have leaped off the bed. The sensation was beyond anything she could have imagined. The muscles low in her belly clenched, her breasts throbbed and her pussy clutched desperately at emptiness. Noah's hand rested on her buttocks, pushing them gently apart and stroking harder with the vibrator. She wanted to beg him to put something inside her. Anything to give her some relief.

Then he stopped. Just stopped.

Taylor wiggled her hips as much as her position allowed, waiting for Noah's touch again.

"More?" he asked softly.

She nodded and at once the vibrator pressed against her flesh again. He retraced the pattern, over and over. Never too slow, never too fast. Around and around, up and down. Pulsing against the highly sensitized area, calling every nerve into play. The spiral of need was coiled tightly inside her, demanding release.

Then it stopped again.

"Oh, no." She couldn't stop the words. "No, please."

But instead of the vibrator, this time it was his fingertips spreading her wide open and his mouth touching her. The rough surface of his tongue lapped at her slick flesh, his mouth drinking her cream. At last, he thrust his tongue inside her. Fucking her. Scraping her inner walls.

My clit, she wanted to shout. *Please touch my clit.*

But as if he knew how much she wanted it, he totally avoided it, concentrating on her other sensitive areas. His thumbs continued to spread her wide open as he teased her and tormented her. Her newly bare sex was ultrasensitive, every current of air like a heavy breeze stimulating it.

And Noah had been right. Losing the sense of sight heightened everything else. Every inch of her body was in an extreme state of arousal. The spiral began to tighten again, gripping every inch of her body, demanding release.

Then he stopped again.

Taylor wanted to sob with frustration. In the darkness, with no distraction, she was focusing completely on the sensations Noah created, every tiny tremor of nerve, every quiver of muscle, every uncontrolled spasm of her slick, hot walls. She could think of nothing except filling the demanding need that was driving her.

"Do you want to come, little girl?" Noah's voice was dangerously soft, heavy with lust but edged with control. "Do you want me to release that orgasm?"

"Yes. Please." She bobbed her head frantically. "Please let me come."

He rubbed both hands over her ass. "Not yet." And he bent over her again. "Do you know why?" he asked in that same soft voice.

She shook her head.

"Because I want you so hot that no matter what I do to you, your body will be ready for it."

She clamped her teeth into her bottom lip, trying to steady herself, to regulate her breathing. He moved slightly, then his hands were back at her ass again, rubbing the firm globes, squeezing them, massaging them. Her breathing began to slow down, the edge of the need subsiding.

Noah trailed the fingers of one hand through the cleft of her buttocks again, teasing at the tiny hole. Streaks of flame shot through her and her walls fluttered in response to the dark stimulation. Oh, god, she wanted his touch there, wanted his invasion. Wanted his cock!

When she tried to clench her cheeks, drag his fingers closer, he simply held them open. He touched his tongue to that dark opening and her body lurched, her stomach muscles clenching. Her swollen nipples felt as if they might explode in the pressure of the clamps even as they craved the pinching touch of his fingers.

What's happening to me? What am I turning into?

He blew against the spot, a light stream of air. When she shivered, he gave that low, rumbling laugh again.

"Does that feel good?" He placed a hot kiss at the base of her spine then licked the skin with the tip of his tongue. "I have something to make you feel even better."

"What…? What do you…?"

"Don't tense," he ordered.

Something cool and thick oozed onto the opening of her rectum, then Noah was slowly stroking it into her. First one finger, then two. First the tips, then down to the knuckle. As the fingers slid more easily into her, he scissored them, stretching the tight tissues. Dark heat washed through her and everything in her body throbbed, every nerve fired.

"Take a deep breath, little girl. We need to get that sweet ass loosened up for me, so I've got a treat for you. Come on, deep breath. When you feel something, push back."

"But…"

He bent low to her head and brushed his lips against her temple. "You can do it, Taylor. Just breathe."

He squeezed more of the lubricant inside her, then something round and metallic pushed against her hole. With one hand, Noah spread her cheeks wide. She took a deep breath and, as she let it out, the warm metal cylinder slowly slid inside her. The pulsating beat she felt deep rose in crescendo.

"Okay?" Noah asked.

"Y-Yes. Okay." *More than okay. Please fuck me. Please, please, please.*

A little more pressure on the vibrator and it began to emit a low hum. Vibrations rumbled through her dark, hot channel, echoing through her body. As she was scrabbling for some kind of focus, trying to adjust to them, he returned the first vibrator to the outer lips of her sex and began tracing the familiar pattern again.

Thought left her. Reason deserted her. She was reduced to a quivering mass of nerve endings, all driving her toward some steep precipice. The wand in her ass emitted gentle vibrations and the one in Noah's hand teased her mercilessly as he held her pussy wide open with his fingers. She was sobbing by now, reaching for the fulfillment he held just beyond her reach.

Her entire body was screaming for release and still he held it just beyond her reach. His fingers did their clever dance along the insides of her thighs and against her heated skin. She writhed as much as her position allowed, tugging hard on the restraints. And still it went on and on and on.

"Do you want to come, little girl?" He had turned the vibrator in his hand up to full strength now.

"Yes," she cried, tears running down her face, her swollen clit begging for attention. "Please, please, let me come."

"All right, then." He slid the vibrator into the demanding walls of her sex and with his thumb and forefinger pinched her clit.

She crashed over the precipice, flying into space, her body shattering, flying in all directions. Her body gripped the vibrator and her hips moved back and forth with the limited range of motion allowed. She yanked on her restraints, trying to anchor herself. Then it was there, the orgasm gripping her with fierce intensity. Noah kept massaging and pinching her clit, drawing it out, one hand at the base of her spine holding her in place. She convulsed and spasmed, her belly clenching, her nipples rasping against the fabric beneath them, screams ripping from her throat.

"Yes," he hissed. "Let me hear it. Let me hear your pleasure, little girl."

Just when she thought she'd reached the crest, Noah pressed on both vibrators and pinched her clit again, scraping it with his fingernail and she pitched forward into space once more. She lost count of how many times he'd made her come when at last he turned off the toys, removed the vibrator and ran his hand over her body, soothing her.

She had no breath left, no ability to move. She was sure her body was reduced to a pile of melted muscle and bone.

"Once more," he whispered, his voice so heavy with desire his words sounded as if they were pushing through cotton wool.

"I can't," she gasped, so spent she barely had the strength to protest.

"Yes, you can," he ordered. "And you will."

As he spoke, one hand slapped her ass with a stinging bite and she jerked at the unexpectedness of it.

"What…?" *Oh, my God!*

"I've been dreaming about doing this to your gorgeous ass from the first time I saw it." His voice was so heavy with lust Taylor almost didn't recognize it. "Watching that flesh quiver under my touch, turn pink then red and seeing the heat streaking from your cheeks down to that wide-open cunt." As if to emphasize, he administered another hard slap.

"It…stings." She was surprised that she could even speak.

"Only for a moment." He voice was low and seductive. "Spanking is an art. The right intensity, the right tempo and it makes you hotter than you've ever been."

Something speared through her. A lightning bolt of apprehension and hunger and all the forbidden pleasures hiding in the secret corners of her mind burst forth. She'd wanted this—all of it—and he was delivering as promised. Her mind wondered briefly if she'd even be able to walk in the morning. Then Noah's hand came down on her ass again and he was right. The pain was an introduction to pleasure, arrowing straight to her core. He set a tempo back and forth and she began to arch into it. But at the moment she settled, he stopped and placed his mouth on her again.

The clutching started up inside her again, spasms she'd been sure her body couldn't begin to react with anymore. She tugged desperately on her restraints, wishing she could move more than the tiny bit he allowed her. Wishing she could squeeze her thighs together, but his body held them apart. The hunger grew in her again, a living thing laughing at her exhausted, sweat-slicked body.

If she thought he'd give her relief right away, that idea flew out of the window as he continued to push her responses unmercifully. Nothing had changed. As before, the clever arousal went on and on, her body reaching the apex of need, hovering on the brink of orgasm until she was sure she would come any minute. Then cessation, leaving her panting heavily. She was balanced on that cliff again, nothing but space before her, body straining to climax.

And Noah was relentless in keeping her on that edge. As the heat from the spankings continued to warm her starving pussy he kneeled behind her, leaned down and, holding her open to him, placed his mouth on her swollen lips. The rough surface of his tongue on her tender opening made her jerk in response. One thrust of that tongue and the coil tightened again in a body she thought already spent beyond endurance.

"You see," he said, lifting his head. "You can come again, after all. Your body is so ready for it, so ripe to explode. Wasn't I right?"

She moaned, helpless in his grasp and in her restraints, as he licked every inch of her inner walls and outer lips with his clever tongue. Rimmed that tiny opening to her soaked channel. When he laved the sensitive tissue between both entrances to her body then flicked her asshole in a teasing movement, the throbbing began again throughout her body.

"Yes. You were right." She was sobbing with need, tears running down her face, her ass and pussy burning. She was not ashamed to beg for the release he held so tormentingly just out of reach. "I can come again. Please, please let me come."

Chapter Fifteen

Noah struggled to control his breathing, unwilling to let the woman spread out before him like a sensual banquet know just how affected he was by all this. That was something he struggled to understand himself. He'd had dozens of women in all kinds of situations. He'd done things far more extreme than anything he'd given Taylor so far. Yet he'd always managed to maintain his signature remoteness, his cool demeanor, functioning almost as an observer to his own actions.

That had been his intention tonight, despite the need that constantly consumed him to fuck the life out of Taylor Scott. Everything he'd done had been carefully crafted to keep him in the role of observer, physically and emotionally disengaged. But somehow his careful planning had backfired. Despite his constant pronouncements to this woman that what they had was a flame that needed to burn itself out—the sooner the better—the fire only seemed to be getting hotter. None of his plans for quenching it were working.

With Taylor, no matter how much effort he exerted, his body responded to every contact with her skin, every cry of arousal escaping her soft lips, every gushing of cream from the most beautiful pussy he'd even seen in his life. Not even with…

Don't go there. Do not go there.

Shaving her exquisite cunt had been a major lesson in self-discipline for him. He still didn't know how he'd managed to keep his hands as steady as he had, except that his fear of hurting her overrode the effect of the sensual impact. He'd wanted nothing more than to open her up as wide as he could and plunge himself into her. His tongue. His fingers. His cock.

And as he'd brought her to the edge of orgasm again and again, he'd marveled at the responsiveness of her lush body. Unlike the other women he was used to, her responses were not practiced, not those learned through experience. No, Taylor Scott gave him the most honest sensual response he'd ever seen. Even more than…

Don't go there!

His cock was so hard he was sure if he bumped into anything it would bend or even break. He'd been gritting his teeth to keep from casting aside everything he'd planned and simply ramming himself home in that hot, wet, slick channel that beckoned to him so enticingly. Where he'd used his bag of tricks with other women to keep himself stimulated, with Taylor they nearly sent him over the edge. Every time he touched that satin-soft skin, slid his tongue or his fingers into her body, thought about finally having his cock in her virgin ass, he almost came just from imagining it.

Jesus Christ, Noah, get a grip. This is no time to lose it. Especially now. And especially with this woman.

He was almost afraid to actually fuck her again, fearful that once that pussy clenched around him, he'd be completely and totally lost. Not a day, no — make that a minute — went by that he didn't damn himself for that night at the hotel. If he'd just walked away from that room — from her — maybe he wouldn't be in such deep shit now. When he'd given in to the throbbing of his cock, his initial intention had been to drive her away, to scare her with the kind of things he knew she'd never done. But the mirror trick had backfired on him. The minute he'd watched his fingers sliding in and out of that delightful pink pussy, rubbing the swelling flesh, her cream coating his skin, he'd been lost.

Tracking her down in Tampa had been a dual-edged sword. He'd prayed every minute of the plane ride that when he saw her again, he'd hate her. That she'd turn out to be either a bitch or a marshmallow, disgracing herself with Arroyo's board and executive staff, and he could move on to implement Josiah's Plan B.

But she'd been neither of those things. Instead, she'd shown a core of steel that had no doubt gotten her through the first thirty years of her life, a sharp mind and the ability to hold her own with anyone. And she'd given him as good as she'd got. He made it blatantly clear he was using her for nothing but sex. That in public he was the person he'd promised Josiah he'd be, her guide through the tangled intrigue that was threatening to bring down Arroyo. But in private he would take her every way she'd ever thought of and many she hadn't.

She hadn't flinched, bringing her own brand of fire to their coupling and scorching him in the process. If he didn't get the hell away from her soon he'd be lost. And he knew more than she did how unlikely a future was for the two of them. She had no idea of what lived in his soul or the barriers to any kind of real relationship between the two of them.

And now, hearing her beg for her orgasm, seeing the imprint of his hand on her ass, seeing the cream from her hot channel coating her thighs, hearing her voice hoarse with need, he thought he'd have a heart attack strangling his impulse to quit playing games with her, throw caution to the winds and capture her for his own as he'd wanted to from the very beginning.

He took a deep breath to steady himself and turned the wand in her anus on to low vibration again. As he plunged his tongue into her, he tugged on her clit with his thumb and forefinger and she shattered. Her usually petal-pink folds, now nearly crimson, clenched around his tongue and her body bucked as much as the restraints allowed. Raising his other hand, he warmed the cheeks of her ass with another series of slaps, each one sending her into another spasm.

He watched her convulse, saw her body jerking on the

bed and heard screams ripping from her throat. His testicles ached with the buildup of semen, his sac heavy against his thighs, the muscles at the base of his spine tensing.

I want her to scream like that when my cock's inside her.

Shut up, Noah. Don't borrow trouble.

He had to have her. Now. When she was still in the grip of her orgasm and the pressure and fullness would be easier for her.

Sliding the wand from her ass, he squeezed the lubricant onto his hand and slicked his cock with it. Spreading open her still heated buttocks, he pressed the tip of his penis against her rosette. The tight muscle resisted at first, but he pushed relentlessly forward until it relaxed and he was inside. The dark heat of her rectum surrounded him and he had to clench his jaw to keep from coming at once.

"Does that feel good, little girl?" he rasped as he began a slow back and forth movement with his hips, his hands holding her in place.

Her orgasm had slowed, but, as his cock moved within her, he felt the ripples begin again and the muscles in her belly clenching at the tips of his fingers. The tendons in his arms corded as he moved her back and forth on his cock until she began to accept the rhythm herself. She was making low animal sounds in her throat as she pushed down on him, her thighs quivering.

His testicles drew up and the tension in his spine increased. The climax ripped up from the deepest part of his body and he shook with the force of it, a loud shout escaping his lips. As his seed shot from his cock into her hot, dark tunnel, he threw back his head and pumped for all he was worth. The more he filled her, the harder she convulsed around him, milking him of every drop until he was sure there would be no fluid of any kind left in his body.

At last, completely spent, he withdrew from her. Managing enough strength to release her restraints, he turned her over to release the nipple clamps. Then, giving in to impulse, he cradled her against him as he fell onto his side. He wasn't sure whose heart beat more furiously, only that they thundered against each other. Taylor lay boneless in his arms, a mass of liquid muscle.

I want to keep her.

The thought exploded out of nowhere.

Well, that was a dumbass thing to be thinking. He should be putting miles of emotional distance between them, not considering how to break down barriers. He knew how disastrous that could be. Had been. Would always be.

It seemed forever before he could catch his breath to speak then he wasn't sure what to say. "I was rough with you," he finally managed, knowing he had been.

"It's all right." Her voice was slurred. "I needed it. At least it reassured me I was still alive."

"Yes, well, I could have found other ways if I'd thought about it."

But I didn't want any other way. I wanted exactly what we did. And more. What the hell am I going to do?

She leaned in to the wall of his chest, her small hand pressed against his skin. "But I didn't want any other way. Remember? Besides, you said you'd planned this before… the other thing happened." She yawned hugely. "Right now I just want to go to sleep."

He forced himself up from the bed, taking her with him. "Shower first."

"Oh, God, Noah, don't make me move."

"You'll be glad of it afterward. Those muscles will be plenty sore without it. Come on."

He carried her into the small bathroom, stood her in the shower with him and turned the water on as hot as she could stand it. She was so boneless he simply leaned her against the shower wall and went about lathering every inch of her body inside and out. He made sure to massage her swollen nipples and the lips of her cunt, knowing even with that she'd be damn sore the next day. Well, at least when this was over she'd have something to remember him by.

Would she remember him when he walked away? He was torn between wanting her to crave him and hoping she'd forget him.

Finally, they were both washed and dried with the big towels he stocked. After he used the small hairdryer he kept there, he carried her back to the bed and tucked her into the covers. When he slid in beside her, he pulled her against him, molding his body to hers. This was the first time they'd actually slept together and it was something else he wasn't sure was such a good idea.

He brushed her hair away from her temples and rested his chin on the top of her head.

"Noah?"

"Mm-hmm."

"Thank you. I think I can sleep now without dreaming."

* * * *

But she didn't. Sometime in the early hours of the morning she woke up screaming, brushing furiously at her back to wipe away the thick feeling of the blood that had clung to her. Raw shrieks ripped from her throat, bouncing off the walls of the room. She thrashed against the arms holding her, pushing and shoving to get free.

"Taylor." A hard, familiar voice. "Taylor, it's all right."

"Let go of me!" she shouted. "Let go!"

"Taylor, it's me."

Strong arms circled her tightly, holding her against a warm hard body, a voice murmuring soothing words to her. The familiar sound of it cut into the nightmare and she opened her eyes to stare into Noah's dark ones.

"What happened?" She shook her head, trying to focus her addled brain. Noah was holding her close to him and stroking her back and she had no desire to move.

"You had a nightmare. I'm not surprised after everything that happened."

"I'm sorry." She was embarrassed and tried to turn away

from him.

He gripped her chin, lifting her face toward him. "Taylor, you had something pretty bad happen tonight, something that I'm damn sure is well outside the realm of your experience. I'm surprised you didn't crack before this."

She started to tell him she had no intention of cracking, but her bruised mind and abused body had simply reached the tipping point. The first tears trickled from behind her eyelashes and in seconds a cascade was washing down her cheeks. Great sobs shook her and she pounded her hands against Noah's chest, cursing and wailing and damning the people hunting her. She cried until her body felt empty.

The erotic sex had reached down to where she'd pinched her emotions into a tight ball, hiding from the horror of the shooting, and brought forth enough tears to wash it all away. Her heart still hurt for Charlie and her guilt wouldn't go away for a long time, but at least she could begin to deal with it.

She gave a little embarrassed laugh when she finally realized they were sitting in bed completely naked and she'd just had a rampant case of hysterics. She swiped at her cheeks with the palms of her hands. Noah took a corner of the sheet and mopped her face, brushing her hair off her forehead and tucking it behind her ears.

"I'm sorry." She struggled to steady her breathing and regain some semblance of control. "I've drenched you and made a fool of myself."

He tipped up her chin again. "I'd be surprised if you didn't have a reaction."

She pulled in another deep breath. "I just couldn't get rid of the feel of Charlie's body falling against me and his blood covering my back. And the realization that if I hadn't bent over when I did, it would be me lying there. And most probably dead."

His fingers bit into her arms. "No thanks to me. But I can promise you this is the last mistake I'm making."

"I didn't mean to imply…"

"I know. But I did. And I'm taking care of it." He got out of bed, unconcerned about his nakedness, and poured her another drink. "Here. I'm not trying to make an alcoholic out of you, but you need to settle your nerves again so you can go back to sleep."

She took the glass without protest and sipped it slowly. Words whirled around in her brain and she tried to put them together in a proper coherent sentence. "Noah, about tonight."

His face tightened. "You don't need to say anything. I crossed a line I shouldn't have. It won't happen again."

"Damn it." She took a healthy swallow of the drink, trying not to choke on it. "Don't do that. I was the one who asked for this. Begged for it, if you remember. Isn't this what you told me I'd run from? Be scared of?" She drank from the glass again, too angry to pay attention to how much she was drinking. "Well, guess what, Noah Cantrell. I'm not scared at all."

Much. Only it's not you I'm scared of. It's me and the door you unlocked in my brain.

"Taylor," he began.

"Don't Taylor me. You had this in mind all along, remember? And tonight I wanted it. Demanded it. I needed this, don't you understand?" She threw back the sheet and strode to the counter, ignoring her own nudity, and refilled the glass. "And here's another shocker for you." She thrust out her jaw. "I want more. Do you hear me, Noah? Am I clear?"

Taylor couldn't believe she was saying this. She knew she was raving, but she couldn't help herself. Her mind was a bubbling mass of emotions and his words and attitude were waving at her like a red flag.

Noah strode to her from the bed and took the glass from her hand. "I think you've had enough of this for tonight."

"Not by half." She reached around him and took it back, deliberately taking a big gulp. She gritted her teeth against the burning sensation in her throat and blinked against the tears in her eyes.

He grabbed it back and tossed what was left into the sink. "You don't know what you're asking for."

"Oh, really?" She stood in front of him, naked, hands on hips, fire raging inside her. "Well, maybe I do, or maybe I don't care."

He grabbed her shoulders so hard she winced.

"Whatever you want from me, Taylor, I don't have it to give." His voice was cold as ice. "I told you that before. We have no future together and the situation just keeps getting worse. If I hadn't made a promise to Josiah I'd walk away right now. But you can be damn sure as soon as this is done, I'll be gone."

Her inner rage was suddenly overridden by something else, something that churned her insides and gave her a desperate feeling.

"Fine. Walk away. But, in the meantime, aren't you the one who said you couldn't keep your hands off me? That all you wanted to do was fuck me? Well, go ahead. That's what I want too. The harder and raunchier, the better."

Her hands were clenched into tight fists and her breath rasped from her throat. When she met his eyes, they were like twin lasers burning into hers. Leaning forward, she brushed her nipples against his chest. She unclenched one hand and closed it around his jutting cock.

His breath hissed out between his teeth. "Jesus Christ, Taylor."

Fueled by rage, alcohol and the lingering effects of the shooting, she kneeled on the floor in front of him, wrapped her fingers around his rigid shaft and took him into her mouth. She used the tip of her tongue to tease his cock. She probed the slit with the tip of her tongue then glided her fingers up and down the silken sides covering the steel shaft. His testicles lay heavy against his thigh and she reached down to cup them lightly, raking her fingernails over the downy soft hair covering the skin.

Noah jerked, fisting his hands in her hair as he tried to

drag her away from him. She shook her head furiously and sucked him even deeper, her lips stretched wide over the broad expanse of his penis. The harder he tugged on her, the harder she sucked, until in self-preservation he finally gave up and just guided her head. His skin was slick now with her saliva and his testicles hardened in her hand. When she reached underneath them and scraped a fingernail across the tightness of his anus, he jerked again and swore.

"Christ, Taylor, do you even know what you're doing to me?"

She slipped her mouth off his engorged cock, licked the tip and looked up at him. "I guess some things just come naturally to me." She bent to her task again, stroking up and down with one hand even as her mouth tried to draw everything from him, the other teasing at his ass and balls.

His breathing became ragged and in the wet heat of her mouth, he grew impossibly harder. When she gently squeezed his balls again, he ripped her head away from him.

"All right, God damn it. But if I'm going to come, it'll be in that soft cunt that's been worked so hard tonight. It should be good and swollen and fit me like a tight glove."

He picked her up and carried her back to the bed, a lethal combination of lust and anger glowing in his eyes. Before she could catch her breath, he had a condom rolled onto his cock and was kneeling between her legs.

"You asked for it, little girl. Okay. If this is what you want, this is what you get."

He spread her thighs wide, bending her legs bent back so far her knees were almost to her chest. He ran his tongue the length of her cleft in one liquid swipe from her anus to her clit. Then he was poised at the entrance to her eager body again, one hand wrapped around his shaft as he pressed against her tender opening.

The head breached her flesh and with a heavy thrust he was inside her. She screamed at the intrusion into her abused flesh, but Noah was merciless. He pounded her, sweat dripping from his brow, his eyes wild. He tugged and pulled at her clit, which was so sensitive just the lightest touch nearly brought her off the bed.

Taylor could find only one thought in her head as Noah's muscles tightened, his hair flying wildly about his shoulders. This was the first time she had ever seen the warrior's famous control snap.

The time for thinking disappeared. Noah was riding her and riding her, filling her impossibly tight sheath with his enormous cock. She gripped the sheet, trying to keep up with him, stunned at the orgasm that was building rapidly inside her. When he leaned down and shoved two fingers into her rectum, she screamed at the intrusion. But his body went rigid and his cock began pulsing heavily in her hot channel.

Hardly believing it possible, as low guttural shouts tore from his throat, she came apart, flying, every part of her body shaking as the spasms rocketed through her. Cream that she didn't even know she still had drenched Noah's cock, the liquid pooling inside her around the thick shaft that stretched her to impossible limits.

As her own breathing slowed and her heart rate began to settle down, she watched Noah through heavy-lidded eyes. He slid from her body and stripped off the condom, the mask in place again. He backed off the bed and headed for the bathroom.

"Go to sleep, Taylor," he threw over his shoulder. "You'll need your rest. I have a feeling tomorrow is going to be a busy day."

A cold knot settled into the pit of her stomach, despair reaching every corner of her heart. Along with dissolving all her inhibitions and introducing her to the most intense sexual pleasure, he'd lodged himself inside her emotionally. She'd had the misguided hope despite Noah's protestations that tonight might have been the start of something for them, but his attitude just now made it very clear. He'd fuck her any time, any way, a hundred different ways, but that was all she was to him. That and a responsibility. She'd take care of that as soon as she could and get Noah Cantrell completely out of her life.

Chapter Sixteen

Taylor woke to sunlight streaming in through the large picture window and the murmur of Noah's voice. Prying open her eyes, she saw him standing in the kitchen, holding a coffee mug and satellite phone. He had pulled on a pair of jeans and a T-shirt that showed every line of his body and his thick hair was still wet from the shower.

Brushing her hair out of her eyes, she sat up in bed, trying to ignore the protest of sore and aching muscles. Every detail of the previous night suddenly flooded Taylor's brain with painful clarity. For a moment she wondered if she'd dreamed it all. Surely the erotic images flashing through her consciousness were totally foreign to anything she'd experienced in her life. That could not have been her. Could it?

Oh, God!

A tremor skittered along her spine at the memory of the uncontrollable responses of her body. Noah had warned her he would give her a hard ride and he hadn't been wrong. She shivered, remembering her sobbing as she'd begged him to give her an orgasm, the desperate need of her body as he teased it endlessly, the feel of his thick cock in her rectum which even now felt stretched and sore.

Was this the real Taylor Scott? A hedonistic wanton who willingly gave her body to a man who cared nothing for her as a person? Who now craved the shattering orgasms he brought her and demanded even more exploration into the dark side of her fantasies?

Damn him, anyway. And damn Josiah for setting him on me.

Noah shifted his gaze to her, the only movement in his

impassive face. "I'll get right back to you," he said softly into the phone. He hung up, walked over to the bed and handed the phone to Taylor. "John wants you to call him. I'll get you some coffee."

"Thank you." Taylor took the phone and punched in the number of the ranch.

"Oh, my God, Taylor, are you all right?" Jocelyn's breathless voice greeted her.

"Yes. I'm fine. Thank you. And praying for Charlie's recovery."

"We are, too. Don't worry about the ranch. The security's been beefed up and everyone's riding armed." Her voice had a slight strain to it. "When you find these people, I might shoot them myself."

Taylor had to chuckle at the thought of the impeccable Jocelyn shooting anyone. "Can you get John on the phone for me?"

"Right away. He's anxious to speak to you."

John Martino reported his findings in his usual even voice, but Taylor heard the underlying excitement and when he'd finished she understood why. The more he talked the tighter the knot in her stomach grew.

"I want to see all of this," she told him. "I've only given the workings of the corporation a cursory look but I have the feeling there's stuff under the rug I need to find. That's why you're here, but I think we might get further now if we combine our brains. Let me see what's possible." She disconnected the call and leaned back against the pillows.

Damn! 'Disaster' was the only word that came to her mind.

"Not good," Noah guessed, watching her face.

"Not good at all." Taylor swallowed some of the coffee, trying to collect her thoughts. "Noah, is there any way we can bring John out here, or the three of us can get together someplace secure?"

"Taylor —"

"Noah, this is my corporation and *your* responsibility.

227

The three of us need to get together."

He was silent for so long she wondered if he was thinking or just trying to find a way to say no again.

"Okay. This is against my better judgment, but I do see your point. Give me a minute to think here."

Taylor dug her nails into her palms to control her impatience while he rolled it all around in his mind.

"I don't want to bring him here," he told her. "And I don't want to take you back to the ranch yet. I know damn well whoever is behind this has eyes on everyone and everything. But I have an idea that might work. It's risky and complicated but…"

"Thank you." She leaped at him and threw her arms around him. When he stiffened she took a step back. "Sorry. Let's hear the plan."

It took a while, and Taylor had to admire Noah's ingenuity in getting them together without leaving a trail of breadcrumbs. At last, however, they convened at Tomas', a place where Noah was as sure as he could be that no one had tracked them. John had his laptop with him as well as the files he'd printed out. Taylor and Noah also brought their laptops and Taylor had her briefcase with the work she'd been doing so far on studying Arroyo. Now, with full coffee mugs, the three of them sat around the kitchen table, looking at the data laid out before them.

"I meant to go back and study the Idaho plant when I had time," Taylor said, the folder open in front of her. "I can't tell you what it was that triggered my brain, but something did."

"Interesting you should pick up on that one." Noah looked at the report he was holding. "Josiah paid scant attention to it. As long as the balance sheets looked good and the production details met his quotas he was happy. He chose to deal with the more complex divisions."

"Which is what made this one a prime situation for whatever the hell is going on," John told him.

"I can't even fault him," Taylor added. "He directed his

energy to the areas that provided the bulk of income for Arroyo and trusted his staff to handle the little things." She studied the sheet she was holding. "Someone named Nate Patterson runs the operation on site."

Noah tapped the paper with his finger. "Supervised by Kate Belden."

"Ah, yes." Taylor sat back in her chair. "The woman who wants to cut out my heart. Nobody's been looking over her shoulder, so she had free rein. And still would, if Josiah hadn't stumbled on that orphaned insurance policy." She looked at John. "Which is why I decided we needed your expertise to dig out whatever was going on there. So, what have you got?"

"I stated checking out both suppliers and customers to see if there was some kind of connection for this." He placed a sheet of paper on the table. "I printed this out so we could all look at it together. The list with all those names on it. The first two I checked don't even exist."

Taylor frowned. "Okay. Let's divide this up and see what we get."

They were barely halfway through the list when Taylor looked up.

"Damn. Just God damn it."

Noah twisted his lips in a grim smile. "I'm guessing you found the same thing I did."

"And me," John added.

"None of these companies or individuals exist." She looked at each man in turn. "Right?"

"Right," John agreed. "And the financial transactions just don't make sense for a legal operation. I keep tracking them and hit a dead end."

"And these reports I've been reading are completely sanitized," Taylor added.

"Did you try calling there?" Noah asked.

John nodded. "Got a very efficient secretary-type person who said their plant manager was unavailable but she would have him call back."

"Let me try." Taylor picked up her cell and dialed the number on the report in front of her.

"Arroyo Agrico," a very pleasant voice answered.

"Yes. This is Taylor Scott, CEO of Arroyo Corporation. I'd like to speak to the plant manager." She looked down at the report. "Andy Genero."

"Oh!" The woman sounded startled. "Miss Scott. Well, it's an honor to speak to you."

"Thank you, but I have some questions for Mr. Genero that need to be answered right away. Can you get him for me?"

Silence hummed over the connection for a long moment.

"I'm sorry," the woman said at last. "He's out in one of the warehouses at the moment. But I'm happy to take a message."

"Who am I speaking to?" Taylor asked.

Another beat of silence.

"M-Mary Lamont."

"Well, Miss Lamont, I suggest you send someone out to fetch Mr. Genero and get him on the horn to me right away."

"A-all right."

Then more dead silence. But this time, Taylor was sure the woman had disconnected.

"She hung up on me." She looked at the two men. "John, you said the financials looked clean, right?"

He nodded. "But as you know, that doesn't mean anything. Someone who knows what they're doing can dummy up the books and if no one looks, they don't have a problem. I'll check for activity under the plant manager's name, but again, I'm damn sure I won't find anything."

"Let's call on Google Earth," Noah suggested.

All three of them entered the information in their computers and watched while Google Earth did a search for the address they'd put in. When the screen brought up the location, they all stared at each other.

Taylor was the first one to say anything. "Empty fields."

"No shit," Noah said.

"So where is the money coming from and where is it going, if not to pay expenses?"

"Someone's running an illegal operation right in the bosom of Arroyo," Noah spat.

"I've got the bank accounts up now," John told them, fingers flying over his keyboard. "I know this will come as a shock to you, but they're in a very small local bank, as opposed to the national one Arroyo uses. Taylor, how the hell did no one spot this as an anomaly?"

"I can answer that," Noah said. "Kate Belden had all the oversight. She could get away with whatever she wanted to."

"Well, what she's getting away with is hiding some kind of illegal operation right under Josiah's nose."

"Because he trusted her," Taylor said.

"Too fucking right," Noah spat.

"So, how do we find out how the project started, where the money is actually going now and where the normal-size profits come from?"

"Give me a few minutes here—maybe a half hour—to go through everyone's travel information and the records of the use of the corporate jets." John was already typing furiously. "I can get you an answer."

The answer, when he had it, made them even angrier.

Noah poured fresh coffee for everyone then he and Taylor sat in tense silence while John did his thing. Each new piece of information brought worse news than the one before. No wonder Josiah had been killed. He was about to rain on someone's very profitable parade. The fake Idaho plant was a project Josiah had asked for to begin with, but it had never existed there. Instead, someone had built a facility in the heart of the Mexican state of Chiapas.

"Mexico." Noah smacked his fist on the table. "Kate used the jet for trips to Mexico."

"All to the same location," John added. "Let me do some more digging here."

Half an hour later, he had traced money to accounts in Geneva and the Bahamas.

"How do you know those are Kate's?" Taylor asked.

"Trade secret." He winked. "If I tell you, I'll have to kill you."

"Please." She curved her lips in a wry grin. "There are enough people trying that already."

"I could be wrong about something else, too," he went on, "but based on what I've discovered in the past year for other clients, I'd say there's a facility in Mexico manufacturing guns for the cartels which get sold to terrorist groups. There's *beaucoup* bucks in that."

"That has to be what Josiah discovered on the plane trip. He must have checked the flight records, too. None to Idaho but plenty to Mexico." A muscle jumped in Noah's cheek. "Whoever's behind this knew about it and arranged to have him killed."

John's face was a hard mask. "I agree."

"We need to see that plant for ourselves," Noah told them, "and, if possible, blow it up."

Taylor's mouth dropped open. "Did you say blow it up?"

Noah lifted one shoulder. "We can't kill the supply train, but we can cripple it if we take out this facility and make the buyers waste time looking for other suppliers. Meanwhile, we can turn them over to Interpol to track."

"And Paul and Kate?"

"If they're in Mexico, we'll bring them back and turn them over to Homeland Security. I want Arroyo's slate cleaned in public, if possible."

"Ditto." Taylor shivered but not from a chill. "I'm going. You're not leaving me behind on this."

"God knows I want to." His voice was edged with frustration. "But leaving you alone isn't an appealing alternative."

"Damn it, Noah—"

"Damn it, nothing. We have no idea what's waiting for us and the last thing I want is for the next bullet to hit you.

I'm calling Greg. I'll have him pick us up here. Tomas' back yard is big enough for him to land the chopper. I'll also have him call the airport to prep one of the planes."

Taylor watched him carefully. Something was bothering him. Until she could find out what, she'd have to avoid any more intimacy. It clouded her mind and her judgment.

What are you hiding, Noah Cantrell? What do you really feel and what's put up those shields again?

Before any of them could say anything else, they heard the *whap! whap! whap!* of the helicopter rotors. From the big window that looked out onto the yard she saw Greg setting down in the clearing. Noah hurried out to the chopper to greet him then motioned for Taylor and John to join him.

"Jocelyn packed a small case for you," he told Taylor. "In case there might be something you need, since she doesn't know how long you'll be gone or where you'll be going."

Taylor smiled. "She is definitely worth her weight in gold. But what about you and John?"

He actually laughed. "I guess our grooming habits are unimportant. Come on, get in the chopper and let's make tracks."

It seemed they had just lifted off before they landed at San Antonio International Airport. When Greg landed almost next to the Arroyo plane the jet engines were already whining. Someone jumped down from the cockpit and walked toward them.

"She's all set," he told Greg.

"Thanks for getting her ready for me." The two men shook hands.

Then Noah hustled them out of one machine and into the other. It seemed just moments before the plane began to taxi toward the runway.

"I told the pilot to file a flight plan for Costa Rica," Noah told her. "Just in case anyone was curious. We'll make a correction once we're in the air."

"Good."

"Buckle up. We're about to take off."

233

As soon as they were airborne, John asked for a satellite phone then looked up a number in his encoded cell phone. He moved to the rear of the plane while he carried on his conversation, but when he sat down again the expression on his face was grim.

"My source is familiar with the facility," he reported. "It manufactures a variety of small arms and shoulder-propelled rockets. The reports Josiah received each month were nothing but a fairytale. A certain amount of money went into the Arroyo coffers, but the bulk of it went to two dummy corporations then to the accounts in Geneva and the Caymans. When we get back," he added, "I can finish the traces I did on Kate Belden and Paul Hunter, so you have hard proof."

Noah had been on a sat phone, as well.

"Okay, we have a place to land." He looked grim. "I think it's the same place Kate and or Paul landed each time they traveled. I've got people meeting us in Mexico with maps and manpower, as well as transportation for us to the site. My contact knows exactly where the factory is located."

She could only begin to imagine who Noah might have called. She wouldn't be surprised if he had either the CIA or a band of mercenaries waiting for them when they landed.

"We should find out where Kate and Paul are now," Taylor told him.

"I'll call Carmen and tell her you want to meet with both of them and to set it up."

But when he finished the call, anger flashed in his eyes. "Neither of them are there. They left word they had an overnight business trip to take."

"I'll just bet they did." Taylor didn't remember the last time she'd been so angry.

She'd fix this, for the father she'd never known and whose memory she wanted to honor.

Damn skippy she would.

Chapter Seventeen

Greg had arranged for a steward to be on board and the moment they reached cruising altitude, he served sandwiches and drinks. As they ate, the three of them went over the information again. The more detailed it became, the angrier Taylor grew. She drew diagrams on a pad of paper she pulled from her briefcase, putting information into the boxes. John did the same thing and they made constant comparisons, with Noah adding information now and then.

Finally she threw down her pencil and leaned back on the couch.

"It's all there, plain as day, if you know where to look for it like John did. Paul drew up all the paperwork for the real estate and the bank accounts as well as the dummy corporations. Kate negotiated for the land and the construction and set up the contracts with buyers."

Noah nodded. "She spent several years working for a corporation in the Middle East. I'm guessing that's where she made all her connections. The rest was easy. They fed Josiah just enough money and information to keep him in the dark." He slammed down his own faxes onto the pile. "Damn it, I read her pre-hire investigation. It came back clean, but I should have pushed and dug harder. If some of this stuff had turned up, then Kate Belden never would have seen the inside of Arroyo."

Taylor poured herself another glass of iced tea from the pitcher on the table. She was trying her utmost at maintaining composure. She worked very hard to ignore the memories of the previous night and the residual soreness in her body.

That took precedence over everything else. She could do it. Being focused was her stock in trade.

"Why would he suddenly ask questions, anyway?" Noah swallowed some coffee. "He trusted her. Maybe not Paul, but certainly Kate. He had no reason to be suspicious until the insurance review turned up the discrepancy."

Taylor stirred sweetener into the tea. "She couldn't have him write insurance on a nonexistent facility. Besides, he'd have to have it inspected and she'd have to give him a copy of the payroll for worker's comp."

"Handling everything herself made sure her little secret was secure," John added. "But when I print out all of this stuff, there'll be no doubt about what's been happening."

"People will do a lot of things for money," Noah pointed out, then shifted subjects. "I'll bet Kate and Paul were both frantically trying to find you after last night. Now neither of them are in the office."

"On their way to Mexico to make sure their resources are safe," Taylor guessed.

Noah nodded. "Rounding up their own troops and making plans to eliminate you. They're damn devious, I'll give them that. I had Tomas put tails on them last night and they both managed to ditch them."

"Comes from being a crook and always looking over your shoulder," John told them.

"No shit." Noah picked up the sat phone again. "I'm going to make one more call. There's an agent with Homeland Security I know very well." The call was short but apparently satisfactory. "He'll be meeting with his bosses and they'll proceed to get the necessary paperwork to bring this thing down."

"That doesn't kill the hydra, though," Taylor pointed out.

"You're right. Only closing down this factory and seizing all the records so we can destroy the tentacles will do that."

"And that's why we're here." Despite herself, she couldn't help the little nervous thrill that clutched at her.

"Exactly."

They all fell silent after that. John sat silently watching out of the window while Taylor fiddled with her drink. She wanted desperately to talk to Noah about the night before but this was hardly the time or place, especially with a third person along. Before last night she could have said, 'yes, it's just sex, so take it and go away.' But now he owned a piece of her soul.

Now, I'm in big trouble.

Noah rose from the couch and walked to one side of the cabin, hands shoved into the pockets of his jeans. The line of tension in his body was like an electric guy wire, taut and ready to spring back if someone released it. Taylor forced herself not to say a word. But something had happened last night, to both of them, and sex was the least of it. They'd each crossed unintentional boundaries and she wasn't about to let Noah hide behind his walls anymore. Nor was she about to run from what she was feeling for him, whatever it was.

Her concentration was interrupted by the pilot's voice over the intercom.

"Miss Scott? Mr. Cantrell? We'll be landing in a few minutes. You'll need to take your seats."

Then they were banking over green jungle heading toward a dirt landing strip. If they survived she was going to lock Noah Cantrell in a room with her and get this settled.

* * * *

Taylor knew very little about the Mexican state of Chiapas, only what she'd read in the newspaper. The Mexican government had established a massive military presence, including many paramilitary groups, to wage a low-level war against the protesting indigenous groups who lived there. Funding the groups often became a problem and many of the paramilitary units turned to kidnapping, drugs and arms as a way to support their operations.

Outside the cabin window they were surrounded by

the greenery of jungle growth and something much more ominous — at least a dozen men in jungle fatigues carrying rifles, belts with bullets and grenades slung around their chests and waists. No one was smiling.

Taylor turned to Noah. "What's going on?"

"Everything's fine."

His mask firmly in place along with the aviator shades that hid even his eyes, he jogged down the stairway.

One man stepped forward and shook hands with Noah. They then embraced and she released her pent-up breath although she was still far from reassured. Noah turned and climbed back up the stairs, the man behind him. Taylor stayed where she was, wondering where she could hide if she needed to.

"Taylor Scott, I'd like you to meet Edgar Villalobos. Edgar, this is Josiah's daughter."

Edgar took her hand and bent over it, his narrow moustache tickling the back of it. "It is my very great pleasure, *Señorita* Scott. Your father was a man of great character."

"*Gracias.*" Taylor managed a faint smile, but she looked at Noah. She had questions for him.

"Edgar was in the Rangers with me," Noah explained. "When I was setting up the new security department at Arroyo he came to work with me for a while. Before his relatives begged him to help them here."

Relatives. Paramilitary. That meant that Edgar was somehow related to the ruling party of Mexico. Was he part of the group Kate and Paul were dealing with? *No.* Noah would know who to trust and who not to.

"Edgar is definitely on our side," Noah said, as if he read her thoughts. "There are several paramilitary groups down here, many of them working at cross-purposes. Edgar says one of them is guarding the facility and working the arms deals with Kate. These men here are all loyal to him."

"That's certainly good to know. So now what?"

Edgar smiled, a flash of white teeth in a dark face, although it held little humor. "Now, Miss Scott, we will gather in the rest of my men and make our way to the site of the factory. Noah has indicated he would not be unhappy if we put it out of business and we plan to accommodate him."

"You and John stay here," Noah ordered. "Edgar will leave some men to guard you."

"Not on your life, you damned arrogant ass. This is my company and it was my father they killed." She looked at John. "But you, my friend, need to stay here."

John held up his hands. "No argument from me."

Edgar just shrugged, then nodded.

Taylor was sure Noah's eyes were filled with murderous rage, but she was past caring. This was her fight. She'd nearly been killed twice, two of Noah's security guards had been beaten almost to death the day of the first attack and Charlie was fighting for his life because of her. No way was she hiding out in the plane. Slipping on her sunglasses, she threw her shoulders back, daring the men to leave her behind.

"I'm ready."

"Fine." Noah's jaw was clenched so tightly the muscles in his face were ridges. "Just do exactly as we tell you and nothing else." He was out of the door and down the steps before she could say a word.

Edgar directed her behind the plane where several dark green Hummers waited. She almost made a comment about the paramilitary business paying well until she remembered that was why they were in Mexico. She clamped her lips together and let Noah assist her into the truck Edgar indicated.

"Exactly where are we, anyway?" That couldn't be too prying, could it? She knew they were in Mexico. "I'm assuming we didn't go through any kind of customs and immigration because we flew in under everyone's radar."

Edgar nodded. "We're in the center of Chiapas, where several long sierras, or mountain rangers, bisect the state. They make an excellent location for clandestine facilities like drug and arms manufacturing. And Chiapas has a common border with the Pacific Ocean, so transporting goods, especially to the Middle and Far East, is not a problem. The villages are so poor they eagerly work for the money people like your Paul Hunter and Kate Belden will pay them."

"Any sign of them?" Noah asked.

Edgar nodded. "A small plane landed on the far side of this sierra not an hour before you did. The blonde-headed woman and the man with gray hair were seen walking into the factory with a few others."

Noah cast a glance at Taylor. "I'd like to take them and the division manager, Jim Haskins, alive if possible and return them for trial. But you do understand that destroying the factory is our prime objective."

"Yes." She forced herself to show a calmness she didn't feel. "Do whatever you have to."

They bumped along through the low vegetation, the massive vehicle riding smoothly over exposed roots and dead plants. Finally the lead Hummer turned abruptly into thick undergrowth and the others followed.

"What's happening?" Taylor asked.

"We can't drive closer than this," Edgar informed her. "We go on foot the rest of the way so we avoid detection. Guards and sensors are everywhere."

"Stay here," Noah ordered, turning to face her.

"You can't—"

"Oh, yes, I can. And I will. We know what we're doing. You don't. Besides endangering your own pretty neck, you might get some of these men killed if you don't know what you're doing."

When she saw it was useless to argue, she simply threw herself back against the seat.

"We'll leave the keys in the Hummer. If you have to, take off and drive like hell. There's a SAT phone on the seat up here so you can call Greg. He'll find you wherever you are."

Edgar pressed something cold into her hand. A gun. "The safety is off." He pointed. "If anyone but one of us approaches, shoot at once. Don't ask questions. Can you do that?"

She swallowed and nodded.

"*Excelente, señorita.*" He took her hand and kissed it. "Before you know it, it will be done." He slid out of the vehicle.

Noah leaned over the back of his seat. "You heard what he said. Any doubts, just shoot."

"Fine. Fine. Just go and do what you have to."

Suddenly he reached and hooked her head toward him. The kiss he gave her was scorching, his hands clutching her head. When he pulled back, she was breathing as heavily as he was. He took one long last look at her, then was gone.

Time moved as if it had chains on its feet and was dragging them through the jungle. Outside, she heard the screech and cry of a variety of birds and saw an occasional flash of color as one swooped through the dense greenery. The interior of the vehicle was stifling and for a moment she thought about running the AC, then decided against it. The engine would make noise and attract attention.

Another hour passed with no movement or sound whatsoever and her nerves were raw with anxiety.

I don't care what they said, I should never have let them leave me here. Surely something should have happened by now.

At last, unable to bear the suspense one minute more, she opened the door and slid out, stretching her legs, the gun firmly in her hand.

"I wondered how many more bugs I'd have to let bite me before you climbed out of that monstrosity. The damned things are bulletproof and I didn't think you'd be obliging enough to just open the door for me."

The voice was like the knife edge of an ice cube, only colder. Taylor whirled to see Kate Belden holding a gun firmly in two hands, the muscles in her face tightened into a frightening mask of rage. Dressed in khaki shirt and pants and a pair of jungle boots, she looked every inch the female guerilla.

Taylor tightened her hand on her own gun, but Kate shook her head.

"Don't even think about it. I can kill you before you even get a sight on me. Drop it. Now."

Taylor stubbornly held on to the weapon, her eyes never leaving Kate's. Where were Noah and Edgar? She hadn't heard any explosions, or even any gunfire. What were they waiting for?

"It's over," she told the woman in front of her. "You might as well quit while you're ahead."

"Over?" Kate's laugh bordered on hysterical. "Too damned right it's over. All because I had that stupid car accident and your damned father — or whatever the hell he was to you — had to go sticking his nose where it wasn't necessary."

"It's his company," Taylor pointed out in a voice she hoped sounded calmer than she felt.

"And it could have kept on being his company. Only a few more of us could have gotten rich along with him." Her eyes flashed blue fire. "And now, since I can't get back to my plane, you're going to take me to yours and have your pilot fly me out of here."

"Where's Paul? Are you leaving without him?"

Kate snorted derisively. "That pussy. All I had to do was fuck him to get him to agree to anything. They can have him. Come on, Taylor. I can't kill you just yet, but I can make you wish you were dead. Drop the gun before I shoot it out of your hand."

Taylor took a deep breath, made as if to drop the gun, then raised it to fire a shot. As she did, she threw herself to the ground. She heard Kate screaming, another shot fired and the fires of hell raged through her body. At that exact moment, before her vision grayed and she fell into a black hole, she heard shouting, the chattering of machine guns and a series of powerful explosions.

She thought she heard Noah's voice calling her name and felt his hands on her. Those marvelous hands that carried her to incredible heights. She wanted to roll into his body and let it surround her, protect her and keep her safe.

Noah!

She tried to scream his name and beg him not to leave her, to stay with her. But the pain stole her breath. She tried to clutch at him, but all she found was air.

Then she went under.

* * * *

She wanted to open her eyes, but the enormous pain gripping her kept pushing her back into the softness of unconsciousness. Fluffy clouds embraced her and protected her, a barrier against pain and unpleasantness. But whirling in the background were loud noises and voices shouting. The unpleasant memory of being moved and jolted made her cry out in her semiconscious state.

"I think she's ready to wake up," a strange female voice said. "I'm giving her some more pain medication because when she does, she'll hurt like hell."

Wonderful. Just what I wanted to hear. Please just let me go to sleep again.

"There." The same voice. "That should help a great deal. And the doctor will be in to check again very shortly."

Doctor? Why do I need a doctor? Why do I hurt?

A large male hand took her small one, fingers rubbing lightly against her knuckles. "Taylor? Come on, little girl. Wake up for me."

Little girl? I know that person. I know him, know him, know him.

"Where's that fire I'm used to? That kick-ass attitude? Are you going to just lie there for the rest of your life?"

"G'way. Leave m'lone."

"You spoke. Excellent. Now come on, open your eyes."

No!

The voice raised a level. "Don't go to sleep again, damn it. Wake up."

Gritting her teeth, she forced her eyelids upward. A man stood next to her, a blurry figure towering over her.

"That's it, little girl. Come on. Don't wimp out on me."

Little girl again. Noah! Oh, God, Noah.

"I'm awake." Her voice sounded like she was grating rocks.

He leaned over her and her vision cleared. There were those bottomless black eyes staring at her, only now they were red-rimmed with dark bruises beneath them. Lines carved trenches in his face and he had at least a three-day growth of beard.

"Welcome back to the living." He was still holding her hand, but he straightened up.

"Water," she croaked. "Please."

"Ice chips only." He picked up a plastic cup from the bedside table and placed some on her parched lips. "Don't swallow too fast. Your throat's still pretty swollen from the breathing tube."

Breathing tube?

She ran her tongue over her lips, licking the last drops of the melting ice. "Where am I?"

Noah's face tightened even more, if that were possible. "You're in a hospital. In San Antonio."

"Hospital? H-how did I get here?"

"Very painfully." He fed her more ice then replaced the cup on the table. "We flew you back on the plane after the doctors in Mexico City got you ready."

She closed her eyes again as broken memories danced through her brain. "I was shot."

He nodded. "Not a smart move to get out of that car, Taylor."

"Kate?" Her throat was closing up on her again.

"Also shot." He couldn't hide the ghost of a grin. He pulled a chair over and folded himself into it, one ankle resting on the opposite thigh. "I'll give you a two-minute version until you're well enough to hear it all."

"'K."

He leaned back in the chair. "Edgar and I waited to take out most of the guards at the plant quietly before getting close enough to set the charges. That took some time. Paul Hunter was caught in the blast."

"Dead?" She could manage just the one word.

He nodded. "But before he bought it, he told us Kate had escaped. Jim Haskins was also killed in the explosion. Edgar and I and the rest of the men were all headed back to the Hummer when we heard the shots."

"And?" She seemed incapable of managing more than one word at a time.

"You hit Kate in the shoulder, shattering it. She fired at the same time. Her bullet plowed into your side and shattered in your body. It did a lot of internal damage and splintered three ribs."

"Bad," she managed.

He nodded. "No shit. By the time we got to you, you'd lost a great deal of blood. It took all of Edgar's political connections to get you into the Mexican hospital and treated by one of the country's best surgeons without any questions or paperwork."

"Thank...Edgar for me."

"I did."

"What...else?"

"My contact from Homeland Security showed up with four men to take custody of Kate. One of the HS forensic teams is still sifting through the remains of the factory. Carl Mortensen, Arroyo's board chairman, is running the company temporarily and keeping things on an even keel until you could return. He was a close friend of Josiah's and is more than qualified."

"Not needed...anymore," she tried to joke.

"Don't kid yourself. They need you now more than ever." He cleared his throat. "John Martino left everything for you locked in the den safe and said to call him anytime. For anything."

She tried to nod, but everything hurt too much. She could

tell the drugs were kicking in again, thankfully. Her eyes closed and she fell back into the soft fluffy embrace of unconsciousness.

When she opened them again, he was gone and Jocelyn Hart was sitting beside the bed. As soon as Taylor opened her eyes, she lifted the ever-present plastic cup and fed her some ice chips.

"They had to do a lot of internal repair work," she explained, "so they're keeping you off even liquids long enough to help you heal."

"How long have I been here?" Her voice sounded marginally better to her ears.

"Eight days."

"Eight…eight days?" Taylor started to sit up in shock, but the pain made her recoil. Even after eight days, it had barely approached a manageable level.

"Just lie back." Jocelyn's hand was cool on her arm. "The ranch is running just fine so you have no worries there. And tomorrow, if your doctor says it's okay, I'm going to wash your hair. After the nurse bathes you, I'll put you in something a little more decorative than these penal colony gowns they give you."

"My bandages…" She gestured at the bulky gauze and tape on her body.

"Kate's bullet did a lot of damage." She took Taylor's hand in her own. "You have a lot of healing to do. Just take it one day at a time, okay?"

She had one more question. "Noah?"

Jocelyn took her time answering. "I, um, believe he's gone on a trip."

"A trip?" Taylor shut her eyes tightly, squeezing against a lone tear that threatened. Noah wasn't on any trip. He was gone. Just as he'd told her he'd be. Silent as a thief in the night.

When she was finally released from the hospital, Jocelyn and Tony came to get her with Greg, preferring the helicopter to the bumping of the Expedition. She set her mind to her recovery, knowing she'd accomplish nothing as long as she was a semi-invalid. She exercised lightly, swam in the pool, took walks. She read everything John had left for her and turned over copies to Homeland Security. They were busy following the many threads to terrorist groups.

She finally had the time to tour the ranch with Tony and get a thorough explanation of exactly how it worked. His knowledge and ability impressed her and gave her a comfortable feeling, knowing the ranch would continue to prosper under his direction and guidance.

Little by little, she worked herself back into the running of Arroyo. On days she didn't make it into the office, Carmen came to the ranch and they worked. She hired a headhunter to find someone to replace Kate and Paul and asked the board to assist with the interviews.

And she tried to put her life back together. She visited Josiah's grave, then ordered a new headstone that said *Beloved Husband and Father*. The picture he'd had of himself with her mother she had blown up and hung it to replace the one of him alone.

But there was still a gaping hole in her life that no amount of work or activity could fill. Every day, she waited to see if he would walk into her office or the ranch. Jocelyn had told her he hadn't left her side at the hospital, but as soon as she'd woken up, he'd left and no one had seen him since then. His house was up for sale, his office had been cleaned out and Arroyo Security had a new vice president for security.

She was sitting in the den, having just gone over some recent reports, when Jocelyn walked in.

"I have to say you look a thousand percent better," the woman told her.

"I feel it, too." When the other woman continued to scrutinize her, she asked, "Do I have smudges on my face or something?"

"No." Jocelyn shook her head. "But I have something for you and I was directed not to give it to you until I felt you were well enough."

She got a bad feeling in the pit of her stomach. "What is it?"

"It's a letter from Noah. I'm going to leave it with you. Call me if you need anything."

She left the room, closing the door behind her.

Taylor looked at the envelope for a long time, turning it over and over in her hands, before opening it.

Taylor,

I should have told you my history long before this. And I should have had the discipline and sense to say away from you, but I couldn't turn away no matter what.

My father was a seventh-generation Texan, descended from one of the original Spanish conquistadores. His family had a huge estancia where he raised cattle for generations, but when he married my mother, his father disowned him.

Taylor stopped reading for a moment, realizing how parallel their stories were.

So he struck out on his own. He worked for other ranchers in South Texas until he saved enough money to buy some land and cattle himself. He and my mother never got rich, but they made a very comfortable living. Enough to send me off to get a college degree, which they both insisted on.

I graduated with a degree in engineering, went into the Army Rangers for four years and came back to San Antonio to a great job with a small but very good firm. The senior partner was like my grandparents, descended from a long line of Spanish nobility. I met his daughter, a bright and beautiful woman, and we fell in love.

We got a little careless in bed and she became pregnant. We were planning to marry anyway, so I took her home to meet my parents.

That was the end of it. Before I could even think, the engagement was off, she'd aborted the child and I was out of a job.

You see, my mother is also from around here. Near

Fredericksburg, not far from where the cabin is. Also a descendant of many generations. Only she's full-blooded Comanche. Just like my maternal grandparents, Teresa's parents didn't want a half-breed in the family. Neither did she. And they spared no language to tell me what they thought.

Again Taylor paused, wiping the tears blurring her eyes.

I didn't drink much then. Still don't. But that night I went out and really tied one on. The bartender knew me and took my car keys away from me, so I started walking home. It was pouring rain and freezing cold, a typical Texas winter night. I finally sat against a building and decided if I froze to death or caught pneumonia I'd be a lot better off. That's when Josiah found me.

The building was where Arroyo had its offices then. He nearly stumbled over me when he came out of the door. I must have been mumbling and he got bits and pieces of the story. He dragged me into his car and took me home with him. I guess he saw his own situation reflected in mine.

He was a stubborn man, your father. He refused to let me give up and die. He bullied me into living, taught me to value myself and ignore the slurs and gave me a job working for him.

I made up my mind after that not to let any woman into my life, at least not for more than sex. I couldn't put myself through it again. Sex, yes. But not anything else. You and I come from opposite worlds, Taylor. Your world would never accept me and in time you'd grow to despise me. Just as Teresa did.

Your family is cut from the same social cloth as Teresa's. There's nothing for us in the future, Taylor. Accept it and move on. This whole thing was a mistake.

Did I want you more than I've ever wanted another woman in my life? I did. Even more than Teresa. I thought if I could fuck you enough, I'd get it out of my system.

That didn't work so the best thing for me is just to walk out of your life completely.

I will only say this once. I love you, Taylor. But we are worlds apart. It would not work.

Noah.

She sat holding the letter, tears running down her cheeks. His pain flew off the page and lodged itself in her heart. It was too much for him, so he'd run. She ached for his tragedy and the sting of rejection by someone he loved, especially considering the reason. She couldn't even begin to imagine what he'd gone through that had robbed him of the will to live. Now she fully understood his loyalty to Josiah. It also gave her a deeper look into Josiah Gaines himself.

She forced herself to eat a light dinner but went to bed early. She lay there, her throat so tight from choking back tears she wasn't sure she'd be able to speak the next day. Tears for herself, for Noah and his lost child, for the father she'd never have the chance to know because of shallow, narrow-minded people.

But I'm not like that, Noah. Why didn't you at least give me a chance? I don't know what we have been but why couldn't you stay around to find out?

The hair on her mound had grown back and she wondered with a rueful feeling what the hospital staff had thought of it. She thought about shaving it herself just to recreate the feeling.

She forced herself to get up the next day and the next. She had a massive corporation to run and she was not one to shirk responsibility. She certainly owed it to the father she'd never known. The ache between her legs grew incessantly stronger and when she showered, she imagined it was Noah's hands grasping her nipples. She wanted him almost more than she wanted her next breath and the thought shocked her beyond belief. When had their adversarial relationship based on nothing but an uncontrollable sexual need turned into something else?

That night in the cabin he'd stolen her soul as well as her body. And he'd taken it with him when he'd left, wrapping it around the pain he'd carried with him for so very long.

She badgered Tomas, who was less than helpful, and

even haunted the security department in case he happened to drop in.

Finally, she had to admit he wasn't coming back, but as far as she was concerned that wasn't the end of it. She knew where he was and she was going there before another day passed.

Chapter Eighteen

The first rays of the morning sun dappled the leaves of the oak trees surrounding the cabin as Noah stood on his porch wearing only a pair of jeans, watching the gray of the night sky fade away. Today, as he'd done every day since leaving San Antonio, he would run his five miles, climb Moffett's Hill and find other activities to push himself physically. Enough to exhaust him so when he fell into bed at night, maybe he wouldn't dream.

Ha! Fat chance!

He barely closed his eyes each night before the image of that miniature Rubens figure with her fall of auburn hair, ripe breasts with plump nipples and tempting curves slammed into him. Green eyes glittered with passion. And that gorgeous cunt, so naked and glistening after he'd shaved it, the pussy lips swollen with need and glistening with the flow of her juices. How many times had he awoken in the middle of the night with an erection that could drill a hole in the wall?

He couldn't help but smile every time he remembered the way she'd grabbed the reins at Arroyo and yanked on them. Or feel his body heat when he remembered the grip of her pussy walls around his hard cock as they climbed the rollercoaster together. Fire and steel under that silken exterior. A woman any man would want to claim as his own.

A woman he wanted to claim.

When he'd seen her lying in that clearing in Chiapas, he'd thought his own heart would stop beating. There'd been so much blood and she'd been whiter than bleached cotton.

Beneath the forced exterior calm, he'd been a madman until they'd had her at the hospital in Mexico City. He'd threatened Edgar with everything including castration if he hadn't gotten the best doctor in the country and made sure Taylor was treated properly.

And the hours spent sitting beside her once they got her back to San Antonio, praying for her to just open her eyes and say something. Anything. Even if it was to tell him to go to hell.

Walking out of her life was one of the hardest things he'd ever done, but that was a road he'd never travel again. Once was enough. No matter what Taylor Scott said, before long she'd realize too strongly their difference and begin to turn away from him. White-bread women like her didn't last with ancient warriors, no matter how good the sex.

So, he'd cleared out. Left Arroyo, called Jocelyn to put his things at the ranch in storage and put his house up for sale. And retreated to the one place he hoped to find some kind of peace.

He'd just poured himself the first cup of coffee of the day when he heard the familiar whapping sound of the helicopter rotors. He looked out of the window and saw Greg landing the Arroyo machine in the clearing. He jerked, and swore as the hot liquid splashed onto his hand.

Damn son of a bitch. I never should have brought her up here. Go figure she'd remember where it was. Can't she leave me alone? I knew it was a mistake to have him pick us up here that day.

If the 'copter itself bothered him, he became even more agitated when he saw the woman jumping down from the cabin. He started out of the cabin to tell her to get the hell back on the bird, but he was too late. She waved at Greg, the 'copter lifted off and there she was, a goddess in the clearing. Her auburn hair, hanging in loose waves to her shoulders, gleamed in the sun. The jeans and blouse she wore outlined a body that had grown thinner than when he'd last seen her.

She smiled at him, a tentative smile. "Hello, Noah."

"Taylor, what in the goddamn hell are you doing here?"

The smile wavered. "Nice to see you, too. Is that coffee you're drinking? I could use a cup myself." She started forward.

"You shouldn't have let Greg take off like that and leave you here."

He was such a seething mass of emotions. He wanted to scream at her to get out of his life at the same time he wanted to wrap her tightly in his arms, caress her and fuck the life out of her.

"Too bad. Now you're stuck with me."

She walked into the cabin, brushing past him as if he wasn't even there.

"Listen, Taylor…"

She ignored him and rummaged through the cupboards to find another mug, which she filled from the carafe. She blew on it then leaned against the counter. Her emerald-green eyes stared at him over the rim.

"So how are you, Noah? Enjoying your own company? It was very rude of you to just walk out on me that way."

"Damn it, Taylor. Didn't Jocelyn give you my letter?"

"Letter?" She waved a hand in the air. "Oh, that. I threw it away."

"What?" He shouted the word. "Fuck. So you know why I left and why you should never have come here."

"I don't know any such thing. Did you really think you could be rid of me with some stupid letter? I got tired of waiting for you to realize what an arrogant ass you are and come to your senses. In Greg's favor, he didn't want to bring me, but I coerced him."

"Then I hope you brought a sat phone to call him and get him back here, because you're leaving."

"Not on your life. No phone, anyway."

They stared at each other across the small space, the heat between them intense enough to combust on its own.

"Taylor, we have no future together. You know that and you know why. Now call Greg back and get the hell out of

254

here."

She set her mug down carefully. "I'm insulted as hell that you think so little of me, to even consider that I'd be repulsed by your heritage. I think if Josiah was here, he'd kick your ass for even saying it."

With fingers that trembled just slightly, she undid the top button of her blouse. Noah gritted his teeth, fighting for some kind of control.

"I thought you had more guts than that. We have something special between us and sex is only part of it." Her laugh was shaky. "Although I have to say, the sex is damn good. Damn good." The second button was opened.

"Stop." He should grab her hands to stop her and button her back up, but he was rooted to the spot, immobile.

"But I sense a real connection between us, a strong one." Another button. "And I'm positive Josiah would approve. Aren't you?" The last button was undone and Taylor opened the shirt and shrugged it off her slim shoulders.

Noah felt his mouth go dry as he saw she wore no bra. Her breasts stood proudly, tempting him, the plump rosy nipples just begging to have his mouth around them.

"Put your blouse back on." But his voice sounded hesitant even to himself.

"I rooted around in his den while I was recovering. Not much to do when you can't get around."

Now he saw the scar, running from just under her right breast and disappearing into the waistband of her pants.

Shit!

She was lucky to be alive. Some bodyguard he was.

"He was an interesting man, my father," she went on. Now she opened the button on her jeans and slowly slid the zipper down. "Courageous. Gutsy. Not afraid to take a chance on life. Even when life stole the woman he loved from him, he went on and built himself an empire."

The rasp of the zipper was amplified in the silence of the room. She pushed the denim down over those lush hips and kicked them to the floor.

Noah nearly strangled on his own tongue when he saw that she'd shaved herself. Her naked cunt stared at him from between her firm thighs. His heart rate kicked up a notch and a thin layer of sweat broke out on his forehead. He set his coffee mug down on the little round table before he dropped it.

"I think he'd be very disappointed that you were afraid to take a chance on something that could be so important in your life. That after ten years, you still kept the past wrapped around you like a hair shirt."

Still keeping her eyes on him, she reached behind her and boosted herself up onto the counter. She spread her thighs wide and reached down to her mound, touching herself with the tips of her fingers.

"I haven't enjoyed life too much without you, Noah. Somehow even being the CEO of a big international conglomerate doesn't have the same spice."

She pulled the outer lips back slightly and he saw all that sweet the pink flesh glistening. His legs were suddenly unsteady and his cock was so hard he was sure it would break right through the zipper on his fly.

Taylor scooted back on the counter, lifted her feet and planted them at the edge so every bit of her sex was open to his view. His heart was beating so furiously against his ribs he was surprised they hadn't broken. When she moistened the tip of one finger with her tongue and touched her clit, he couldn't stand it anymore. His body finally got the signal and he moved forward.

Thank God!

As Noah began to move toward her, Taylor breathed a silent prayer of thanks. It was taking all her courage to put on this performance for him. If he didn't respond, she was sure she'd die of humiliation.

Her body already ached for him, the victim of the long nights in an empty bed. She'd tried to figure out how to break through his self-imposed barricades and this was the only answer she could come up with. When Greg had dropped her off, he'd winked and wished her luck. She'd need every bit of that.

Now she watched him as he approached, her bronzed warrior with the dark eyes and the silken fall of black hair loose around his shoulders. She could see every one of his ancestors reflected in his body and his face and at that moment felt sorry for anyone who couldn't appreciate the value of Noah Cantrell as a man.

As he moved between the vee of her legs she held her breath, waiting for him to make the next move. When he dropped his gaze to her gaping sex and slid one finger along the wet length of her, she almost shouted with joy. She had him now.

"Noah—"

Anything else was cut off as he pressed his mouth to hers with bruising intensity. He licked the soft inside of her bottom lip before plunging his tongue inside to the roof of her mouth, the velvet of her inner cheeks, the roughness of her own tongue. He gripped her shoulders, his fingers biting into the soft flesh as he drank from her mouth. He left no inch of that hot wet cavern untouched.

When he lifted his head to look at her at last, his eyes glittered with hot flames of desire.

"You kill me, Taylor." His voice was thick with desire. "You have no idea how much I want you."

"Then take me," she cried. "Please stop this nonsense that's cluttering up your head. I know you loved Teresa, but maybe she wasn't for you. Maybe she couldn't love you as much as you loved her." She took a deep steadying breath and let it out. "But I do." Her voice shook so much she could hardly get the words out. "I love you, Noah, and I think you love me."

"A nice white-bread girl like you wants to mate with a savage?"

"Stop it. Just stop it." She wanted to pound his chest with her fists. "You are what you are and that's who I love.

Please." One lone tear rolled down her cheek, despite her attempt to contain it. *I won't cry.* "I'm not Teresa. I'm Josiah's daughter and that makes a world of difference. And, yes, I want the savage, because he's part of the man." She wet her lips. "The man I love."

Please, please, please.

"We'll both be damned if this doesn't work out, but I can't turn away from you. Not again."

And just like that, the shields cracked and the walls crumbled. His face was alive with naked desire and need and for the first time, she saw real emotion in his eyes.

He lifted her from the counter and carried her to the bed. In seconds he had his jeans off and was kneeling between her legs. "I have to taste you. God, I've missed your taste so much."

He separated her folds, pausing a second before lowering his head and sliding his tongue from her anus to her clit. Again he did it and again, holding her thighs wide apart to give him greater access as he drank his fill. He licked her outer lips slowly, dragging his tongue along the shaved skin then plunging it into her wet heat, eagerly lapping her juices that were now flowing in rivulets.

Streaks of desire raced through her body and all her pulses throbbed. She thrust her hips at him, urging him to suck harder and deeper, but he lifted his head instead and moved up her body.

"Such pretty nipples," he whispered, taking them between thumb and forefinger and rubbing them gently. "They're like ripe berries, just there for the eating." He captured one with his lips, teasing the tip with his tongue before swirling around every inch of it and drawing it deeper into his mouth. As he sucked on the one, he tormented the other, pinching and tugging and squeezing until Taylor was sure she would come just from his attention to her breasts.

When he had teased one beaded nipple until it was thoroughly swollen, he turned his mouth to the other, giving it the same treatment.

Taylor gripped his arms and pressed her open sex to his chest, silently pleading for his mouth again, but he was relentless in his attention to her nipples.

"Please," she begged, rubbing her naked cunt against the crisp hairs on his chest.

"Please what?" His voice was a hoarse whisper.

"Please fuck me, Noah. Please let me feel your mouth on me again, feel your fingers inside me."

He sat back on his heels and draped her legs over his thighs. With great care, he opened her pussy so he could see it all — the inner and outer lips, the glistening hole just begging for his cock, the juices running down into the cleft of her buttocks. When he slid one finger inside her, she bucked at the touch. It wasn't enough. She wanted more. With a sensual grin he slipped one then two more fingers inside her and began to stroke them in and out, curling them to rasp the sensitive flesh.

When he lifted her hips higher, his fingers penetrated deeper and the pulsing picked up in intensity. She began riding his hand, feeling the spasms begin slowly in her womb. He moved his hand so he could gently scrape one finger against the area between her opening and her anus. The streaks of electricity jolted her, releasing another flood of cream.

"You're so ready to come for me, aren't you?"

She nodded, unable to speak, only wanting to reach that elusive peak dancing just beyond her grasp.

"Then come. Now."

He moved his hand slightly and jammed his pinkie into the tight ring of her anus.

Her orgasm exploded over her and her body jerked and convulsed. Her vaginal walls gripped his fingers, her ass pushed against the intrusion and she poured into his hand, a long, undulating wail escaping from her throat. He wouldn't let her come down, using his other hand to massage and tug at her clit, taking her over the edge of one cliff to another.

She thrashed, gripping the sheet, pushing her hips forward as hard as she could.

At last he removed his hand but the aftershocks still claimed her. Her inner walls rippled with need.

When he started to move away from her she gripped his arms with a fierceness she didn't know she had.

"No."

"Taylor, I have to get a condom. If I don't get inside you in the next thirty seconds, I'm going to come all over your body and that's not what I want."

She was drawing in great gulps of air, trying to find her voice. "Are…? Are you clean?"

He frowned for a moment, trying to decipher what she meant. Then he nodded. "I haven't been with anyone but you in months and I get tested regularly." He grimaced. "When you play in as many playpens as I do, it's a necessity."

"I am too. I haven't had sex with anyone but you in three years. Please. I don't want anything between us. I need to feel your naked cock inside me."

Those onyx eyes scrutinized her. "Are you sure?"

I'm sure, I'm sure. Hurry up.

"Yes. Just hurry."

She had no more time to think because, with a powerful thrust, he was inside her, filling every inch of her quivering vagina. He held himself motionless for a moment, pinning her with his eyes.

"Say it, Taylor. I need to hear you say it and know you mean it."

"I love you, Noah. I truly love you. Please, please, please fuck me. Now."

And the last wall cracked and fell. "I love you, too. God help us both."

Then he was moving, stroking in and out, leaning forward so he could capture one nipple with his teeth, pushing her toward fulfillment. She moved with him in a rhythm so natural she wondered why he'd ever doubted it. She locked her ankles at the base of his spine, pulling him tighter, holding him inside her, thrusting her hips to meet every motion of his.

She wanted him to hurry, the need to come with him so great it was consuming her, but he wasn't to be rushed. He bit and nipped at her nipples and the soft skin of her breasts, then moved one hand down between them to capture her clit, rubbing the tip maddeningly as she clenched, demanding release.

Just at the moment she was sure she'd lose her mind, he shoved two fingers into the hot darkness of her ass and she came. She felt his release at the same time, his hot semen splashing into her and she screamed his name.

"Noah!"

Endless spasms gripped them both until he collapsed on top of her, his sweat-slicked skin pressing into hers, his breath fanning her cheek. She wrapped her arms around him and held on for dear life, afraid that if she let go the whole thing would be a dream and vanish like a cloud.

At last he rolled to the side, taking her with him, his cock still inside her. She felt the thud of his heart pounding against her in rhythm with her own. He pressed his lips to her forehead, then her cheeks, her nose, even her chin. Then he bent slightly and traced the scar with his mouth.

"You frightened the shit out of me."

She grinned. "Me too. Let's not do that again."

"There are so many things I want to do to you," he said. "With you. God, Taylor, I've been out of my mind with wanting you."

She swallowed back the tears of relief that clogged her throat. "I know you'll still feel the pain of Teresa's betrayal and the loss of the child for a long time. But we'll make our own babies and build a good life together."

For an instant, his voice hardened. "And what of the people who work for you, socialize with you, see you as Taylor Scott, Arroyo's CEO?"

"Actually, I'm hoping to change it soon to Taylor Cantrell," she teased. "And anyone who's foolish enough to disdain you won't be around for very long." She ran her fingers through the black silk of his hair. "I can't do this without you, Noah. We do it together or not at all. Let it go, Noah. It's time."

"I've lived with this a long time," he said.

"Long enough to get past it now."

"Are you sure this is what you want?"

She swatted at his arm. "If you ask me once more, I'll shoot you instead of marrying you."

"I'm not an easy ride," he warned.

"Good," she laughed. "Because easy rides aren't worth taking."

"And I won't be Mr. Taylor Scott," he warned.

She smiled at him. "I don't think there's anyone who will ever doubt just who's in charge in this relationship. So how soon can I convince you to marry me? I won't take a chance on having you walk away again."

"If you're absolutely sure, how about this weekend? We just have to arrange to get the blood tests and a license."

"And some clothes. I came here with nothing."

"Excellent." He held her tighter. "I plan to keep you naked for the next day or two. Maybe then I'll let you out of bed."

She laughed with the joy of it and inside her his cock was hardening again. She looked into his eyes and knew for both of them, this was right. This was good. This was perfect.

This was home.

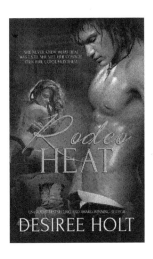

Rodeo Heat

Excerpt

Chapter One

Grace Delaney could sense the excitement in the enormous coliseum building, the one where the rodeo vendors had set up right next to the huge rodeo arena. The air was filled with a raucous blend of shouts and laughter, the air heavy with the mingled scents of horses, cattle, manure and hay that drifted in through the massive open doors. Grace Delaney figured there were at least two thousand people jammed into a space where half that number could barely fit comfortably.

She stood in front of the makeshift mirror at the vendor's booth, tilting the cowgirl hat she was trying on this way and that. Her western-style shirt and prewashed jeans felt like an outfit she'd borrowed from someone else and her new boots were pinching her toes. Torn between a suddenly emerging need for adventure and a lifetime of playing it safe, she'd let her closest friend, Melanie Keyes, drag her to a western store and outfit her, then agreed to come to the rodeo with her. Now the habits of more than twenty years were rearing their heads and misgivings were crowding in on her, nearly smothering her.

"I wish I knew how in the hell I let you talk me into this," she muttered.

"Because you need to have some spice in your life." Melanie Keyes lifted a hot-pink hat from the display stand and set it firmly on her tousled blonde curls then turned to Grace. "What do you think?"

"I think I should have stayed home," Grace told her, removing the hat she wore on her own head. "I must be crazy. This isn't me. Hanging out at rodeos and displaying myself for the cowboys just isn't my style. You know that, Mel."

Melanie grabbed her by the shoulders and gave her a stern look.

"Listen, Grace. We've been friends since fifth grade and you've never taken a chance in your life. I watched you dive into a 'safe' marriage, one that wouldn't unlock the part of yourself I know you hide inside."

"But I loved Joe," she began.

"I know, I know. But it was a safe love, whether you want to admit it or not. I watched you pull yourself together when Joe died and build a life for yourself and your kids. I watched you choose a 'safe'—make that dull—career in accounting so you could put numbers in squares just like you've done with every day of your life. And when, after eighteen years, you finally decided to date again, you picked men twenty years older than you. 'Safe' again. I'll bet they can't even get it up without a big supply of those little blue pills. Come on. 'Fess up. I'm right, aren't I?"

Grace blew out a breath. Sometimes she didn't know whether to hug Melanie or kill her. The problem was that, in this instance, she was completely right, and Grace hated that. So what if she was forty-four and boring? It was better than being divorced three times and running around with one gorgeous but unreliable man after another like Melanie did. Wasn't it? Well, wasn't it?

But even she had been smart enough to know her life needed something besides spreadsheets and men with clammy hands. Joe had died before they'd ever had a chance to fully explore their sexual relationship and for more than twenty years she'd been completely celibate. One day, when she'd been passing an adult entertainment store, her car had turned into the parking lot as if it had a life of its own. Shocking herself, she'd left with a collection of erotic books and movies that would have made a hooker blush.

Driven by her suddenly awakened curiosity, she'd huddled in her bedroom each night, reading until her eyes had blurred and watching the movies until her eyes had popped out and she'd found heat creeping up her cheeks. Like an addict seeking more drugs, she'd returned to the store again and again, her secret collection growing as her brain had struggled to absorb the things people did with and to each other in their sexual encounters.

The things the authors described hadn't even been on her radar. She'd never be brave enough to try any of them in real life, but at least she was expanding her horizons. If she couldn't do it, she could read about it. But as she'd lost herself in page after page and in scene after scene, she'd found herself aroused, turned on, squeezing her legs to still the throbbing between her thighs, so she'd invested in a couple of toys that she used to relieve the tension when she needed to.

"Glad to see you spicing up your life," the clerk had told her the last time she'd rung up her purchases.

Grace had lowered her eyes and nearly run from the store. What was it with everyone wanting to 'spice' things up for her? Was she flashing a sign that said 'boring'?

Now, however, she had quite a collection of books and movies, each one introducing her to new and exotic sexual pleasures. She kept the books and DVDs hidden in her closet, dragging them out at night with the bedroom door locked. Not that there was anyone left in the house to even pay attention. She'd been reading her latest, appropriately titled *Ride Me, Cowboy,* with a naked cowboy on the cover, when Melanie had called to talk her into this little excursion and she hadn't been able to say no.

So here she was, decked out in her new threads, being pushed for the first time in her life into something daring and wondering what kind of fool she'd make of herself. Or if she even had the courage to try. Her mind and body were busy doing battle with each other. But…she guessed she had to start somewhere to step outside the lines, even it was only buying a new outfit.

"That hat is so you," Melanie gushed. "I'm buying it for you. Put it on again."

"But—"

"But nothing. I'm still spending Langford Keyes' more than generous divorce settlement. Take it while I've got it, honey."

"I thought we were here to see the rodeo." Grace hurried to keep up with her friend who was sashaying her way—that was the only word for it—through the crowds of people. "So far, all we've done is shop."

"We will, sweetie. We will. But shopping's half the fun. I want to stop at a little booth I hit every year. This woman sells the most fantastic jewelry, some of it very old. And she always has a story to tell about each piece."

Grace shook her head but followed Melanie halfway around the barn until her friend found the vendor's booth she was searching for. She and the woman greeted each other like long-lost friends, hugging and gushing. Grace sighed and distracted herself by examining the jewelry displayed on the table.

"Oh, miss." The woman reached out and touched her arm. "Look. This is perfect for you. I feel a connection."

She held out her other hand, palm open. An exquisite

pin in the shape of a boot nestled there. A tiny silver rowel clung to the heel, which was scored to show the lines so commonly seen. The brilliance of newness had faded with age and now it glowed with a smooth patina that sparkled and warmed. As if pulled by a string, Grace reached out for it and at once felt a heat on her skin that raced through her body.

What the hell?

"It is for you," the woman told her. "You must have it. I tell you, I feel the connection for you. This pin has a long history of bringing lovers together."

"Oh, no," Grace protested. "I'm not—"

"That's true," the woman said with a knowing look. "But there is a hidden longing, a sense of desire. This pin will unlock those doors you hide behind."

Grace wanted to run away. How dare this woman talk to her in such a personal manner?

But the woman gripped her hand. "I will charge you very little, but if you pass it up, you will miss meeting the most extraordinary man ever."

Grace stared at the pin, mesmerized by the feel of it, at the same time thinking, *it will take more than a pin to do something about my pitiful sex life.*

Not that the choice wasn't hers. As it had been for the past twenty years. But her new taste in reading had made her do some uncomfortable thinking. Somewhere she'd lost her sexuality and searching for it was a task that would move her out of her comfort zone, a terrifying thought.

"Oh, buy it, Grace," Melanie enthused, interrupting her reverie. "No. Wait. I want to buy it for you. You're so practical you'll walk away from it."

"Sensible," Grace corrected. "And I'm not looking for an 'extraordinary' man."

I don't even know what 'extraordinary' is anymore.

"And that's the problem," Melanie said. "It's well past time you found one. There. Now we just need to follow its lead." She fastened the pin onto Grace's shirt, patting it.

The moment the pin touched her again, the same blaze of heat shot through her, stirring her pulses and making her weak-kneed. Grace had never believed in omens or good luck charms or anything so fanciful, but somehow, she couldn't make herself remove the pin.

"Okay, let's go." Melanie tucked her purchase into her purse and took Grace by the arm. "Now, we hit the big barn where the guys eat. I promised a special honey that I'd pop by and give him a kiss."

Grace tried to huff and walk at the same time. "I swear to God, Melanie. Is this another one of your boy-toy trophies? And what do I do while you and he make eyes at each other? Or whatever else you plan to do."

Melanie laughed as she headed for an exit. "He's an old acquaintance, honey, who I've enjoyed a lot of good times with. And while I'm reminiscing with him, you'll be scoping the room for your own trophy. And it's surely about time. Just remember the pin."

How did I ever let Melanie talk me into this?

They were in a hallway leading to the next building, Melanie bouncing along in front of her, chattering a mile a minute, when Grace spotted a rodeo poster tacked on the wall and stopped dead. A dark-haired, dark-eyed cowboy in the classic pose on a bucking horse, arm extended in the air for balance, stared down at her. If he wasn't the naked man on the cover of the book she'd been reading just last night, he was so close they could be twins.

The pin on her blouse seemed to blossom with heat and, in an instant, she was once more engrossed in the pages of the story, in the scene she'd read over and over again, wishing the heroine was her.

* * * *

"Sweetheart? You upstairs?"

His footsteps on the stairs made her pulse ratchet.

She was waiting for him at the door to their bedroom,

wearing nothing but a big smile. His eyes widened as he spotted her and a huge, wicked grin split his face.

"This was definitely worth waiting for, sugar." He lowered his head to lick her nipples and ran the fingers of one hand through her almost bare slit. "Mmm," he moaned and licked his fingers clean. "Delicious, as always, but the first thing I have to do is wash away all the cow stink. I don't know how I'm going to control myself long enough to do that."

She reached out a hand to him. "Lucky for you, I've got that covered."

She led him into the bedroom where she quickly stripped away his jacket and placed his hat on the dresser. While he toed off his boots, she unbuttoned his work shirt, taking her time to run her fingers through the fine pelt of dark hair on his chest and graze her fingernails over his nipples. He tried to reach for her hands, but she batted him away.

"Uh-uh. This is my show." She stood on tiptoe to nip at his chin. "Happy anniversary, my love."

When she had the shirt completely unbuttoned, she yanked it from his jeans and tossed it to the side with his jacket. As she went to work on his belt buckle, she bent her head and took first one then the other of his nipples into her mouth, nibbling at them then lapping at them with her tongue.

He gripped her shoulders hard. "You're killing me, sugar. Please let me just get rid of these clothes and jump in the shower. I can't stand not to touch all your sweet, naked flesh."

"Be patient," she teased, pulling the belt free of its loops. "There'll be plenty of time for touching. And other things."

The sound of his zipper being lowered was loud in the room. Kneeling down, she licked a line across the top of his waistband then pushed the denim fabric down his hips, taking his boxers with them. His hot erection sprang proud and free from its sheltering nest of curls, the broad head already deepening to a dark purple. A teasing smile curving her lips, she wrapped her small fingers around his cock, bent her head and swiped her tongue across the velvet surface, catching the drop of fluid that sat atop the slit. For good measure she probed the slit with the tip of her tongue then sucked the head into her mouth.

"Jesus!" He pulled her head away from him. "In a minute, I'll forget myself and fuck you right here on the floor."

She looked up and let his cock slip from the tight clasp of her lips. "Now that would spoil all the fun, cowboy."

She stood, took his hand and led him into the huge bathroom, part of the new master suite they'd recently added on. Fat candles shimmered on every surface, filling the air with traces of vanilla and fragrant steam rose from the large hot tub they'd had built in.

"Every cowboy should have something fancy in his life," she told him. "I thought this would be nice for our anniversary."

"You're all the fancy I need," he replied. "No shower first?"

"Oh, yeah." She winked at him. "You bet."

She turned the handle in the big shower and jets misted water at them from a dozen directions. She held out her hand and drew him inside, licking her lips as she took in the sight of him. When she'd splashed water on every inch of his naked body, she grabbed the shower gel and squeezed a generous amount into the palm of one hand.

"You just relax, cowboy, and let me do the work."

When she'd worked the gel into a thick lather, she began spreading it over his body. First his arms and the hollow spots beneath them. Then his chest, swirling the bubbles around his nipples, pinching them lightly. With careful strokes, she rubbed the gel into the line of hair arrowing down to his groin. When she closed her hands over his rigid cock, a low moan rumbled from his throat.

"Holy God, sweetheart. Careful, or this will be over before it starts."

"Don't you worry about a thing." She grinned. "I've got

it all in hand."

He laughed. "I'd say so."

She soaped his erection from root to tip and up again then massaged lather into the heavy sac between his thighs. She covered his legs from hip to ankle and nudged him to turn around and went to work on his back, beginning with his shoulders and working her way down.

When she reached the cleft of his buttocks and slid her soapy fingers into it, his muscles tightened in response.

"You know what that does to me," he reminded her.

"Exactly." And she continued massaging the gel into his flesh, probing the tight ring of his anus, penetrating it with just the tip of her finger.

By the time she'd finished lathering his entire body and rinsing him off, she knew he was hotter than a match and ready to flare. Just the way she wanted him.

She didn't even dry them off, just stepped into the bubbling water of the hot tub and held out her hand to him. She wet her lips with the tip of her tongue as she swept her gaze over every powerful masculine inch of him. Tonight, she was in control and she would relish every minute of it.

When they were submerged to their shoulders, facing each other, she scooted between his wide-spread legs, running her hands over his muscular thighs. With a teasing touch, she caressed the soft skin between them, cupping his balls and rolling them in her fingers.

"Don't move," she told him. "This is my show."

His muscles tightened with sexual tension and heat flared in his eyes. From the first day they'd met, the fire between them had never lessened. She hadn't thought it was possible for their sexual activities to get better, but he was always inventive, always thinking of new ways to bring her to climax. Tonight, it was her turn to pleasure him.

She wrapped the fingers of her other hand around his stiff shaft and moved both hands in coordinated rhythm, feeling him pulse in her grip.

"Would you like to touch me?" she asked, an impish tone

in her voice.

"You know damn well I would," he growled.?

"All right. You may play with my nipples."

She hitched even closer to give him easier access to her, to pull and tug on her hardened tips, heat flashing in his eyes as she slid the hand toying with his balls even lower. With the water up to her chin, she eased her fingers into the crevice of his ass and searched for the puckered skin of his anus. She'd discovered how much he loved this, although he'd been embarrassed to admit it the first time they'd experimented. Now, sometimes, she even made him beg for it. But not tonight. Tonight, it was all about him.

The muscles of his buttocks clenched when she probed at him with a fingertip and his breath hissed between his teeth.

"Holy God," he growled. "You're driving me crazy."

"That's the idea."

He rocked back and forth on the dual stimulation, the rapid movement of her hand on his cock and the sensation of the finger she eased slowly into his ass. He sucked in his breath when she rubbed the sensitive tissues, exploring deeper and deeper, adjusting her position to allow her the greatest access to his rectum. The water bubbled softly around them and the blend of aromas floated in the room, creating an erotic cocoon that stimulated their senses.

She increased the pace of her hand, up and down his shaft while she plowed his ass with her slender finger fucking in time to her movements. When he tightened his fingers on her nipples, squeezing them hard, she knew he was close. She pushed her finger deeper inside him to find that spot that drove him over the edge, his body tensing in response.

"Now," she whispered.

His balls tightened against her thighs and his cock pulsed in her hand.

"Happy anniversary, sweetheart," she murmured. "Let it go. Come for me now."

He exploded, the muscles in his neck cording, his head

thrown back, and beneath the scented bubbles his semen jetted over and over onto her stroking hand and fingers.

"Grace!" he yelled. "Grace… Grace… Grace!"

* * * *

"Grace. Damn it, Grace, do you hear me?"

Grace shook her head, hearing Melanie's voice rather than her sexy cowboy's. He wasn't the one calling her name. Where had he gone?

"Can you hear me, Grace?" Melanie demanded. "Are you all right? You've been standing here staring into space as if you were in another world. What is the matter with you?"

Heat flooded Grace's face. The poster had thrown her into an erotic daydream right there in broad daylight, blanking out everything else. How long had she been standing lost like this? What had people going back and forth in the hallway thought of her?

Without thinking, she lifted her hand and touched the pin, feeling it warm against her skin. Maybe that woman had been right about it. Was that a good thing or a bad one?

"Sorry." She let out a breath. "I guess my mind just wandered for a minute."

Melanie looked at the poster on the wall and once again at Grace. A slow smile tilted the corners of her mouth. "Well, no wonder. Want to meet him in person? Or at least the closest thing to him?"

Grace adjusted her hat and hitched her purse strap up on her shoulder. "I'm fine, Mel. Just fine. I don't need to meet anyone. Let's go."

But Melanie just kept grinning at her. "Now, that's where you're wrong. We didn't come here so you could hide in your usual corner. Let's go see if we can get you laid somewhere except in your mind."

"Wait. Wait. Are you crazy? I just—"

Melanie had a grip on Grace's arm like a vise and was practically dragging her into the huge barn that had been converted into the modern version of a chuck wagon for the rodeo contestants and workers.

"Uh-huh. Right. Forget it. I know the right cowboy is just waiting in here for you."

Oh, shit. I am in such big trouble.

More books from
Totally Bound Publishing

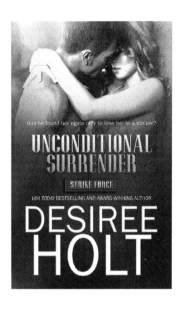

Book one in the Strike Force series

Had he found her again only to lose her to a stalker?

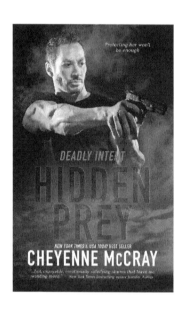

Book one in the Deadly Intent series

Danger, desire, death.

Some things are best left forgotten.

Book one in the Heat series

For Murdoch, women are bad news. Trying to stay alive in war-torn Andalusia, tracking a vanishing femme fatal, hunted by The Brotherhood, the last thing he needs is love…

About the Author

Desiree Holt

A multi-published, award winning, Amazon and USA Today best-selling author, Desiree Holt has produced more than 200 titles and won many awards. She has received an EPIC E-Book Award, the Holt Medallion and many others including Author After Dark's Author of the Year. She has been featured on CBS Sunday Morning and in The Village Voice, The Daily Beast, USA Today, The Wall Street Journal, The London Daily Mail. She lives in Florida with her cats who insist they help her write her books, and is addicted to football.

Desiree Holt loves to hear from readers. You can find contact information, website details and an author profile page at https://www.totallybound.com/

Home of Erotic Romance

Printed in Great Britain
by Amazon